Pride Publishing books by Angel Martinez and Bellora Quinn:

AURA
Quinn's Gambit
Flax's Pursuit

I0663000

AURA

KELLEN'S AWAKENING

ANGEL MARTINEZ
AND BELLORA QUINN

Kellen's Awakening
ISBN # 978-1-78651-959-7
©Copyright Angel Martinez and Bellora Quinn 2016
Cover Art by Posh Gosh ©Copyright May 2016
Interior text design by Claire Siemaszkiewicz
Pride Publishing

Published in 2016 by Pride Publishing, Newland House, The Point, Weaver Road, Lincoln, LN6 3QN, United Kingdom.

Pride Publishing is an imprint of Totally Entwined Group Limited.

KELLEN'S AWAKENING

Dedication

This one's for our betas, for all those folks who took the time to write reviews, and for the fans of this quirky series — thank you for taking a chance on a bizarre idea that hit two authors in the head one evening. Thank you for staying with us.

Chapter One

Dry ground in any city park in October was something of a rarity. When Ness tested the grass in the little park across the street from his apartment and his hooves didn't squish, he was ridiculously pleased, and reclined his equine half near bushes set back from the sidewalk.

People walking by could still see him, which wasn't always a good thing, but he wanted to be able to glance up at his apartment window from time to time as he read. He straightened the bottom hem of his sweater and the matching paprika scarf. Not that he really needed either, but he had to wear something on his top half for the sake of decency. Besides, Sin had bought these for him, saying the color was 'absolutely the bomb' with Ness' olive complexion.

Sin said some odd things. Nonhumans who had spent time living on the streets picked up more colorful language, he supposed. So long as they understood each other, it wasn't important in the least. Ness flicked his tail and got his book and his glasses out of his messenger bag, before settling in to read.

The ebb and flow of scents around him were a constant current of semi-distraction but it was a low-level thing, like background noise. Unless something that was familiar or threatening came into his range, in which case the scent 'volume' hit his awareness as a loud note. He was turning the page when such a note drifted into his sensitive nose and caught his attention. Ness lifted his head to catch it again, conscious that it was a particularly equine gesture. Sin had told him he thought it looked hot. Ness hadn't been sure if he was teasing or not at first, but experience with what Sin found arousing taught him that his incubus had been entirely serious.

The note became louder, although stronger was probably the more appropriate term in the human tongue. He had a hard time thinking of scent that way, though, because it didn't become *more*, instead it suddenly slotted into the proper category and was then distinguishable from the myriad other scents clamoring for attention. This one was not a danger, just familiar, and a moment later, its source came walking down the sidewalk with an armload of produce in a bag.

"Quinten," Nestor said when he came closer.

The young man stopped and blinked, then smiled. "Ness! Hey, how are you? I didn't see you there."

"I'm well, thank you. Just waiting for Sin."

Quinn left the sidewalk to sit on a nearby rock. *Of course, yes.* The ground would be too cold for him, even with clothes on his lower half. "Waiting for him? Don't you live right there?"

"He's, ah…" Ness' cheeks grew warm. "He has his weekly appointment. I prefer…not to watch his feedings."

"Oh. Yeah, I get that." Quinn squinted at the ground, obviously chasing a thought. "So he's with...er, someone you know?"

"Yes. She's an escort. She enjoys Sin's company and doesn't charge us so much." Ness shifted his forelegs, not entirely comfortable with the topic.

Quinn blinked at him, obviously surprised by his reply. "But, Ness, you're a cop," Quinn said. "And you're buying your boyfriend a hooker?"

Ness closed his book and pulled his human torso up straight. *Don't be defensive. Don't, for all the gods' sakes, whinny in offense.* "There's legal precedent. *Kalia vs. the State* established that succubi and incubi paying prostitutes constitutes a legal purchase. The court ruled that it's necessary for survival and so he's paying for food, not sex."

"Oh," Quinn said again, looking uncomfortable himself. "Sorry, Ness, I didn't mean to offend you, honest."

Ness shrugged. "I get a little defensive where Sin's concerned. I suppose it does get to me a bit, too, though I tell him it's fine. It is. Fine. He has to feed."

"So...um...why can't he, you know? From you?"

"Incubi construction. He needs to feed from female sexual energy. The way Sin explains it, yes, he can snack on any sexual energy, but it would be like me eating nothing but a handful of raisins every day. Eventually, he would sicken and die."

"Right," Quinn said, apparently rolling that idea around in his head. He looked like he might be about to ask Ness if he was really okay, then thought better of it. He cleared his throat and asked, "So, what are you reading?"

Ness suppressed a sigh. He always dreaded that question. "It's, ah, Jane Austen. *Northanger Abbey.* I think it's better than some of her novels that get more attention…" And there he went again, sounding like some weird conglomeration of wimpy things. "I know. Big centaur reading old romances."

"It's a romance? Does it got naughty parts in it?" Quinn winked at him.

"Ah…ahem." Ness really wished he didn't blush so easily. "It's not that sort of romance. The older sort, with carriages and grand estates and everyone being terribly proper, so it was harder to get to the love part. People had to work for it."

Quinn stared at him for a long moment, opened his mouth, shut it and looked away.

"What? Go on. Ask. I can tell you want to ask me something," Nestor said.

"Well, it's just, does it bother you the way people treat horses in those books? Or in general? I mean, I know you're not a horse, but some people can be such idiots. I'm sure you've run into someone wanting to treat you like you should be strapped up to one of those carriages."

Ness put the book away carefully, took his glasses off and folded them. "There's a lot of centaur prejudice. Yes. Though I suppose I could ask you if it bothers you how chimpanzees are treated in zoos." He tapped his glasses against the palm of one hand. "But you're asking two different things. Does it bother me when someone mistreats a horse? Yes. It bothers me to see anyone mistreated. I'm not a horse. But, yes, humans often see me as one."

"Like the kids wanna pet you?"

"Hmm, yes. Often without asking. Though the adults are more wary. Lumping all centaurs in together because a few are violent drunkards."

Quinn grinned at him. "Well, you have to admit a lot of your brethren do like to party. There's a new centaur-run club opening up every other week."

He didn't want to get angry with Quinn. He liked Quinn. So instead of responding to what he felt was close to a racial slur, he asked, "Quinn, why do you think I'm a cop?"

Quinn shrugged. "Same reason anyone becomes a cop, probably. You're willing to stick your neck out to make sure the world doesn't get overrun with assholes."

"There's certainly something to that." Ness nodded. "I get a lot of satisfaction out of my job. Thing is, when I applied to AURA, I applied to Research. They rejected me."

"There's probably a dozen reasons why that's a good thing, considering what happened to most of the previous research team, and concluding with not having to work for the world's bossiest drow, but I get the feeling you're not mentioning it just because you want me to commiserate with you."

"True." Ness frowned at the memory and shook his hair back from his forehead. "This was before Kai, of course. Under the old, mostly human regime. I was told that a centaur would be... How did they put it? *Too energetic* for the department. Too restless and possibly disruptive. In other words, *Bugger off, pony boy. You're too stupid to do simple math and you'll wreck the place.* If this sort of rejection were given to a human? I'd probably have grounds to sue. As a centaur? I have no recourse."

"The stereotypes suck, I know," Quinn said. "And I'm sorry if I offended you, again."

"You didn't offend me, Quinn," Ness said more gently. "The assumptions people make, especially people in power, offend me. I just... I guess I just wanted someone to spin it out to. Not many humans would listen."

"Yeah, well, most humans are jerks," Quinn said cynically. "That's probably a stereotype too, but it's also the truth. You okay, Ness? Want to go get a coffee or anything?"

Ness smiled for Quinn and put his glasses back in their case. "I'm fine. There's my Sin at the window, so he's all done for this week. And most likely a little frisky."

Quinn arched an eyebrow at that but made no comment. "It's a strange world we live in, isn't it, Ness? I'll let you get back to your man, and I better get home to mine too."

"Can't imagine a stranger one." Ness rose and bent a foreleg to plant a kiss atop Quinn's head. "Thank you for listening. We'll see you at work."

Traffic stopped for him as he crossed the street. Motorists saw the equine legs and no matter what Ness wore, they stopped in a conditioned response to mounted police. The normal pattern—cars stopped, drivers realized he was just a centaur in a crosswalk, horns blared, catcalls started. Today, there were three offers to fuck him and one to buy his sweater. At least that was something new.

In the lobby, he stopped at the row of metal boxes to retrieve the mail, said a pleasant good afternoon to the woman hastily pulling her child away from him, and retreated to the stairwell. Most days it didn't bother him too much. He wasn't a natural occurrence here. Some days, though, he missed his herd, missed his siblings and his friends. Missed his mother.

She had been a centaur of fiery intellect, of purpose and drive. If she'd come through an Event into this world, she would've started an organization for the advancement of centaurs by now.

Ness was lucky some days if he could muster the drive to eat breakfast. He walked up the stairs to the seventh floor to avoid the dirty looks he got when he took the elevator, and arrived at his door just as it opened to allow a beautiful dark-haired human woman in a smartly tailored suit to exit.

"Hello, Maggie." Ness leaned down so she could kiss his cheek even though he knew he had already flushed scarlet.

She smiled and smoothed a stray lock of hair behind his ear. "Hello, Ness. Nice to see you." With a hand still on his arm, she turned to call back into the apartment, "You behave yourself, gorgeous!"

"Never!" Sin's warm laugh drifted into the hall.

Maggie patted Ness' chest and strode off on her expensive heels. She never slunk or sashayed as the streetwalkers did. She walked as if she owned the world, head up, shoulders back. *Queen of sex workers.*

"Sin?" Ness called as he closed the door behind him with a back hoof.

"In the kitchen!"

Well, that's a relief. The first few times they'd tried this arrangement, Ness had returned to find his Sinistrus sprawled out on the bed, looking decadently replete, naked and horny, and he had tried. He really had. It had simply had too much of a feeling of sloppy seconds. Ness hadn't been able to muster his usual enthusiasm, and Sin's feelings had been hurt. Apparently, they were learning.

Now, Sin showered after his feeding, even though penetration was never involved. Today, his thick black hair was still wet and mussed, his huge, leathery wings drooping behind him to let them dry, but he had pulled on sweats.

"Hey there, tall, dark and shiny-hooved," he purred as Ness came to give him a peck on the cheek.

Ness let Sin lean against his side as he sorted the mail. *Junk. Junk. Bill.* "Good feeding?"

"Always. You wanna drink? Oh, hey… What's in the fancy-schmancy envelope?"

"Hmm? Drink? Yes. Beer, please." Ness pulled the lovely vellum envelope out of the stack of cheaper paper as Sin went to pour himself a whiskey and pop a beer for Ness. "Oh. Huh."

"What, huh?" Sin tried to peer over his shoulder, which wasn't quite possible with the difference in height. "Good 'huh' or bad 'huh'?"

"Just, interesting. It's the invitation to Kai and Tenzin's wedding."

"Well, okay." Sin gave up and leaned a hip against the counter instead. "We're friends. We get invited. That's normal. But I'm not wearing any damn neck noose."

Ness cupped his cheek and leaned down for a kiss, indulging in those wonderful, soft lips for a moment. "I'm sure we can find something nice for you to wear without a tie. It's not the invitation that's a surprise. It's the location."

"Yeah? Kai's having it at the Metropolitan or somewhere snooty, I bet."

"Apparently, they're having it in Central Park. Near the Azalea Pond."

"Really? That's weird. Last I heard, Kai was campaigning hard for a snooty-place wedding and Tenzin was pushing for something mountain-y. And Kai has this strange relationship with the park. He never has anything nice to say about it. Okay, he doesn't have much nice to say about anything except Tenzin."

"Now that's not true," Ness murmured, distracted by the pretty designs and all the different *parts* to the invitation. He'd never received one before and hadn't realized they were so complicated. "He says nice things about Quinn and about Breon. And he loves the opera."

Ness glanced up to see that fond, indulgent smile on Sin's face, the one that said he was being wool-headed and going off track. "All right. True. The park has some bad memories for most of us. But it sounds like a compromise. Maybe it was Tenzin's idea."

Sin shrugged, which made his wings rustle. It was a restless sound. Funny how he could do that. He spoke almost as much with his wings as he did with his mouth, which was looking decidedly kissable right now.

"Who knows?" Sin said. "Are we going?"

Ness put the invitation down on the counter and tugged off his scarf. "I'll have to check to see if I can get time off. But you will too." He put a finger under Sin's chin and tilted his face up. "Busy med tech that you are these days."

Sin lifted his arms, looping them around Nestor's neck, and pressed close to him, folding his wings in tight. "Never too busy for you, my love," he said, his voice dropping to a husky purr.

"Mmm. Good thing." Ness wrapped his arms around Sin to lift him and Sin obligingly wrapped his legs around Ness' waist. "You have the most beautiful eyes. Have I told you that?"

"Never, not once." Sin smiled as he blatantly lied. "You have amazing shoulders, do you know that? So sexy."

"You may have mentioned it once or twice," Ness said with a soft smile. He nuzzled Sin's throat and kissed a line up Sin's jaw. "You smell so good."

Sin tipped his head back and made a soft, aroused sound in his throat, flexing the muscles of his thighs and buttocks, rubbing up against Ness' front. He shivered and groaned when Ness' lips touched a particularly sensitive spot. "Mmm, I love how you do that. When you touch me there."

Ness chuckled and nipped at the spot on Sin's throat. "There?" When Sin let out a deliciously sensual moan, Ness thought his legs might buckle. "Sin... Do you want to... I mean...whatever you'd rather...but could I get the table out for us?"

"I don't know if I can wait that long. But yes, I want to," Sin said, still flexing and rubbing up on Ness, almost catlike.

"You can wait," Ness whispered in his ear. "You're practically a god of sex. I think you can find a little bit of control."

Sin whimpered. "Stroking my ego will get you everywhere."

"There's a lot of you I want to stroke." Ness set Sin on the countertop and wandered out toward the front closet, stripping off his sweater and letting his hind quarters sway as he went. The beautiful dragon wing pendant Sin had given him stayed on, wings spread on either side of a teardrop ruby. That never came off, no matter what.

Sin squirmed and tracked Ness' movements for a few moments, but that was as long as he could take before he hopped back off the counter, slithered out of his sweats, and followed Ness. He watched those wonderful centaur muscles stretch and flex as Ness reached into the closet to retrieve The Table. The custom-made monstrosity always had capital letters in Sin's head.

He suspected it had cost a small fortune with its over-engineered, truss-enforced folding metal legs and its special padded top, but Ness refused to say and had been gently offended when Sin offered to pay for part of it.

Ness pushed the sofa aside with a back hoof, locked the table legs in place, and set the thing upright. He smiled for Sin, that shy smile that said he was so turned on but still a little embarrassed to say, and patted the top. It took a couple of running steps to vault up since the top was about chest high on Sin, but that was part of the fun. He plopped down on his ass to face Ness, who moved between his legs to kiss him.

"Do you know when I first wanted you?" Ness asked softly as he stroked Sin's still-damp hair from his eyes.

"When you saw me from across the bar, but were too chicken to proposition me?"

Ness laughed, his serious face transforming from handsome to radiant in that moment. "No. It was when I first saw you in the hospital."

Sin arched an eyebrow at him. "Umm…okay? When I was all beat up and crawling past your door like some pitiful video game brawl refugee? Dragging a wing? One eye swollen shut? Really?"

"Oh, you'd be beautiful no matter what." Ness ran his hands down Sin's ribs, kissing along his shoulder. "But it was your determination. That sheer, gods-be-damned persistence that said you were going to find somewhere you didn't have to be alone if it killed you."

"Funny. The social worker always called it being intractable and noncompliant."

"It melted my heart." Ness pulled him close for a fierce embrace. "So brave. So alone."

"You're such a sap," Sin murmured, wrapping wings and arms around his centaur. *Damn pony boy, getting me all emotional.* "Don't you even think about crying. You know I'm not good with the whole tears with sex thing."

Ness had obviously recovered, though, as he reached between Sin's legs to cup his now aching balls. "What *would* you be good with, love? What do you want today?"

"I want you, I want everything," Sin said, kissing him again. He ran his hands over Ness' broad shoulders and powerful chest, his fingers tickling through the soft curls. At some point in the past, he had thought of men with hairy chests as 'furry', but he couldn't think of those coarse curls as fur any longer. Ness' real fur started at the small of his back, where his human torso met the equine. It was dense and velvety soft there and on his hips, running up in a fine line from between his front legs onto his belly and stopping where his belly button would be if he were human.

Sin knew a lot of powerful people, powerful in magic, intellect, skill, authority, but few matched his Ness in sheer physical strength. He was so gentle in his manner that he doubted most people who knew him had any idea what he was actually physically capable of. The muscles in his arms and torso made him look quite buff, but still he knew his coworkers underestimated him. Ness' upper half appeared human, but the way he used his body was not, and the strength in him was not.

Ness leaned in to feather kisses down his throat, just along the pulse line where it drove Sin crazy, his large hands stroking around the sensitive joinings of Sin's wings. It was precisely that gentleness, that tenderhearted compassion that made people see less when they looked at Ness. Just because a centaur showed emotions, they thought it made him weak. Their loss.

"*Everything* is a little vague," Ness murmured as he nuzzled Sin's ear.

A hard shiver of anticipation rushed through Sin and he squirmed at the delicious rush of blood to his cock. He ran a foot down Ness' withers, petting with his bare toes. "I want my gorgeous stallion to mount me and fuck me. Better? Specific enough?"

Ness slid strong arms around him and held him close as he sucked on Sin's earlobe. "Definitely gives me a direction."

"I really hope that direction is going down." Sin arched his back as Ness' lips trailed across his collarbone. He brushed his fingers over Ness' nipples and pinched, encouraging him further.

"Need you…" Ness trailed off on a moan, rubbing his chest against Sin's. "I wish—"

"I know, it's okay, shh." Sin took that earnest, handsome face between his hands and crashed their lips together. Yes, they'd had that discussion, more than once, the one where Ness lamented that they couldn't do some of the things bipedal couples did, that Ness couldn't hold him if he were going to be inside Sin. It didn't matter. For Sin, it was all glorious, and the holding was just as nice after.

"Lie down for me, love? On your front?"

Sin folded his wings in close to make it easier to turn. He kissed Ness again, more tenderly this time, before he shifted and resettled. He left his wings spread out once he was on his front, mantling like a possessive raptor in his excitement.

Ness kept a hand on him, stroking his back and the sensitive membranes of his wings as he circled around to the end of the table. A soft whinny and a clatter of hooves, then Ness' front hooves settled on the shelves designed for them on either side of Sin, slightly below tabletop level. One of these days, he was going to convince Ness to record this. It had to be a magnificent sight, his centaur rearing up, powerful body covering him.

Sin's wings snapped back, curving over Ness' sides in a unique caress. His lover's skin was sensitive, every inch of it, and Sin never missed an opportunity to play that to its fullest. He wriggled back, sliding along the soft fur of Ness' chest and underbelly. A back hoof stamping on the carpet let him know that Ness was trying his best to be patient. He didn't *have* to be, Sin could take just about anything. Though sex with that dragon once? That had been a mistake. But Ness was terrified of hurting him and would never rush.

The other thing about centaurs? Poor things couldn't reach their own cocks, so they did tend to get anxious about getting things lined up. Hence the lube dropped onto the table beside Sin.

"Stay still, big guy. I'll take good care of you." Funny how the male on top was usually the one to say that. Sin chuckled to himself as he reached back to slick Ness up. Good thing he was ridiculously flexible on top of being a sex god. His wings caressed Ness' fur, so much softer than horsehair, every shiver of his equine muscles telegraphing down through the table.

Above him, Ness gasped and stamped again as Sin got him where he wanted him, a duet of moans joining the creaking of the table as Ness pushed inside.

That was an incredible feeling, so completely and utterly filled. Ness moved with him but carefully, much more carefully than Sin knew he wanted to. That was okay, though, at least at first. He might be a deviant, and experimental didn't begin to cover it, but having to take the time to heal was a pain, literally and figuratively.

Ness' strangled moan was so damn sweet, partly because he was so obviously holding back and reining in his frustrations so hard. "All right?" Ness gasped out. "Love, talk to me. Please."

"It's more than all right," Sin exhaled, inching his way down and moving a little faster now. "It's perfect, wonderful… You are so amazing." If Ness lamented a certain lack of intimacy in the way they had penetrative sex, Sin did try to make it up to him verbally. Sometimes the sensations were just so intense he forgot how to speak though, and Ness had to remind him. "You can go faster now, Ness, harder."

"Sure?"

"Hell, yeah, I'm sure. Go for it, babe."

He knew that Ness would never lose control in this position. Ever. But it did send a spike of pleasure through his core when Ness let out a wild yell and thrust in more forcefully. Sin grabbed on tighter with his wings and held on white-knuckled to the edges of the table so he wouldn't be shoved up with each thrust. He wasn't kidding or exaggerating. It was amazing.

Sin had already been primed from feeding earlier and he knew that as much as Ness enjoyed this, he enjoyed holding him and doing other things with him even more, so he didn't hold back anything once he got Ness to this point. His body reveled in each sensation at every point of contact. Relaxing let him take even more—he arched and moaned as he was so thoroughly mounted. The padding underneath was not just for comfort. He could press the front of his body into the yielding surface and he rubbed and humped eagerly as he was impaled again and again.

Between the leather at his front, the fur at his back and Ness, glorious Ness, he was overwhelmed with sensation. When Ness finally gave in and drove deep enough, the hard pounding against his prostate nearly sent him into convulsions of ecstasy.

"Close?" came the desperate, panting question from above him.

"Oh, yeah… Any second, babe… Just a little… Oh, goddesses… *Ness*!"

Certainly not the longest he had ever lasted but it didn't matter, the release felt too damn good, the feeling of being stretched so far and impaled so deep while his body spasmed and shuddered was the best feeling in the world. Well, almost the best. Being loved and cared for by his beautiful lover was the absolute best.

Ness cried out above him, his powerful body moving in short, jerking thrusts as his own orgasm overtook him. The flood of Ness' cum was hotter than any human's, giving the illusion of branding him from the inside, but it was just his own oversensitive body that made it seem so. Then Ness stilled, the harsh panting of his laboring lungs the only sound in the room.

Sin lay limp, his wings drooping to either side. As Ness slowly eased back, he knew he should push himself up, not take advantage, but he also knew if he just lay there, Ness would scoop him up, and he liked that feeling. He gave in to it and didn't move or resist when Ness lifted him in his arms. He wrapped his own arms around Ness' neck and snuggled close.

"You really are amazing. I love you so much."

Ness' breath hitched. He was often a little more vulnerable after sex. But he seemed to catch himself, nuzzling into Sin's hair. "I love you, too. Bed?"

Well-fed and well-fucked, Sin smoothed the hair back from Ness' forehead. "Bed. And don't you even look at the table and say we have to clean up first."

"Just this once," Ness said with a soft smile, and clopped through the apartment to their bedroom with the extra-large, custom king-size.

Chapter Two

A watery morning light cast the room in a dull murk as Kellen woke. He blinked and squinted his sensitive eyes even in that wan glow. Groaning softly, he stretched and yawned. This diurnal lifestyle was going to be the death of him. Still, having to be awake and mobile while the sun was in the sky was more than a fair trade for the life he'd left behind. Living in the crowded, noisy stink of New York City was far preferable to the place from which he'd come. He was unusual in that regard. One of the few crossovers ripped from his home world who was happy to be here, and not there.

Quietly Kellen rose and made his way down the hall to use the bathroom and have a quick wash. That accomplished, he went to the kitchen, which was his favorite room in the house. It was small, dark and warm, which weren't the reasons he liked it as much as the jars of honey in the cabinets. All different flavors, from rich, dark buckwheat to light, tangy orange blossom. This morning he chose a golden clover honey and took the jar and a spoon to sit at the table. He had learned from experience that humans found it odd when he ate spoonfuls straight from the jar, and he usually tried to find a quiet spot alone to eat when he was at work.

Kellen spooned up a good amount and savored the rich, sweet taste. So much food here it was hard to get used to having so much. The absence of hunger sometimes took him by surprise. He had more to eat since his crossing than he'd ever had in his life on the other side and he'd finally reached his full size and a healthy weight. The human physicians still thought of him as thin, but Kellen had put on pounds, actual pounds. His ribs no longer stuck out so prominently and his body showed the contours of his lean muscles rather than his bones. The steady diet of honey and milk whenever he wanted had improved his health in other ways as well.

For as long as Kellen could remember, his hair had been shorn to the scalp. He hadn't cut it since he'd crossed over, and now it was a rich, lustrous burnished auburn that hung in thick waves to the middle of his back. Kellen wasn't ashamed to be a little prideful of his hair. It was the first time he'd ever had anything to be proud of, and he relished both the look and the little sparks of happiness it brought him.

A glance at the clock told him he had better hurry or he would be late. Stuffing one more spoonful of honey in his mouth, he let it melt on his tongue as he went back to his bedroom and found clean hospital scrubs to wear. Some of the species he had met at the AURA headquarters medical facility modified their clothing to accommodate nonhuman shapes and sizes, but Kellen didn't have to.

He was small but the scrubs came in smaller sizes and yet were roomy enough that he could fold his wings flat and the shirt fit right over them. That was another thing that tended to worry humans. They thought his wings would be brittle and fragile because they looked like they belonged on an insect, albeit the largest dragonfly anyone in the modern world had ever seen. They were far from delicate, though, no matter how they looked, and Kellen had no trouble tucking them out of the way or even sitting on them. It did get uncomfortable keeping them folded under the shirt all day, but people didn't stare as much, and the staring made Kellen more uncomfortable than a bent wing. He grabbed a large wrapped ham from the refrigerator and his keys from the countertop then locked up behind him.

The building he lived in was old and shabby. In a former life, it had been a factory building and after the business had gone belly up, it had sat empty for many years before a developer had converted it into apartments. The building itself was squat and ugly and after an initial success as a pseudo artist community, it had slowly fallen into disrepair and the financial ruin of the owner had ensured its inevitable downfall until it had obtained the dubious status of one of the filthiest and most dangerous tenements in the city, even by New York standards. When a fire had gutted most of the lobby, it had finally been condemned and slated for demo. That had never happened. After some bureaucratic delays and wrangling, the city had decided that with a bit of repair and a paint job the place could be turned into housing for displaced crossovers. The first new resident had been a troll.

Trolls got a bad rap and deservedly so. Large, powerful creatures that smelled like a cross between an open sewer and a charnel house, but not nearly as stupid as most people assumed—their glee in destruction and chaos ensured most of them were imprisoned or killed if one came through an Event. Tok was quite different. He seemed to lack the innate trollish nature that drove his brethren to malicious destruction. Soon after moving into the building, he declared himself head of maintenance and took care of the janitorial duties and repairs. The building was as clean and safe as he could manage, and the crossovers and mages who started moving in soon overcame any reservations they had about the maintenance troll living in the basement.

Kellen took the elevator to the ground floor. He crossed the foyer then opened a door on the opposite side to a set of stairs that led down. His nose was nearly as sharp as an elf's and the faint musky, slightly rotten odor of troll wafted up to him despite all their efforts to kill the smell. When Kellen had first moved in, he almost couldn't bear it, and he'd helped Tok work out a system to reduce the pungent aroma. Once a week, Tok scrubbed the entire basement and stairwell with a strong disinfectant so the odor didn't cling to the walls and once a month Kellen gave him a supply of pixie dust that Tok mixed into a paste and rubbed all over his body. The combination worked pretty well. Humans could barely detect him at all, and those with a keener sense of smell like elves and pixies picked up on it, but weren't overwhelmed.

"Tok? I'm coming down," Kellen called when he reached about midway. At the bottom of the stairs were a set of steel double doors and ordinarily his light tread and even his call wouldn't have alerted anyone on the other side, but trolls had an exceptional sense of anyone approaching their lairs. It was damn hard to sneak up on one. Kellen heard the click of the latch on the other side being drawn back and the door opened silently on well-greased hinges. "I brought your meat," he said, lifting up the package.

Tok's gray-skinned face loomed above him, the lines carved into his forehead and the sides of his mouth deepened, which was Tok's version of a smile.

"Bone?" Tok asked.

"Yes, I got one with the biggest bone and the most fat I could find," he said, handing the package over, along with the smaller pouch of pixie dust.

"Milk?"

"No thank you, I can't today. I'm already running late for work."

Tok gave a little grunt of acceptance and Kellen waved over his shoulder as he trotted back up the stairs.

* * * *

Val scrubbed at his face with both hands as his phone rang for the tenth time in fifteen minutes. Small emergencies, often situations his staff could have handled, insisted on finding him instead. While it was wonderful to be needed and to have people want to rely on you, the constant barrage of bureaucratic nonsense was enough to drive an elf police captain insane.

"Hartgrove," he growled into the receiver, too irritated for niceties or diplomacy.

"Captain, this is Tenzin." Oddly enough, the yeti's voice sounded on the edge of irritation as well, and nothing besides his fiancé ruffled Tenzin.

Val sat up and cleared his throat. "Ah. Sorry, Tenzin. What can I do for you?"

"Your physical was scheduled for two this afternoon. Are you coming down to medical?"

Great fields and stones. Of course. He'd forgotten again. "I'm so sorry. The day got away from me. Could we reschedule?"

"Mandatory physical, Captain. We've already rescheduled you twice. Honestly, it's not as if the enforcement department is the only one that's busy."

Even though Tenzin said it kindly, Val cringed. He had become so wrapped up in the day-to-day handling of this crisis and that one, he'd been terribly inconsiderate. "I'll be right down."

"Thank you, Captain."

He left his suit jacket hanging over his chair since they would ask him to remove it anyway, and tried not to glower as he hurried through the department and down to medical.

* * * *

Generally speaking, Kellen enjoyed his job. Tenzin was an excellent supervisor and kept things running smoothly even in the midst of chaos. Not that there was usually a lot of chaos, unless there was an Event gone wrong.

AURA had sectioned the medical wing into areas designed to accommodate different maladies based mostly on whether the injury was physical or magical, and staff were assigned according to ability. Kellen was a class-three medimage, which meant he could work in the most dangerous sections. Today there were no curse victims to cleanse or magic burn sufferers to treat and so he had volunteered to help out with the enforcement department's staff physicals, which was very much appreciated as no one much liked dealing with grumpy officers who were 'wasting their time' in medical while there was real work to do.

"We're done then? Clean bill of health?" Officer Aello asked him. The siren had been fidgety and snappish, but at least she hadn't raised her voice this time.

"On the physical portion, yes, as far as I see," Kellen said. "Of course, other test results will take a day or two at the lab. You're cleared pending those results."

Kellen walked her out into the small waiting area near the front desk and handed the chart over to Tenzin's assistant.

"Is that the last for today?" he asked.

"One more. Captain Hartgrove is on his way."

Kellen felt a sharp twitch in his shoulder blades as his wings tried to give an agitated furl.

"I've got this one." Sinistrus sauntered up to snatch the folder from the rack but Tenzin covered the top of it before he could pull it free.

"No. I want Kellen to do the captain's exam," Tenzin said firmly.

Sin grinned at the yeti. "You sound as if you don't trust me to be entirely professional, Tenzin. I'm wounded. Just crushed."

"You might be if you try to needle the captain about his physical. It was difficult enough to get him down here."

"Aw, c'mon, Tenzi! A little ribbing's good for him. All stiff and starched all the time." Sinistrus pointed a thumb over his shoulder at Kellen. "And besides, the twerp's just about having a stroke thinking about conducting his physical. I can tell."

Kellen was glad his wings were safely tucked down. Things like embarrassment and annoyance were easy enough to control in his expression, but his damn wings always gave him away if they were free.

"I assure you I'm in no danger of a stroke," Kellen said calmly. He reached out to take the folder but Sin still had one hand on it and so did Tenzin. He lifted an eyebrow at the incubus, as if to ask if he were really going to make the matter a challenge.

Sin's frown was fleeting, soon replaced by his dazzling smile. He flipped his huge black wings and backed up, both hands in the air. "All righty, then. Little twerp it is. I'm overdue for break, anyway."

Before Kellen could retrieve the file, Sin bent down and whispered in Kellen's ear, "You be nice to that big hunk of beefcake. And try not to look at the goods too much. Though he's got a lot in the goods department. Hell, yeah."

With that, Sin straightened and swaggered away, whistling.

Kellen waited until he was around the corner and out of sight before he let out his breath. He had no idea why Sinistrus had taken a dislike to him but it had been like this since Sin joined the department. Tenzin had assured him it was nothing he had done and it was more to do with Sinistrus' personality. Kellen tried to avoid him as much as possible.

"Do you want me to speak to him?" Tenzin asked him as Kellen finally picked up the folder.

"No. Please don't. It's nothing," Kellen said.

The captain strode in not two seconds later, his quick steps and the fidgety way he toyed with his shirt cuffs screaming that he wanted to be gone as soon as he'd arrived. "Tenzin. Good to see you. Again, my apologies. Couldn't I simply sign a waiver or some such? I'm in perfect health. Better than I have been in years."

Before Tenzin could answer, Kellen stepped in. Tenzin had a soft spot for the captain and would hesitate to insist for fear of seeming as if he were haranguing his friend.

"You signed a waiver the last time, Captain," Kellen pointed out, tapping on the piece of paper in question in the file. "The rules say we can't give two in a row. If you'll follow me, I promise to have you done and back to work as quickly as possible."

Captain Hartgrove's jaw tightened, and he gave every indication of being about to refuse.

"Val," Tenzin said softly. "If I can get Kai to sit still for *his* annual, I'd certainly expect someone as disciplined as you to be able to."

"Ha. Shaming me into it, are you?" Val shook his head, but his annoyance seemed mostly at himself. "All right. Lead on."

Kellen hurried down the hall to the first available exam room and hid his nerves by shuffling through the papers in the folder. In some ways, the human world had wonders of medicine that were far beyond anything imagined in his home world. On the other hand, magic itself couldn't really be measured and gauged by these marvels. While humans and elves looked physically similar, they were still different species and he himself, as a pixie, was actually closer physiologically to an elf than a human. Still, things like the machines that measured blood pressure and thermometers to measure temperature were excellent in determining a baseline, once those baselines had been determined for each species.

Kellen had probably done a dozen exams that day, and not once had he even had a stray unprofessional thought, but he couldn't help remembering Sinistrus' words as Captain Hartgrove removed his shirt and laid it across the back of the chair. Damn him and his talk of *goods*. He stuck his nose back into the folder and stared at a blur of words just so he didn't have to look at the long, lean lines of the captain's muscular back for a moment.

Get your act together, Kellen!

He fumbled with setting out equipment on the countertop to avoid turning around. "Please have a seat on the table, Captain," he said in as cheerful a tone as he could manage. He heard the rustle of paper and finally took a breath, though when he turned, he nearly dropped the lightscope.

Good Goddess, he's perfect.

And very much taken, Kellen recalled. Everyone knew that. "All right, just a few pokes and prods and we'll have you out of here," Kellen nattered.

"The ribs are a bit sore still from that wild wyvern we came across last week." Captain Hartgrove gave him a crooked smile. "Please don't poke too hard. Really should leave winged crossovers to winged staff, I suppose. Though Sin and Hal were right there to take her down."

"Oh? Neither of them were injured, though, I take it," Kellen said conversationally as he managed to pull his eyes away from the perfect expanse of Captain Hartgrove's chest and drop back into professional mode. He examined the bruising along his side with a gentle touch. "Last week, you said? That must have been some hit you took. Are you not spending enough time with your mate? Do you need a healer to sing for you?"

The captain chuckled. "Thank you, no. They're nearly healed. I expect wyverns to attack tooth and claw and she *head-butted* me! Of all the things… I didn't expect it. She broke three ribs."

"Mm-hmm, I see. Still, I'd like to see this further along. You should spend the evening with your mate, and maybe tomorrow as well."

"Not a hardship, Kellen. None at all."

Kellen used the lightscope to peer into Captain Hartgrove's ears, being careful not to brush against them. Then he listened to his heart and lungs, tested his reflexes with a small rubber mallet, and all the while hummed softly under his breath, using the tones to weave in and around his patient's energy and check for any weaknesses or deficiencies. By all appearances, other than the rib injury, he was as healthy as he claimed.

The last portion was a blood sample, which Kellen accomplished quickly then pasted a little bandage over the puncture that was already closing, just to be thorough.

"See? That didn't take long at all," Kellen said, jotting a couple of notes in the file. He ran his finger down a column. "Just as a reminder, it's been three months since your rotation to donate blood. When your ribs are healed, please make sure you find some time to come back down."

"Ah. Of course." The captain pulled his shirt back on, covering up that wonderful expanse of muscle, much to Kellen's relief. "Really should talk to Tenzin about another blood drive." With that, he was striding down the hall again, all steadfast purpose and unstoppable drive. "Tenzin!"

Kellen twitched but stopped himself from flinching. Even so, he was glad the captain's back was turned to him. He had worked hard to stop cringing every time someone raised his voice, he didn't do it nearly so much anymore. In fact, the only time the old panic gripped him was when—

"There you are. I need your signature, physical signature, on these documents releasing Wolfheart from duty next week for the project. Apparently the wonders of technology were only invented in this world rather than embraced to the fullest, and an email won't suffice." Kai Hiltas waved the sheaf of papers he was holding at Valerian before he had even made it back to the front desk.

Kellen froze, clutching the file so tightly his knuckles ached. His stomach did a swooping dip and his breath locked in his chest. Oh, this was going to be a bad one.

No. This is stupid. He's not going to hurt you, idiot!

Kellen forced himself to breathe and paste a smile on his face that felt rather sickly. He stayed where he was, immobile. They would talk and leave, or leave and talk—either way they would take no more notice of him and that was exactly as it should be. There was nothing to fear here. He went through the mantra in his head. *Nothing to fear here.* No one would hurt him. He was free while he was at work.

The drow happened to glance up from pointing out where to sign, caught sight of Kellen, and scowled. "Oh, for pity's sake. I don't bite. Much. Anymore."

This time Kellen couldn't prevent the flush of embarrassment from creeping up his cheeks. He twitched his shoulders and his wings rustled softly. "I know. Pardon me." It took an effort of sheer will to make his legs carry him forward and actually pass the dark elf… The drow. He struggled not to drop his head deferentially but that was one battle he'd not been able to win yet. The subservience had been ingrained in him too many years to erase, no matter that Kai Hiltas personally hadn't made him feel that way. Kellen couldn't explain that to him, though, not when he could barely speak around the drow. And would the truth really make him feel any better? Kellen doubted it. Better to let Tenzin's lover believe he was simply terrified of him.

He thought he caught an irritated puff of breath after he passed by, but that might have been his overactive imagination. And, oh joy, there was Sin at the end of the hall to see the whole thing.

"There's our lovely drow!" Sin called out in a playful tone, though his gaze rested squarely on Kellen. "How's it hanging, gorgeous?"

"Quite well, thank you, my dear." Kai, clipboard tucked back under his arm, hurried down the hall toward the front desk, and, to Kellen's absolute shock, stopped to kiss Sin's cheek as he went by. "No time to talk. I'll see you a bit later."

Kellen immediately felt a wash of relief as the drow swept out of the doors, and on the heels of the relief was a wash of guilt. Kai Hiltas was not just a respected member of AURA and the head of the research department, he was also marrying Kellen's boss. He should have been able to face him without practically cowering on the floor at the sight of him. It was ridiculous and humiliating, and no matter how well he tried to hide it, Kai always saw right through his efforts, and he wasn't the only one.

He handed over the folder at the front desk. "Captain Hartgrove is cleared for duty, pending test results," he murmured.

"Kellen," Tenzin said softly. "If there's someone you need to talk to, we can make an appointment. The therapists downstairs are very understanding. No matter what it is."

Kellen shook his head. "I'm okay, thank you. If that's the last patient, I'll just take the samples over to the lab."

"Thank you, Kellen. Have a good night." Sometimes it was hard to tell with yeti expressions, but Tenzin was clearly worried. Kellen didn't have the slightest idea what to do about that.

He didn't have time to worry about it either. The day's samples had been labeled and packed in refrigeration and Kellen transferred them to a cooler marked with biohazard symbols along with dry ice. It probably wasn't necessary to go through all that when the lab was only in the basement of the building, but it was procedure. As a senior medimage, he didn't have to take the cooler himself, one of the aides could handle it, but Kellen always took the samples down.

As always at the end of day shift, Triton was leaning on the counter in the basement lab, drumming his fingers, watching the clock on his computer. The satyr usually managed to concentrate on his job during the day, but as five o'clock neared, his mind wandered to wine and orgies. Not his fault. Satyrs needed both to stay healthy and sane. Kellen simply understood his nature well enough to benefit from it.

"Hey there, I got some samples here. Not that you couldn't see that, huh?" Kellen joked. A pretty lame joke, and one he'd said before, but Trifon laughed anyway. "Where are you headed tonight?"

Trifon tossed his curled-horned head in an impatient gesture. "I've got a pair of nymphs waiting for me, Kell. Twins, can you believe it? And they say they have a couple of little faun friends too who'd probably stop by later. Damn it, I got so lucky I can't stand it, and I'm stuck here. I need a freaking shower at least before and…you know."

Kellen smiled, yes — he knew. Satyrs were very driven creatures on the whole. "You need a hand?" he asked, then quickly shook his head. "I mean with work."

"One of these days, Kells, you're gonna want to tap this." Trifon waved a hand at his whipcord-lean body. "Nah, I get it, bud. Just kidding. Would you mind taking the expired shit to the biohazard bin for me? While I get your samples checked in?"

"Sure. No problem." Kellen set the cooler down while Trifon rifled through papers and grumbled. The waste was kept in the locked walk-in fridge, but Kellen had done this often enough to know precisely in which corner of the top desk drawer Trifon kept the key and he snagged it before heading to the walk-in.

There was an antiseptic smell to the cold air inside the fridge. Stainless steel shelving lined the walls and neatly stacked parcels were labeled with the contents both mundane and magical. The medical wing of the AURA building was technically supposed to function only as an emergency facility and clinic, not a full hospital, but more often than not the human hospitals weren't equipped to deal with many magical creatures and AURA's medical staff took the brunt of those.

Consequently they were well stocked in treatments of a magical nature, and many of those items locked in the cooler would fetch a good price on the black market.

Kellen spotted the red and black bin marked in bold letters *Med Waste — Biohazard* on the floor, picked it up, then locked the walk-in behind him. He dropped the keys off on his way back through. Trifon was muttering and scribbling on papers as he logged in the contents of the sample cooler.

"Have a good night."

"Oh, I intend to, Kells." Trifon stopped his logging long enough to shoot Kellen a grin. "It's gonna be fabulous. You have a good night too. Do whatever pixies do for, you know, fun."

Kellen laughed and waved as he walked out. Funny how Trifon's teasing never bothered him. Not the same way Sinistrus' teasing did. He took the stairs up to the ground floor and walked to a service entrance at the back of the building. The doors were not locked from the inside, but had no handle on the outside so if he let them swing shut, he had to walk all the way back around to get back in. There was a brick right outside the door that was there for just that reason. He propped open the door and took the waste bin over to the depository. This too was gated and locked, with only a small space where the bins could be shoved through for pick-up by the incineration company. The space was also magically protected so anyone that got it in mind to shimmy their way in there would not be able to shimmy their way back out, and would sound an alarm to boot. Not that Kellen intended to do any shimmying. He placed the bin on the ground next to the slot and broke the sealing tape. The bin contained six bags of expired plasma, each labeled with species and blood type. He lifted out one bag of elf blood and one that was labeled faun and tucked them into his shirt, then closed the lid and pushed the container through the slot.

A wave of guilt hit him, bigger than the one he'd felt earlier after Hiltas had left medical. Technically, even if the expired blood was going to be destroyed, it was still stealing. If anyone found out about it, he would be fired. Hell, he might be jailed. He didn't know. That would be terrible. But it wasn't as if he had much choice. And besides, the waste wasn't being used to hurt anyone.

Chapter Three

Sin shifted the bottle under his other arm as he waited on the last landing for Ness. They *could* have taken the elevator up to Kai and Tenzin's condo. It was big enough for a centaur, but Ness hated the nasty looks he got from the other snooty tenants. They always took the stairs.

"Hey," Sin said as Ness maneuvered himself around the final turn, looking far too hot for visiting friends in his tight burgundy Henley and his black leather jacket.

"Hmm?"

"Have I told you how gorgeous you are?"

Ness laughed and took his hand as he ducked under the doorway out of the stairwell. "Not tonight. Not yet."

"You are, though. And I'm having a hard time not being able just to rush back home and ravish you." Sin made a show of adjusting himself. "A very hard time."

"Behave, you horn dog." Ness laughed as he said it and Sin took it as a compliment. "A few hours. You can manage."

Huge, enthusiastic yeti hugs and somewhat more reserved drow ones greeted them when the condo door opened and Sin handed over the bottle of wine once he could breathe again.

"You need help in the kitchen, Tenzi? How are you both?" Sin took Kai by both shoulders and got a good look at him. "The big bad drow looks exhausted."

"Dinner will be out in a moment, Sin. Stay there," Tenzin called from the kitchen. "And the big bad drow has been obsessing over wedding details and not sleeping as much as he should."

"I suppose we're not shocked," Ness said from where he was carefully easing down onto the cleared spot of carpet beside the oversize coffee table. Eating at a human-height dining table was awkward for him, so Kai and Tenzin always made certain there was room for him to recline his horse portion on the floor.

Kai sniffed in mild offense. "It's not the easiest thing, melding traditions. Of course, I won't insist on the bloodletting a drow bonding ceremony would include. And Tenzi has graciously agreed to omit the throwing of large rocks from a cliff that a yeti marriage requires. But it's not an easy thing."

"Obsessing over the exact shade of chrysanthemum for the aisle vases is taking it too far," Tenzin said gently as he began bringing in covered dishes from the kitchen.

There may have been some muttering about Brianna not being satisfied either as Kai hurried to the kitchen to help, but Sin couldn't quite catch it. He chuckled as he settled next to Ness and snuggled up to his furnace-warm side.

"Before Kai gets lost in regaling you with wedding details..." Tenzin settled, then grunted as several flower fairies immediately popped into view around his head to land on his shoulders. "Our lovely Sin, now that we're among friends and not at work, can you tell me why you insist on tormenting Kellen so terribly?"

"Oh, I dunno." Sin picked up a spicy fried mushroom with his claws and popped it in his mouth. "I think I'm pretty good at tormenting him."

Ness nudged him. "Be serious, love. Why do you pick on him? Even I've seen it."

"Look, I just don't like everyone, okay?" Sin spread his hands when everyone gave him side eyes. "Took me a bit to warm up to Val, right?"

"You had good reason to be angry with Val," Ness said as he reached for an oat muffin. "I don't think Kellen ever actually caused you harm."

Sin heaved a dramatic sigh. "Fine. He's absolutely useless as a paramedic."

"Not everyone is suited for emergency field medicine," Tenzin said gently.

Ness leaned over to kiss the top of Sin's head. "You are because you're brave and don't stop to think."

"Hey!" Sin swatted at an equine flank.

"Oh, dear. I didn't mean it that way." Ness flushed darkly while the others laughed. "You don't overthink. When someone needs help, you just do instead of overanalyzing. Not everyone can be that sort of heroic."

"Good recovery." Sin grinned up at his flustered lover. "Yeah, I get it. He's not the first responder kind. But the little guy's just sneaky. He doesn't look people in the eye. He flinches at the weirdest times. I don't trust him."

Tenzin frowned as he ladled vegetable panang onto a plate and set it in front of Kai. "Eat, beloved, before you waste away. About Kellen. I believe it's deep-seated trauma, something so terrible that he doesn't want to have to talk about it, since that would mean acknowledging it."

"Tenzi's so often right about these sorts of things." Kai took up his fork, toying with his food rather than eating yet. "But this time, I have to disagree. There is something uneasy about him. Something beyond old fears."

"You hardly see him thirty seconds out of any week," Tenzin protested. "What could you possibly base this on?"

"Ah, love. A drow knows deception. There's something not quite right about that pixie."

Tenzin sighed and pointed to Kai's plate. "Eat. Or I'll feed you myself. In front of company." He waited while Kai actually started on his food, then said, "Even so, his work is exemplary. Whatever he's hiding must be personal and it's none of our business. I'm asking as a favor, please, Sin. Just try to be a little less contentious. Pick on someone who can return the teasing."

"Great, wonderful. That means I have to go bug Wolfheart every day." Sin tried for a grin but no one was buying it. "Okay. All right. I'll try. No promises, but I'll try."

The rest of dinner was, indeed, all about wedding preparations, and that was fine with Sin. He could sit back and think and the only conclusion he could draw was that the little twerp had complained to Tenzin about him. The old Sin would've held a grudge a mile wide. The new, happy Sin? He wouldn't pursue vendetta, but he was going to keep an eye on that twerp. If the pixie was kicking off drow instincts, there was sure as shit *something* going on.

* * * *

Rask Tiranis lived in a modern condo building of shining glass and steel in Manhattan's upper west side, only a short trip by subway from AURA Headquarters. Kellen was glad the trip didn't take long. It gave him less time to dread arriving. He hated the feel of the plastic plasma bags against his skin, but he didn't dare transfer them to his messenger bag in case someone snatched it. Not only did he not want the blood to fall into unknown hands, that might do who-knew-what with it, but he didn't want any weird rumors to start, no matter how unlikely it would be connected back to him in a city this size. Not to mention the consequences of arriving at Rask's place without the blood.

The late-afternoon sun was low enough in the sky to turn the whole building into orange flame so bright it was hard to look at. As clean, beautiful and spacious as the interior of condos were, Kellen wouldn't have traded his own rundown home. The people who lived in his building were almost all crossovers, and they didn't look at him suspiciously or avoid eye contact like they did here.

The security guard stopped him and looked at his ID, despite having seen him there before, and slid the keycard on the elevator for him only after he'd called up to Rask to make sure he was allowed to go up. Kellen tried not to take it personally. The man was only doing his job.

The elevator doors opened on a private hallway with lush carpeting, expensive designer paper on the walls and even more expensive modern art pieces. He approached the door at the end with reluctance. Just as he lifted his hand to knock, the door opened and Shawna was there, pulling him inside. "Hurry up, the master is waiting for you."

Stereotypical drow tastes would have tended toward a gothic nightmare in decorating—black, heavy furnishings, rich fabrics, macabre designs. Not for Rask. Everything in his condo was lean, modern, streamlined and elegant, much like the owner.

"Did you get it?" Shawna asked him.

Kellen resisted the urge to ask if she really thought he'd show up without the blood. Pissing her off was not as dangerous as pissing Rask off, but she was part of the coven and he was only a lowly familiar. Talking back would not bode well for him.

"Yes, I have it. Elf and faun blood this time," he told her, removing the bags from inside his shirt with some relief. His own body heat had warmed the contents from the cool temperature of the refrigerator and he hated the feel of it warm against him almost more than when it was cold.

Shawna took the bags and sauntered into the living room, holding them aloft like a prize. Kellen was pretty sure that Rask despised her and her frivolous, greedy attitude, but with Shawna came wealth. She was the one who'd made it possible for him to buy the penthouse condo.

"Look what he brought—elf and faun," Shawna said, as if Rask and the others in the room hadn't been perfectly able to hear him say that himself. She dropped them on the table and flounced down on the long sofa with an overly dramatic sigh. Kellen could almost feel the muscle under Rask's eye twitch in annoyance, but his expression was bland when he turned from his computer.

Rask could have been a brother to Kai Hiltas, but then many of the drow held similar traits. The long, white hair and coal-dark skin were the same, as were his milk-pale eyes with hints of opalescence. Those unfamiliar with the drow might not have seen any difference at all, but Kellen had lived among them long enough to see how Rask had more of a tilt to his eyes and his cheekbones were sharper, his chin more pointed. Overall it gave him a harsher look, and Kellen thought it fit him well.

"More elf blood? I told you to bring something more exotic," Rask said, the smoothly neutral tone sending a shiver down Kellen's spine.

"I would have if there had been any available, master," Kellen said.

Rask drummed the tips of his claws on the arm of his chair. "You know how important this is, *peshk*, and yet you continue to fail in this very simple task I ask of you."

Kellen remained perfectly still. Not a swallow or a nervous twitch to give him away.

"Rask…" Miris, the sylph, picked up the bag of elvish blood. "This is Vasse blood. It is rather different from those common Aelfe."

Kellen became so still he hardly drew breath. If they had still been back home, Rask would have shredded her for daring to speak out of place, for daring to sound almost as if she were defending a lowly slave. They were not home, though, and Rask simply gave her a cool smile.

"Of course. We shall see how it reacts."

Miris, oblivious as ever to the seething rage Rask hid so thoroughly behind his mild expression, smiled at Kellen. He didn't acknowledge it, he never did. These others hadn't known Rask from before this world, not like Kellen. They had no idea at all of what he was capable. Sometimes he envied their naïveté. Mostly he just did what he was told and tried not to do anything to draw Rask's attention.

"What else?" Rask prompted him.

Kellen reached into his pocket and pulled out a small, clear container. The contents were visible, a fine shimmering powder, mostly white with some purple specks. No one actually recoiled, but there was a subtle drawing back. None of them wanted to risk accidental contact with the pixie dust, especially not his dust.

Rask stood and took the container from his hands. He was not foolish enough to open it right then, but he did give it a little shake, causing Shawna to squeak and clutch her necklace.

"This is all of it?" The question was spoken softly while his cold, cruel eyes pierced Kellen, pinning him to the spot.

"Of course, master," Kellen answered in a respectful murmur.

Rask reached out and grabbed a hank of Kellen's hair as fast as a snake striking its prey. He backed him up two steps until Kellen's backside made contact with the wall and he held the container up at eye level for Kellen to see.

"I know precisely how much dust a pixie your size sheds, *peshk*. Do you think to play me for a fool?" Rask hissed in his face.

"No! No, master... I swear, that's all of my shed. It's this world, this climate." Kellen winced and gasped as Rask let go of his hair in favor of the curve of his ear. His whole body shuddered with pain and fear. The feeling was not akin to a blow to the groin, but not so far off in intensity. The nerve endings of his ears were every bit as sensitive as an elf's and the twist of pain went through him head to toe.

"So you have said," Rask murmured while Kellen tried not to squirm or cry out. "If I find you are lying to me, *peshk*, I will skin you. The customs of this world be damned."

Kellen bit back a cry as Rask twisted his ear cruelly. "I swear I'm not, master," he gasped out.

"As if your word is worth anything." Rask hissed. He shook the container lightly one more time, as if he could weigh the amount of dust with his hand alone, then shoved Kellen to one side, making him stumble and fall to his knees.

Shawna sighed and shook her head. "You just have to go and put him in a bad mood, don't you?"

Kellen didn't bother to answer. There was no point in contradicting her, since she worshiped the ground Rask walked on and buried her jealousies in barbed comments.

"Get up and get ready for the ritual. At least do something worthwhile tonight."

"Sir?" A soft voice came from the doorway to what Rask called his library. "I have the data analysis you asked for. Did you want to see it? Before?"

Niles didn't even glance Kellen's way — his eyes were all for Rask. The young human was tall and painfully thin with white-blond hair and eyes such a pale gray they were nearly silver. Shawna often taunted him that he was just a drow wannabe.

Rask wordlessly took the sheet of paper Niles was holding. Kellen remembered a time several months ago when Niles had handed him a tablet with his data results and Rask had sneeringly taunted him about his reliance on electronics. He'd gone on to rant about the lost arts of creating on paper. It was nothing but a tantrum meant to make Niles feel inferior but it had worked.

But now Rask ran a claw through Niles' hair and murmured soft words of praise in his ear. It was either genius or sociopathic ugliness, but Rask made it work, keeping his followers on edge, belittling them when they became too comfortable, praising them when they sank too low. All the while, he made certain to set them against one another, which he did now as Shawna seethed at the attention he paid Niles and Niles nearly melted into a puddle of pleased goo.

Kellen had to wonder at their blindness. They saw Rask as brilliant and powerful, the one person who would lead them all to their hearts' desires, and ignored his cruelty and narcissism—whereas Kellen had no choice but to stay in Rask's thrall. They willingly chose to stay. He couldn't understand that.

There wasn't much more time to ponder the inner workings and psychology of the coven, however. There was work to be done. They all adjourned to the ritual room, Kellen following last. Clothes were removed and robes donned while Rask carefully mixed the dust Kellen had given him into a paste that would be used to protect them for any escaping magical backlash. A circle might ordinarily be used to keep any harmful energies at bay, but a circle would not be cast tonight. Their purpose wasn't to contain, but to release.

Kellen removed his scrubs and set them down. There was no reason he couldn't also wear a robe, or even keep his clothes on, except Rask preferred to keep him naked. He knew it was supposed to be humiliating, but in their own world he'd spent so much time naked at Rask's feet it no longer mattered to him.

Rask glanced up from his mixing and heaved an irritated sigh. Someone was still missing. "Otori!" he called, the tone sweeter than his expression would have suggested.

A scrabble of claws on marble came from the hall and the kitsune careened around the corner, half a chicken leg stuffed in his mouth. Otori's several tails waved madly behind him as he removed what may have been dinner or a toy for him, and whispered, "Flowers. It's all in the flowers. Even though you don't always see it. Purple. Sure. Can be. Not always. Oh, no."

"Of course, Otori," Rask soothed. "We're getting ready. Put your chicken away and take off your kilt."

Shawna had finished undressing and had slipped on a silky black robe, which she left open to show off voluptuous curves and creamy smooth skin. She usually only had eyes for Rask, flirting and vying for his attention, but tonight she was unnervingly focused on Kellen. She walked over to him, hands on her hips, and Kellen braced for whatever unpleasantness she was about to unleash.

"That hair is very unflattering. I want you to cut it."

"No," Rask said before Kellen could think of any reply. He turned around and pinned Shawna with an unblinking and merciless gaze. "I've grown to like it. It provides a use." He smirked at her and Kellen could practically feel the crackle of her anger sizzle off her. Rask needed her, needed her money, but that did not mean he was willing to indulge her to the point she gained any power over him. He used her jealousy skillfully.

"How crude!" Shawna spat at last.

Otori, now stark naked, ran a hand over the fall of hair at Kellen's back. "Pretty, pretty, pretty. Sunfire fur."

"Place, Otori," Rask said sharply and the kitsune scurried to his spot for the ritual. Power radiated from Otori in waves, but something in his crossing had put cracks in his sanity. He was one of those beings who had slipped through AURA's support system, and Rask had found him collecting plastic bottle caps in a den he had made under a footbridge. Sometimes he had flashes of sanity, but this didn't seem to be one of his better days.

Kellen wasn't sorry in the least for the distraction.

Even though they were forgoing the magical protection of a cast circle, they still gathered around to form one out of convenience and habit. Kellen took his place at Rask's left side. His part in the rite was simple. Be silent and do as he was told. This included swallowing the contents of the vial Rask handed him. He grimaced at the bitter taste and took a steadying breath. He had enough experience as a familiar by now that he probably didn't need the potion, but Rask insisted. In order for him to become the conduit they needed, his personality must be thoroughly suppressed so there was no risk of him taking control and directing the magic. In truth, if he had to do, this he preferred the numbing influence of the elixir.

As they all settled in and began to shift their awareness, Rask went around with the paste he had made from Kellen's dust, drawing protective sigils on each of the coven members. Pixie dust had several magical properties, depending on the pixie. Kellen's dust was rather unique. It didn't heal or bring luck or even charm people into lust or love. His dust dispelled magic, and if mixed correctly, could be used to either break a hex or prevent magic being cast onto someone or something. Very useful stuff for a coven that was about to force their collected wild magic through him.

He started to drift as the soft chanting began to weave together and grow in power. He blinked and the chalices seemed to appear from nowhere. He'd lost time, he knew, but didn't really care. The blood was being poured and he willed the numbness to take over completely. He didn't want to see them drink, didn't want to feel the flood of magic coursing through him uncontrolled by him. He closed his eyes and drifted passively. In the morning he would wake, dress and leave, alone, and he could go back to work and have his pretend life until the next ritual.

Chapter Four

Ever since Kellen had finished his training courses and had begun work at AURA, he had not once taken an unscheduled day off work. He liked his job and he liked the people he worked with, generally, and since he was rarely ill, he never saw the need to miss work. Today was the first time he had considered asking if he could leave early.

Sinistrus had gone from his usual loud, teasing, slightly bothersome self to a feigned politeness that was downright chilly. Kellen knew at once that Tenzin must have spoken to him, even though Kellen had asked him not to. The way he joked and chatted with everyone else as they went about their work and either completely ignored Kellen or used only clipped, direct sentences if he had to speak to him was almost unbearable.

To make matters worse, Rask had left a reddened bruise on his ear and one of his claw tips had scratched him just below on his neck. Per medical department policy, he had to keep his hair braided at work, so there was no hiding the marks. Since there were not many elves in medical and he was the only pixie, he didn't have to endure too many coy knowing looks or half-hidden snickers. But there were some, and Sin obviously knew a thing or two about elves and pixies if the way he pointedly looked at Kellen's ear, then smirked at him before going back to ignoring him was any indication.

By lunchtime he was imagining every laugh he heard was about him, and he was certain the off-color joke he overheard Sin telling one of the nurses about elves thinking tattoo shops that did ear piercings were the equivalent of some sort of perverted sex club was a jab at him. For a moment he pictured himself swaggering over to them and grinning, maybe even flirting, letting them think they had discovered his 'secret'. He could wink and hint that was what he liked to do in his off hours, find a partner who liked rough sex and kink. Maybe then they wouldn't treat him like such an outsider.

The little fantasy fell apart and he let it go. He didn't know the first thing about swaggering, and he was sure Sin wasn't about to teach him. He turned around at the door to the breakroom before they noticed him and decided to go for a walk in the park instead.

By human standards, the park was a bit of wild hemmed in by the city—a huge, green space to break up the unrelenting concrete. It was a lovely place, pockets of beauty and peace, but it was not in any way wild. That was something Kellen did miss about his home, the vastness of the wild. He had to admit, though, that his memories of that wild were dimmed by the years he'd spent underground before crossing over. If he closed his eyes it was easier to remember.

He flexed his shoulders as his wings twitched restlessly in the confines of his shirt. That would be so nice, to flit from tree to tree again. It had been so long. Sighing, he found a spot he liked that was tucked away off the main trail — it was usually empty and quiet, and today was no different. He settled down amid the roots of a tall oak and closed his eyes. Thinking of the wild and the feel of the trees under his hands and feet and the wind under his wings never failed to soothe him.

* * * *

Sin watched the pixie leave the department with a puzzled frown. He was being polite — he hadn't teased him at all today — and it wasn't making anything better. It was making things worse with Kellen. What the hell was he doing wrong? Twitchier than ever, the twerp wasn't just shutting down when Sin was in the room. He was *cringing*. Damn, damn and more damn.

Snarky comments? No, none of those. Professional criticism? Nope. He hadn't made any. Jokes at Kellen's expense? No. Stupid nicknames? None of those either. As Sin ticked off the list of things he hadn't done, something hit him. *The ear. The damn ear...*

Yeah, for Sin, sex was all the yummies in life. Food and fun, companionship and fulfillment. But he wasn't naïve. It wasn't that way for everyone. What if the pixie kid was in a destructive relationship? Abusive? What if that was what made him skittish and weird?

Drumming his claws on the counter by the front desk, Sin rustled his wings in agitation. Did he tell Tenzin what he suspected? Was that what you did in a professional setting? Wait…no. Tenzin was the most compassionate being in the universe. If an abusive lover was the problem, Kellen wouldn't be able to hide it from Tenzi. Yeah. That sounded right. Tenzin was the supervisor and it wasn't any of Sin's damn business.

He just wished his stomach didn't hurt thinking about it.

"Well. Fuck." Sin gulped down the last of his coffee and checked the appointment calendar before hurrying after Kellen. Not that he thought the twerp would run into trouble on break. Just to be sure everything was as it should be.

Kellen wasn't far ahead, a bit down the block and across the street, heading for the park. Still not a problem. Most AURA folks took breaks in the park sometimes. They all needed to get out of the concrete and steel towers. But, yeah, the park was for other things besides sitting on a bench, soaking up some rays. Grumbling under his breath, Sin hurried across the street after him, then slowed. The pixie wasn't looking around but seemed to have a definite destination in mind. He had a moment of inner debate. He really should make himself known, but he had a feeling that if he did that, Kellen would turn around and go back, or change wherever he was going, and Sin wanted to know what he was up to.

Following him was easy, until he turned off the path. Even someone as oblivious as Kellen appeared to be would certainly hear Sin moving through the leaves and brush, so he waited. Gave him a good head start, then followed him in. He didn't know what he expected to find, secret rendezvous maybe, or something that confirmed his suspicions that Kellen was up to something nefarious. What he didn't expect was to find a tucked-away nook and Kellen leaned up against one of the big old oaks looking either asleep or maybe meditating.

Now Sin just felt sneaky and stupid. He rubbed a hand over the back of his neck and cleared his throat. "Hey. Um. Nice day. Out here. For being out here."

The pixie didn't jump or yelp or even cuss, but his eyes popped open, the pupils fully dilated, and his whole body went rigidly tense then slowly eased down a notch. It was the most controlled startle reflex Sin had ever witnessed.

Kellen looked left and right, like he expected Sin to have followed him out here with backup or some absurd thing, then he stood quickly and fluidly, like a cat stretching.

"Am I late? I—I thought I only closed my eyes for a second."

Sin narrowed his eyes, wondering what the hell he was missing. If the kid needed sex, he could've dealt with that kind of read. But he wasn't good with everything else. "Nope. Not late. Just came out here myself."

Kellen shifted his eyes again, as if still expecting others to bleed suddenly out of the surrounding brush. "Here?" He was clearly confused. "Why? Um, I mean, I didn't know anyone else came here."

So, you come here often? Sin managed to bite back the lame joke. "Just stumbled through, looking for a quiet spot."

Squeak.

"Um…" Sin blinked at the pixie. "Did you squeak?"

Kellen's eyebrows drew together, like they did when Sin teased him. He started to shake his head then stopped as they both heard another squeak-chirp.

Frowning, Kellen looked down at the leaf litter. There was nothing at their feet, but they heard the sound again, and Sin watched Kellen slowly turn and track it, taking a few careful steps around the roots of the tree, then stop.

"Hello, oh…" Kellen said, crouching and gently reaching out a hand. "Oh no… You're far too little to be out on your own," he said, standing with something tiny and furry in one hand. He looked up. "It's a squirrel. He must have fallen out of the nest."

Sin leaned in to peer at the little fluff ball. "Huh. Poor little guy. Hold up."

Without waiting for Kellen to tell him it was a stupid idea, Sin tucked his wings in tight, leaped, and snagged the lowest branch on the oak. He swung up and shimmied up to the messy bunch of sticks and leaves most likely to be a squirrel nest. When he reached it and peered in, the chain of events became painfully obvious. Bits of fur and…squirrel lay scattered in the nest. Some messy predator had made short work of mom and siblings. The little one Kellen held had escaped by falling out into the leaf cover below.

He blew out a long breath, let himself hang from the branch and dropped to the ground. "Um. Well. Hate to tell you, little guy, but Mommy's not coming for you."

Kellen looked at him with those big green eyes and blinked, then looked down at the baby squirrel that had just barely grown his fur in. "He'll die on his own." He stated the obvious. "We keep infant formula in supplies, I wonder if he'd take some of that."

"Dunno." Sin scratched fretfully at the base of one of his horns. "Don't know much about babies. He's a cute little bugger, though, isn't he?" He backed off a step, too aware suddenly of how far he'd invaded Kellen's space. "Not that I care much about baby tree rats. But, you know, I guess medical staff can't let a baby just *die*."

"Rats are very intelligent creatures, you know, if that was meant to be an insult."

"Oh, for the mother's sake." Sin rolled his eyes. "I've known a lot of rats personally. Happens when you're homeless, out of your mind, and living in a dumpster. It's a joke. I got nothing against rats."

Kellen lifted his head and stared at him. He looked angry, his eyes flashing and his lips pressed together. He was cradling the little thing carefully to his chest and Sin realized it was the first time Kellen had actually full-on looked him in the eye. Then he swung around and stalked off toward the path. "I'm going to take care of him."

"Well, good for you." Sin caught up in two long strides. "You're acting like I said you shouldn't. Which I didn't fucking say. What your problem with me is, I don't know. Don't really care right now. But you need to take baby tree rat to Tenzin. Sure, we got formula. But it's not *squirrel* formula."

Kellen didn't stop moving but he shot an incredulous look Sin's way. "*I'm* not the one with the problem. *You* are the one with the problem. You make comments. You call me *twerp*. You *tease* everyone, but when you tease *me*, you mean the words you say."

"Fine. I don't like you. I said it." Sin shrugged with both shoulders and wings. "I don't have to like you to work with you."

Kellen did come to a halt then, for just a moment. His face paled then flushed bright red all the way to the tips of his ears. For one horrible moment, Sin thought he was going to burst into tears but then he started walking again. "Fine. I didn't ask you to like me."

"You didn't have to go telling Tenzin to talk to me either," Sin said.

"I didn't. I told him not to." He shook his head. "You mean he did anyway? Is that why you've been so…so *polite*, today?"

"For all the fucks' sakes! I'm just trying to be *professional*! I'm so damn sorry if that offends you." Sin stopped his wildly waving arms and stuffed his hands in his pockets. "Look. If you want me to be rude, I can do that. If that works better. Tenzin said to lay off. That I was picking on you too much."

"I don't want you to be rude. I don't want you to be polite. I just want you to treat me the same as you do everyone else."

Sin didn't stop walking, but he pulled a hand out of his pocket to point at Kellen. "Then stop being a twitchy, sneaky, clammed-up little twerp. I never know what you're thinking. I never know what's going on with you. I don't tr—" He stopped himself, wondering if saying he didn't trust Kellen was going too far. Way over his head here. Just making things worse, probably.

They had been walking faster and faster as they talked, argued, and now Sin noticed they were almost at a jog. Was he just in a hurry to get the tree rat tended to, or was Kellen literally trying to run away from him? All right, enough. He needed to talk to Ness. He was the only one Sin could trust to tell him if he'd gone too far, or was within his rights. Against his instincts that told him to keep on the pixie until they got to the bottom of the issue, he stopped, and Kellen continued without another word.

Yeah, this called for a Ness visit. Sin let Kellen rush back to medical without him and instead went up to the AURA enforcement squad room on the sixth floor.

Sergeant Nestor, in all his uniformed, in-charge glory, was at the command center, engrossed in something on his screen.

"Hey, babe?" Sin gave a cheeky wave to the dispatcher and leaned on the counter beside Ness. "You have a second for a poor, socially challenged incubus?"

Ness glanced up over his glasses, a move Sin always found ultrasexy for some weird reason. "Hello, there. I'm trying to get scheduling done for Kai and Tenzin's wedding this Saturday. Took a bit of juggling, but I'm almost there. What did you do?"

Sin tried to keep from squirming under Ness' serious gaze as he told him about the weird morning with Kellen. "And then he dashes off. I mean, I know I made it worse. I don't know how to make it better. Should I be trying to make it better?"

"Oh, my darling sex demon, what am I supposed to do with you?" Ness stomped a hoof softly and gave an equine snort. "For now, I'd say leave it. He's upset and you'll only make things worse. You went out with the best intentions, since you were concerned, but really? Maybe let Tenzin know what you suspect and let him deal with it. Or not."

"So I fucked everything up and you're saying I shouldn't do anything?"

"Don't sulk. It's adorable and we're at work." Ness reached over the high counter to tuck a strand of hair behind Sin's ear. "Just give him some space. Try not to treat him differently than anyone else. It'll be all right. Eventually."

Sin rolled his eyes. "Thanks for that. But okay. I'll do the whole 'this is my dance space, this is your dance space' thing with the kid."

"Doubtful he'd get the movie reference," Ness said on a laugh and turned back to his screen. "I'll see you after work, love. I really need to get this finished."

Well, okay. Sin could admit when he'd been an ass. He'd even consider apologizing, but Ness had said to leave it alone. He had to stop being like a little kid picking at a scab and leave it the hell alone.

* * * *

Kellen caused a small flurry as he rushed into medical. Usually when someone was moving that fast through the doors it was an emergency. It *was* kind of an emergency. He didn't know how long the squirrel had been out of the nest but he felt cold and weak, although Kellen's hands were giving him back some warmth.

"Tenzin! I need your help!" The tall, broad yeti was usually so serene that people mistook him for being slow, but he could move extremely fast when he needed to and he was beside Kellen at once. "I found him in the park, fallen out of his nest, and I don't know how badly he might be hurt," he said, lifting a shaking hand to show Tenzin the small creature he held.

"Poor little thing." Tenzin's shaggy white head temporarily obscured the squirrel and Kellen's hand as yeti magic glowed over the little orphan. "You have a baby girl, there, not a boy. She doesn't appear injured beyond some bruising, but we really should try to return her to her mother, Kellen. That's always the best thing."

Kellen swallowed hard when Tenzin glanced up at him. He didn't know why it was so difficult to say that the mother was dead, but Tenzin understood without a word.

"Oh. I see. Well, I suppose we're the mother now." Tenzin gestured toward the front desk. "Sit with her a moment. Warmth and hydration first."

When Tenzin returned, he had a little box filled with a nest of washcloths, one of the tiny feeding syringes they used for injured flower fairies, and a bottle of Pedialyte. He gave Kellen instructions on how to get his foundling rehydrated, sent one of the human aides out to pick up puppy formula, and went back to work, leaving Kellen with his tiny bundle of squeaks.

It was a quiet afternoon, thankfully, and Kellen spent most of it catching up on paperwork while tending his new 'patient', who was soon looking quite a bit livelier than when Kellen had found her. He tried not to hover protectively when the other nurses and staff wanted a peek at the fuzzy baby but eventually he relaxed when the squirrel didn't seem in any distress over the attention. As the afternoon wore on, though, he did have other duties to attend to besides feeding the squirrel. He was reluctant to leave her, even in Tenzin's capable hands. While he was sure the yeti would take excellent care of her, if there was a sudden emergency or they got unexpectedly busy, Tenzin wouldn't be able to pay attention to a baby squirrel too. He solved the problem by tucking her into his breast pocket and taking her with him to do rounds. She was quite content to sleep in the snug pouch.

At the end of the day, he started to realize he had a problem. He could take her home, but he couldn't leave her alone there if he was summoned to Rask, and he certainly couldn't take her with him *there*. Tok could probably watch her for him, but underground in the dark was no place for a baby for long. He was going to have to give her to someone who could care for her around the clock, and he was surprised to find how upsetting the thought was.

"Tenzin, I can't take her home with me. They...don't allow pets." It was a small lie. He could have a pet if he paid a deposit, and even if he didn't, Tok wouldn't care, but it was more important that he find someone who would keep her safe.

"Ah." Tenzin folded his hands in front of him as he thought. "She's certainly welcome to be here during the day where medical staff can look after her. But after shift, with fewer staff... Hmm." He raised his head and spoke to the air. "Brianna?"

Not five seconds later, the air around his head erupted with flower fairies in jewel-bright tones. One in bright pink hovered in front of Tenzin's face, zipped in to give him a kiss on the nose then resumed her hover spot.

"Good afternoon, beautiful Brianna," Tenzin said with a smile. "Our Kellen found an orphan squirrel baby this morning. And while we're happy to watch over the baby during the day, I wondered if I might ask you and your troop to babysit at night for a bit?"

Brianna zipped to her troop where there was much excited chittering. As one, they swooped down on Kellen, peering into his pocket with little cooing noises and zipping up and down in front of Kellen's face.

"What are they doing?" Kellen whispered.

"They're assessing." Tenzin chuckled. "To see if you're a worthy substitute squirrel mother."

Tapping her foot in the air, Brianna hovered directly in Kellen's vision. She nodded, shook her finger at him, then zipped back to Tenzin, chittering.

"She approves, but says she's watching you. And they'll be happy to babysit." Tenzin listened a moment more. "Excellent thought. Kellen, she says to bring the baby down to the woodland counseling room at the end of the day. They'll stay there with her."

It was such an odd mixture of relief and reluctance Kellen felt as he took his squirrel down to counseling and tucked her into her box.

"You'll keep her warm, won't you?" he asked the chittering fairies. "I know it's temperature controlled in here but..." He tapered off as Brianna hovered in midair and still managed to tap her foot on an imaginary surface. "Right. Okay... I'll just leave her in your hands then," he said, glancing back over his shoulder a few times on the way out.

By the time Kellen was jogging up the stairs from the subway, he was already wondering if Brianna would take it amiss if he had someone from medical go and check on them, and deciding she would probably be insulted. He really needed to think of a name too. He couldn't just keep calling her 'the squirrel'.

He was distracted enough with his thoughts that he was only two blocks from home when he felt a tingle run up his spine. Foolish. He knew better than to lose track of his surroundings. He might live here but that didn't mean he was immune to the dangers of the area. He glanced behind him, expecting to see someone following. He'd dealt with muggers before, so he wasn't too frightened. What he saw though froze his blood. That was no mugger.

It looked like some cross between a hyena and a wild boar, only twice the size of both, and it wasn't alone. *Vargs,* his mind whispered. Ruthless pack hunters, both vicious and keenly intelligent. It was only as he caught sight of them that he finally heard the wail of the sirens in the distance. These things definitely shouldn't be wandering around. They couldn't have been here long without having caused a swath of destruction. Had they just come through an Event? If so, why was he hearing sirens so far off and the vargs were here? Did anyone even know about the pack?

All of those thoughts went through his head in about a second as survival instincts kicked in. They were stalking him, but not loping toward him, yet. That was about to change, he could feel it, and there was no way he was going to make it to his building before they were on him. He turned his head and started to sprint as the lead varg bayed a challenge.

Kellen had seen packs of vargs hunting. They didn't harry their prey like wolves, they overwhelmed them en masse, taking whatever was in their path down and ripping it apart. The memory of a huge stag being torn in two almost the second it was caught lent more panic than speed, but he was already running as fast as he could.

The snarling and scraping of hard nails on concrete could have been a block away or right on top of him, Kellen wasn't sure and didn't dare look back. He whipped his shirt off and dropped it. His wings were meant for short flights and it was much easier to drop from a height than it was to take off from the ground, but it could be done. He leaped, letting his wings snap open and push downward in one movement, and he was up as the lead varg reached him. It jumped, intending to bring him down, and teeth snagged his pant leg, sending him spinning off course.

"Hai!"

It was an elvish voice that reached him, both challenge and battle cry, just before he smashed into a nearby storefront. Hooves accompanied the yelling and for a moment, Kellen expected an elvish knight on a war steed. Maybe the reality wasn't too far off.

Officer Flax Wolfheart rode crouched on Sergeant Nestor's back, knives drawn. As the centaur bore down on the charging vargs, Wolfheart leaped onto the back of the lead varg, knocking it off course. They went down in a tumble of flashing teeth and blades, snarling and cursing.

When he spotted Kellen, Sergeant Nestor wheeled to put himself between him and the remaining vargs, rearing and threatening with his hooves. Between those and his nightstick, he beat the vargs back long enough for Kellen to rise.

"Kellen! If you're able to, run! Get inside somewhere!"

He could do better than that. Faster at least. He jumped, letting a wingbeat carry him up, and lightly pushed off the broad back of the centaur to get more elevation. He was up on the ledge of the second story of the store in a heartbeat. In that time, Flax had already killed two of the vargs and Ness was working on driving the others back. Kellen barely got his feet on the ledge before the remaining five rushed them, dividing to come in at their sides and try to drive the two combatants together so they could swarm over them both. Nestor kicked one and clubbed at another, smashing its skull with a powerful blow. Flax moved in a blur of spinning blades but three vargs were a match for anyone and Kellen watched in horror as one leaped for Flax's neck. Without thinking he dove down, knowing if he did nothing, those teeth would make an end of the officer. It happened so fast Kellen was sure he made no conscious decisions, but somehow he had grabbed on to the only thing available to him, a large and heavy flowerpot on the windowsill, which he threw with all the force of his dive directly at the varg's head.

It shattered in a spray of dirt and pottery and the beast's legs buckled.

"Attaboy, Kells!" Flax shouted even as he swept a blade up and sliced open a varg throat. He spun and buried his other blade in the last varg's eye, twisted to make certain Ness didn't need help, then stood head down, panting.

Ness pranced in agitated steps, snorting and making odd whinnying wheezes. On high alert, he seemed surprised to have run out of opponents.

"Easy, easy." Flax put a hand on his withers. "You hurt?"

"No... No, I'm fine." Ness pulled in a shuddering breath. "You're bleeding. And that one varg is still breathing. I can hear him from all the way over here."

"Yeah. Guess he is. Call for a cage van?"

Ness nodded and walked free of the carnage to put the call in through the radio clipped to his shoulder while Flax looked at the blood trickling from his shoulder with a sigh. "Damn it. Ash is gonna have a fit."

"I-I have a first-aid kit. In my bag," Kellen stammered. "Hold on, I'll get it." He headed up the street to where he'd dropped his things. It felt strange to be outside with his wings free and he folded them down out of the way while he retrieved his bag and shirt and walked back to where Flax stood guard over a litter of bodies.

"I have some antiseptic here, but you really need to get that washed out as soon as possible. Vargs carry some nasty filth with them." He prattled as he went right into emergency care mode. He squirted the liquid onto the wound and pressed a sterile pad over it. "Hold this while I bind it. What happened? I could hear the sirens over that way, how did this pack get so far?"

"Huge fucking Event broke through in the park. Like a whole wild hunt pulled through. Tribe of kelpie out varg hunting. Whole thing got yanked through. These guys here, they decided they wanted easier pickings and hightailed it out of the park. Captain sent me and Ness after them. Damn it, that stings."

"Sorry," Kellen said. "Did you say a *tribe* of Kelpie? Hunting a *pack* of varg? And they all came through? At the same time?" That was hard to believe. Nothing that big had happened since the release of the Suppression.

"Yeah. Damnedest thing I ever saw." Flax pulled his cuffs out, considered the still-living varg's paws, shook his head and put them back. "We were afraid it was another weird Event explosion, but our precogs say no. It was just one big-ass Event. Kai's probably having fits."

The officer grinned at that, which Kellen didn't think was really appropriate, but Ness came back to join them.

"Might be a few minutes. They're still wrapping up. No one to spare for us just yet. You need medical?"

"Ness, I *have* medical standing right here." Flax waved his hand at Kellen.

"Not what I meant."

"Sorry. Sorry. No. I don't need transport. It's not enough to take me down and just enough I'll get fussed over when I get home." Flax's grin softened a bit at that.

"It really needs to be flushed out as soon as possible." Kellen spoke up. "I'm not joking about the filth. It'll get infected without care. I, uh, live just over there. I can wash it out for you if you don't want to go back to headquarters?"

"Um, all right?" Flax flexed the shoulder and grimaced. "We gotta wait for backup, though. I'm not leaving Ness out here alone with a mess of vargs and possible crowd control issues."

Kellen chuckled and spread his hands slightly to indicate the distinct lack of another living soul on the street. "In this neighborhood? Even a whiff of trouble and everyone scatters. It'll be morning before anyone ventures out."

"Not talking about the people, little guy." Flax pointed a knife toward the nearby alley where rats were beginning to show an interest. "We'll get relief in just a few."

True enough, a squad car soon pulled up and screeched to a stop along the curb. With the situation explained to Officer Kensington, Flax waved a hand toward Kellen in a *lead on* gesture.

When they reached the steps of the building, Kellen remembered how elves reacted when entering. "Um, listen... Don't freak out about the smell, okay? Tok's kinda sensitive about it." He let that cryptic comment hang as he punched in the code on the main door and opened it.

One step inside and Flax shoved Kellen behind him before he whipped out his varg-bloodied knives. "Holy fuck... Quiet now, Kells. There's a troll in here."

"Yeah, that would be Tok," Kellen said. "He's our maintenance troll. He lives in the basement. We do what we can to kill the odor, but elves can still pick up on it no matter what."

"No shit." Flax looked back at him with a raised eyebrow but he didn't relinquish his defensive stance. "And he *lives* here? And that's…okay with you?"

Kellen shrugged. "Tok is a reformed troll. He likes to fix things instead of being destructive. He's a nice guy. The only thing he won't do is put WiFi in the building, but that's okay with most of us. Come on, let's get you cleaned up."

Flax still eyed the stairs heading down to the basement dubiously, but he sheathed his knives and followed Kellen up. There may have been a little wobble to his steps as he reached the top, but Kellen wasn't going to mention it. He'd been around officers and emergency situations long enough to recognize adrenaline crash.

Once in the apartment, Kellen nudged him into a kitchen chair while he put water on to boil. That was for tea, not for the wound. For that he dug out the larger first-aid kit in his bathroom and some towels. He took the hasty dressing he'd applied in the street off and clucked his tongue. Already the wound was looking red and angry.

"See what I mean? You heal fast, but almost too fast. Not enough bleeding to wash it all out. This is going to hurt, I'm sorry."

"Don't suppose you give out lollipops after?" Flax gave him a crooked grin. "Hey, do what you have to. I've been through worse. And you can tell me why an AURA employee is living in the slums to distract me."

Kellen went to the sink to get water so he didn't have to answer that immediately. Which was probably not a good idea, since Officer Wolfheart was bound to know he was buying time to think. He should have just laughed and blurted something, but Kellen was too used to being careful with his words.

"I like it here. Most of the people in the building are crossovers." Kellen arranged the towels to his liking under the wound. "Hold this up," he instructed.

"There are other buildings with crossovers," Flax pointed out. "In nicer neighborhoods. Safer neighborhoods."

Kellen held the glass of water just above the top of the wound and lightly but firmly pressed his fingers to either side of it to open it while pouring. Wolfheart hissed but Kellen kept going until the glass was empty and the blood was flowing again, along with a bit of blackish stain. He went to get more water and repeated the process.

"Yes, but they cost a lot more," Kellen said, as if there had been no pause in the conversation.

"Yeah…but you're a pixie," Flax said, as if that was supposed to be a revelation. Kellen knew exactly what he meant though. Pixie dust was a rare thing in his own world, and even rarer here. The pixies that sold their dust made an excellent living doing nothing else.

"Not all pixies have the same kind of dust," Kellen murmured.

Flax snorted on a hitching breath, in obvious pain. "I know that, Kells. Just because I'm blond, it doesn't mean I'm an idiot. But you're vulnerable here. It's kinda worrisome."

Kellen prodded a bit more, despite Flax's winces, and poured another full glass of water over the seeping wound. The towel he held under it was soaked through and red with blood and other things, but he didn't see any more black coming out.

He pressed another clean bandage over it and took the blood-soaked towel away, then started to wrap gauze around Flax's shoulder to hold it in place. He gave Flax an amused little grin. "There is a troll that lives here. I think it's safe to say security is pretty good."

"Ha. Okay. You got me there," Flax panted out. "Hey, thanks for this. Even though it pretty much guarantees less fussing when I get home tonight."

Kellen smiled, a genuine smile that felt good. "I'm sure if you limp a little, and make a show of cleaning the blood off your blades, you have all the fussing you'll need."

Flax laughed at that, and it was a good laugh, guileless and free of the mean-spiritedness Kellen often faced. He pulled his shirt back on and patted Kellen's shoulder. "Thanks again. You're one of the good guys. Stay inside tonight just in case we missed any of those big suckers. And make sure you come down to the squad room and give a statement tomorrow, okay?"

Kellen nodded, because that was what was expected, and closed the door behind Officer Wolfheart, returning him to his bright, unambiguous, heroic life.

Chapter Five

The vargs were nearly loaded, six in the coroner's van and one in the department's cage van, when a voice came from above.

"Ness! Damn it all!"

Ness spotted the dark shape winging toward him, huge midnight bat wings slicing through the air. He smiled and lifted a hand to wave. Sin landed in an open spot of sidewalk and rushed him, causing several lab techs to squeak and scurry out of the way while Ness braced and opened his arms to receive two hundred pounds of charging incubus.

"Ness." Sin wrapped arms and legs around Ness' human torso, burying his face against Ness' shoulder. "Are you all right? There's so much damn blood."

"A little scratched, love. I'm fine. Hey…" Ness held his lover tight, concerned over his shaking. "I had Flax with me. And Kellen helped too. What's this all about?"

Sin heaved a long breath, his voice muffled against Ness' shirt. "It was pretty fucking awful. All those vargs they had to kill. We just finished transporting the injured, I really need to get to medical. But Val said he'd sent you and Flax off after a whole pack *alone*—"

"It wasn't a whole pack. Only seven."

"Only?" Sin slid down to stand beside Ness, though he still held on tight. "I'm gonna punch Val in his handsome face. I swear I will."

Ness chuckled. "I'm trying not to be hurt by your lack of faith in me. I know fighting isn't my first choice, but I'm not incompetent."

"You? No way! You're a fucking badass centaur cop. But *vargs*, big guy! I was worried!"

"I see that." Ness bent down to kiss him softly. "Go finish up at medical. We're wrapping up here. I'll see you at home soon."

Sin gave him a last hug before he stepped back. "Kellen helped? 'I'm afraid of my own shadow' *Kellen*?"

"Yes. He flew up and beaned one with a flowerpot. Just in time to save Flax from being decapitated, I might add."

"He did?" Sin blinked at him. "Well, fuck me with a tentpole."

"That doesn't sound fun at all." Ness turned him and gave him a little swat. "Go on, flyboy. Go get things sorted out. I'll tell you everything later."

* * * *

'Later' ended up being four hours later, after they'd both dragged themselves home filthy and exhausted. Ness insisted that they share the oversize shower and Sin was more than happy to be naked and climbing all over Ness to help him wash.

"I don't like that you didn't get this seen to." Sin frowned at the claw marks on Ness' flank. "You're not an elf, you know."

"I had it cleaned and one of the healers sang over it on site, love. Coming into medical seemed a little redundant." Ness bent down to scrub Sin's back and soap up his gorgeous ass, a little clumsy with Sin's wings flipping and twitching all over the place. "Here. Turn. Let me wash your wings so we can go get warm under the blankets."

Sin moaned at having his wing membranes gently washed. Tricky for him to do it himself and the soft skin was incredibly sensitive. He turned the water off when they were both rinsed, helped towel Ness down, taking particular care with his legs, then went to brush his teeth while Ness got ready for bed.

He was propped up, reading with a mug of tea in one hand when Sin finally crawled under the covers to snuggle close. The king-size monstrosity of a bed was Scandinavian, a little longer than an American bed, with a sloping headboard so Ness could rest his horse half on its side and lean his human half in a modified sitting up position against the padded leather.

"Kellen really took down a varg?"

Ness looked up over his glasses, his forehead wrinkling. "It's not as if I'd make that up, you know."

"Yeah, yeah. I know." Sin let out a contented sigh as he rested his head on Ness' chest. "But I'm gonna give Wolfheart all sorts of shit about being saved by a pixie."

"Of course you are." Ness put down the book and turned out the light. "You wouldn't be you if you didn't."

"Hey!"

Ness hugged him tight. "Hush. I love you. Every bad inch of you. Now go to sleep."

"Love you too, pony boy," Sin mumbled, but he was already on the edge of snoring, completely relaxed and comfortable.

Ness wouldn't have had it any other way.

* * * *

Kai flinched involuntarily as the varg slammed up against the glass again. Unbreakable, so he was told. He didn't have much faith in such things. It had been just over a week since the massive Event that had dropped the creature, along with its brethren and an entire tribe of kelpies, into their midst.

"An entire pack, Quinn. Not a mere handful, but a full pack of thirty beasts," he murmured to his human friend. "Why this? Why now?"

Quinn was seated in a hard-backed plastic chair, which he was leaning back on two legs as he contemplated the caged beast. He didn't say anything for so long Kai finally turned and looked at him expectantly.

Quinn blinked at him. "Oh, you wanted an answer? I wasn't sure if you were just doing that talking to yourself thing."

"You are oh so helpful," Kai said dryly.

Quinn shrugged. "I don't have an answer any more than you do, Kai. To be honest, I haven't had much time to pay attention to new crossovers. The last couple months have been a circus freak show gone nuts. I've been sent out nearly every day last week to trap various critters gone pillaging through the neighborhoods. I can't keep track anymore."

"Pillaging? What manner of pillaging?" Kai tried to keep the chill from his voice. This wasn't Quinn's fault. "And why wasn't I informed?"

"Informed of what? That we've been busy? You know that." Quinn snorted. "I don't know. It just seems like everyone went bonkers over the summer. Val's putting a task force together to look into the gangs of goblin kids who've been shaking down local businesses. There's been, like, six arrests over the last few weeks of drunk centaurs trashing bars, sometimes their own damn bars. The last time I had to go out was to set a trap for some brownies who had started shit with some fairies and declared 'war' on them. It's like everyone's pissed off."

Kai paced, the varg's head swiveling to follow him. "I need specifics. Reports. Data. Quinn, something's not right. Don't you feel it? Don't you have a sort of itch under your skin that you can't quite reach? What's happening here?"

"Only thing happening is a nosy drow who's losing his mind 'cause he's getting hitched this weekend." Flax strode down the corridor toward them between the detention cages, Sage close on his heels. "Hey, Quinn. Hey, Mr. Nosy Drow. Sage wanted to see the varg. He never saw one before last night, and you don't really get a good look at shit that's trying to kill you."

"Don't know why you'd want to," Quinn said. "That thing is nothing but hate and teeth."

As if to prove his point, the varg lunged at the newcomers, a fresh gout of slobber smearing across the glass where it smashed its snout against the barrier.

"It's always good to know as much as you can about potential enemies," Sage said. "Killing them is one option, but if we can prevent an attack before it happens, that is better."

Quinn shook his head. "Yeah, I guess that's a good point, but I don't think you're going to get too far convincing these things to chill out."

The varg was watching again and followed Sage's movements as he crouched in front of the glass. Top lip pulled back, its dagger canines bared and back bristles standing fully upright, it snarled and snapped at him, but seemed to be wondering what his next move would be. Puzzled. It definitely was that.

"Perhaps," Kai said, his thoughts leaping in far too many directions at once. "There are beings who use them as steeds, after all. There must be something besides maw and stomach." He waved an impatient hand. "I must speak to Val. It's incomprehensible to me that I've not been kept informed of developments. There must be patterns here. Something. I don't know. Something. But I need more to look at before it will come clear."

"Who's in charge of taking care of the varg?" Sage asked, ignoring Kai's muttering entirely.

"Well, there are a couple of rock trolls who patrol down here," Flax said with a head tilt to match the varg's. "I guess it's them?"

Sage snorted. "I wouldn't be surprised if the beast is smarter than the rock trolls."

Quinn snickered but squelched it. "Don't let Val hear you say that. He'll have you in 'sensitivity training' before you can say you're most humbly sorry."

Sage nodded. "Still, someone that will do more than throw meat in its cage should look after it, or put it out of its suffering."

"It's not hurt. Other than what it's done to itself," Quinn said.

"It's in a cage. That's suffering enough," Sage insisted.

"Well, talk to Val about it. I don't think he's going to let you take it home, though."

Kai narrowed his eyes, observing the keen interest the varg had taken in Sage. "They are pack animals and this one is now without pack. I do wonder…" He spun on his heel and strode for the stairs. "Officer Wolfheart, it sounds to me that your young whelp of a lover is volunteering. Perhaps you should instruct him in the dangers of volunteering for things."

And I must speak to Val. About several things. But mostly about why I've not been getting reports on these increases in violence. It's not right. Even in an unusually hot summer, which it was. It's not right.

* * * *

The medical department wasn't particularly busy on Friday, but it sounded like a damn hive of bees. Everyone kept gathering at the front desk with congratulations and advice and questions for Tenzin. Honestly? Sin thought the big guy should've taken the day off. Working the day before your wedding, or trying to, was obviously a losing proposition.

All the chatter was giving him a headache, so he drifted back toward the counter and computers where the techs and EMTs did their charting. Much quieter, and there was always paperwork to sort out.

Unfortunately, he wasn't the only one. Kellen was back there too, hunched over something. Sin stood on tiptoe, trying to see over the counter, and of course blocked enough of the light to alert Kellen to his presence.

The pixie didn't look up, but there was a soft, dry rustle, a sound Sin had gotten used to. The sound of a wing flick trapped under a shirt.

"Can I help you?" Kellen asked as he continued to jot in the chart he was working on.

"Um, hi." Sin leaned an elbow on the counter, trying for nonthreatening and casual. "How's it going?"

Kellen finally looked up, and the usual evasiveness Sin sensed in him was absent for once. He looked stressed, a little distracted. Several strands of burnished red hair had worked free of his braid and fanned over his forehead and cheek. His eyes though looked positively exhausted.

"Busy," Kellen answered. "Brianna and her troop have things to do this weekend, obviously, but I found another sitter for Lola."

Sin raised an eyebrow at that. It wasn't busy. Their department was the opposite of busy that day. But he decided to let it go and pointed to the box near Kellen's right arm. "Lola, huh? I like it. Can I see the baby? You know, 'cause I haven't in a bit."

"Oh, so you think you can just desert her and then saunter back in and play dad when you feel like it, huh?" Kellen said.

For a half a second, Sin thought he was being serious, but then he noticed the little twinkle in those green eyes and the slight tilt at their corners. A joke? Was Kellen actually joking with him?

"Well, yeah. That's what good deadbeat dads do, you know. Come on, Kells. I did buy the last case of formula, didn't I?" He waited patiently while Kellen gathered Lola up from her blanket nest and handed her up to him. Sin used both hands to cradle her so Kellen wouldn't have a fit and, yeah, he knew his smile was all goofy when she started to snuffle at him and snuggle up to his chest. "Who's a good girl? You're getting so big. Soon you're gonna be running this place."

Sin glanced up to find Kellen watching, and immediately returned his gaze to Lola. "So, um, thanks. For the other night. With the vargs. And Ness. For helping him."

"It was more like he helped me. Him and Officer Wolfheart." Kellen paused. "I'm just glad it was me they were chasing, and not anyone a little slower."

And what were you doing out so late that night? In that neighborhood? Sin couldn't help the stray thoughts. It had been bugging him all week and it was none of his damn business. "Ness was just doing his job and Wolfheart thinks he's a damn army. The extra pair of hands saved his cocky bacon bits. So thanks for helping so that my Ness didn't get all sliced up working with that maniac."

"I didn't really do anything except get out of their way," Kellen said.

"Really? I thought I heard something about a flowerpot being dropped on the head of a varg about to take Wolfheart out?"

Kellen actually grinned slightly and shook his head. "It was reflex. It was coming in behind him."

"Okay, see, this is how this is supposed to go. I say, thank you, Kellen, for helping the love of my life. I'm ever so grateful. And *you* say, you're welcome. Go on. Try it."

Kellen laughed, and to Sin's surprise, it was not a self-deprecating chuckle but a genuine rich trickle of sound.

"All right, you're welcome. I'm very glad Nestor and Officer Wolfheart are both all right."

"Perfect. See? That wasn't so hard." Sin held Lola up to his face to nuzzle noses with her. "You are the cutest little tree rat, aren't you?"

Kellen beamed and seemed to swell a bit with pride. "She is. Tenzin says she's nearly old enough to start on solid foods. Lysander says she's welcome to stay in the sanctuary when she's grown, until she's ready for the wild again."

Sin was just about to suggest that perhaps he had judged Kellen a bit harshly the other day and ask if they could start again, if for no other reason than he wanted his suspicions either confirmed or put to rest for good, when a loud bang and crash interrupted. The big double doors across from the front desk slammed open, and what looked like some kind of demented ancient Greek orgy scene spilled through.

A tall, black centaur clattered through, bellowing and snorting, hooves stamping, blood running bright red down his chest. What could have been mistaken for two smaller versions of Sin, except with tails, flew agitatedly around him, one of whom favored a wing. As if this weren't enough, they were closely followed by two satyrs cursing and yelling something about whose lover belonged to whom while the imps hissed at them. Both satyrs showed signs of claw marks on their faces and shoulders.

"Oh, freaking lovely," Sin muttered and picked up the phone beside Kellen. "Yes. Sergeant, this is medical. We have what looks like the remnants of a bar fight down here. Thanks much."

He turned to the imps and bellowed, "Oi! You two! Over there and have a seat."

Kellen hastily took Lola from him, put her in her box and tucked her safely out of harm's way. Tenzin had stood and was telling the satyrs to please lower their voices and step to one side. As they moved to do so, one got a little too close to the centaur and the satyr gave him a kick, to which the centaur replied in kind, only his kick was much more powerful.

The imps shrieked and dive-bombed at the heads of the two satyrs.

Sin moved one way and Tenzin the other around the oval-shaped desk and Kellen was right behind Sin.

Just as the centaur tried to charge the satyrs, Tenzin stepped between and got his arms around the centaur's waist. "Not in here, my friend. If you wish for assistance, you must stop fighting."

The imps were chattering and screaming and Sin launched himself, sweeping them both into the confines of his huge wings and bearing them to the ground.

The satyrs took advantage of the distraction to regroup and retaliate, fists raised as they tried to get around Tenzin's considerable furry backside to reach their target. Kellen jumped lightly up onto the desk then dropped down between them and Tenzin.

"No you don't, that's enough of this," he told them. "If you don't stop, you'll be escorted out!"

Sin had a struggling imp under each arm and he'd had quite enough. "Knock it the hell off, all of you! I've got officers on the way down and we can either see to injuries or we can have the lot of you arrested!"

As he spoke said officers arrived, the clatter of Ness' hooves joining the nervous prancing of their injured arrival, along with Wolfheart, Captain Hartgrove, and bringing up the rear, Quinn.

The imps squeaked at the sight of uniforms and immediately subsided. The satyrs, not so much.

Kellen didn't give any ground when they rushed forward and consequently took the brunt of their charge. He went down as one grabbed him around the waist and the other leaped to get around Tenzin.

The centaur reached behind Tenzin and punched the satyr square in the face, sending him crashing down to the floor on top of his friend and Kellen.

Ness half reared, striking his hooves out in warning and backing the centaur up while Val waded into the fray and picked up the more bellicose satyr by the back of his neck to bellow in his face, "Enough! Sit down or I drag you to holding for assaulting a medical officer."

The satyr finally lost some of his fight in the face of Val's authority and stilled while the other struggled to his feet.

"They started it!" he shouted, but wisely didn't punctuate this statement by anything more menacing than crossing his arms petulantly.

"I'm sure the officers will be happy to take everyone's statements. But we can't allow you to disrupt medical," Tenzin said and began pointing. "Sin, imps in exam rooms one and two. Sergeant, if you please, the centaur in three."

"And what about us? That great lummox kicked Epeius right in the knee," the satyr Val wasn't holding on to said.

"I'll take him in to X-ray," Kellen said as he was picking himself up.

Val deposited the satyr in question, Epeius, in the wheelchair beside the front desk. If he wasn't exactly gentle about it, Sin couldn't blame him one bit. Bunch of chuckleheads.

For the next hour or so, Sin was occupied with treating the imps for various minor injuries and a more serious wing ligament strain. After he was through with them, he joined Tenzin, who was just finishing up with the centaur who had a rather large and nasty gash from one shoulder down to nearly his belly, but no other injuries. Seeing Tenzin didn't need his help, he moved on to find Kellen, who was just coming out of one of the exam rooms.

"Nothing serious with the satyrs," Kellen told him. "X-ray didn't show any fractures. They're mostly just scratched and bruised."

"Any of these idiots say what happened?" Sin scratched at one horn. "And are you all right?"

Kellen looked a little gray and that couldn't be good.

"All I got from them was a bunch of *he said, he said*. I don't know. Yeah, I'm okay, just got the wind knocked out of me for a — Oh... Oh no." Kellen's eyes went wide and he dropped the clipboard he was holding. "Oh no," he said again in a horrified murmur, lifting his arms and turning them over. The insides of them from wrists to elbow shimmered a dull pearl color, the lights catching on little hints of color, mostly in a purplish cast. "I have to go!"

"Kellen!" Sin called out and gave chase. "What the hell? What's wrong?"

"I'm dusting," he said, not slowing down. "I have to get home." As he ran down the hall, Sin saw tiny sparkles beginning to form around the nape of his neck and on his cheeks.

"Hey!" Sin used the unfair advantage of larger wings and cut off Kellen's exit. "Kells, you're already shedding. You're not gonna get there before you spread dust all over the city. Take one of the empty rooms. Tell me what you need."

"This isn't supposed to happen for a few days… It's early." Kellen bit his lip so hard it looked painful. His eyes held sheer panic.

"It's okay, we can handle this," Sin tried to reassure him.

"No… No, you don't understand." Kellen took a shuddering breath and his shoulders slumped. He went from looking utterly panicked to utterly dejected in one deep breath. He did let Sin guide him into an empty exam room, though.

"I need… I need a sheet, a plastic one. So it won't escape," Kellen said haltingly.

"Okay, all right." Sin patted the air with both hands. "Be right back."

He returned with one of the large plastic sheets for covering up the imaging equipment during room cleanings and laid it out on the floor. "I don't know why it's so important, but I get it. It's important. There you go, Kells. Anything else?"

"No…" Kellen was already stepping onto the sheet and removing his clothes. Shoes and shirt at the same time, his pants and undies next, he was tugging the band off the end of his braid when he said, "Wait…yes. A container. A specimen jar would work."

Sin dove for the closet where they kept routine screening supplies and snagged a couple. Just in case. Most of Kellen was sparkling now and if Sin wasn't quite so freaked out, he might have been able to appreciate the pretty sight. Pixies were quite pretty, and Kellen was one of the nicer-looking ones he'd seen.

He shoved the specimen jars at Kellen, looking the other way.

Kellen took them and held on to them. "Thank you," he said quietly, and Sin could not miss the dejection in his voice. He had gone from briskly efficient to seemingly shattered in the space of a few minutes and Sin couldn't figure out why. It couldn't be the end of the world to shed a couple of days early, right?

Maybe it was a privacy thing?

"Um, should I...?" He made a little gesture toward the door but Kellen had his eyes closed and his head bowed, he had brought his arms in close, and his wings were still tucked down tightly even without his shirt on. He was silent and still, and Sin noticed the sparkling was more like an opalescence now, a sheen over all of his skin. Tiny little sparks began to float slowly down, so small they were hard to see, except the lights above made them sparkle as they fell. It was something like watching a slow shower of glitter sifting down around him.

It also felt very private all of a sudden and Sin reached for the door handle.

"No... Don't," Kellen said in a barely audible whisper. "Too much air."

"Okay," Sin whispered back and made himself into as small an object as he could on the tall lab stool by the door. With his wings plastered against his back, he tried not to breathe too hard, watching and trying not to watch because it just seemed rude.

As the shed began to reveal Kellen's normal skin underneath, Sin spotted an odd blotch on his hip. *No... Not a blotch. A tattoo? No, not that either. Oh. Oh, crud.* That was a brand on Kellen's hip. An old one, bearing the runes and signs of a drow house. Probably a powerful one, but Sin had never learned to read drow. *Slave. Damn it.* Kellen had been property. Was that why he was so skitty? And maybe drawn to dysfunctional, abusive relationships? Was it something that simple?

Ever so slowly and carefully, Kellen brought his wings up, a pair of them on each side of his back, nearly transparent but gleaming with hints of rainbow colors, like a dragonfly's wings. More of the dust sifted down from them and he moved them oh-so slowly. A final shake of his red mane brought the last of it shimmering down to the tarp below.

"Don't move yet, please," Kellen said. "It blows around very easily."

As dainty and graceful as a nymph, Kellen stepped out of the little ring of pixie dust around his feet. He didn't bother dressing before he crouched on his haunches and gathered the ends of the tarp, bringing the corners in and making the circle become a pile. He lifted and manipulated the edges until he had a funnel of sorts, or as close as he could get, to try to pour the dust into the specimen jars.

Only when the lid was finally on did Kellen take a deep breath again. "Thank you, for your help. You should take a shower as soon as possible, before you leave work. I need to take the tarp to biohazard to have it disposed of."

"Um, all right. I guess?" Sin unfolded carefully from the stool, still afraid to move too fast. "Is your dust cursed or something?"

Kellen lifted his head and gave him a lopsided little smile. "No. The opposite, in fact. It will remove magic from anything it touches. Well, most magic. If any witch ever gets mad and decides to hex you…" He held up the little jar. "This stuff will take care of it."

"I'll keep that in mind." Sin put his hand on the doorknob. "And, you know, if I have one night where women aren't trying to maul me on the subway going home, I'm okay with that too."

Kellen nodded and reached for his clothes, and Sin left him to dress. He hadn't gotten a really in-depth look at that mark on Kellen's hip, but he remembered most of it and intended to see if he could get a certain drow he knew to tell him what he made of it. Not tonight though, and not tomorrow either, but certainly before Kai and Tenzin took off for their honeymoon.

Chapter Six

Distress caused Kellen's wings to rustle restlessly as he hurried up the stairs from the subway to the street. It was bad enough that his dusting had come early, not to mention humiliating that he'd had to ask Sinistrus for his help then had had no choice but to let him sit there and watch. Even worse was that Rask had summoned him as soon as he'd gotten off work. He'd told Rask that he couldn't get any blood but Rask didn't care, he wanted the pixie dust as fresh as possible.

It wasn't as if the dust went bad. It would be exactly the same a few days or weeks from now. But Kellen suspected that wanting him to come immediately after a dusting had nothing to do with freshness and everything to do with the amount of power the coven was pulling. It seemed to be growing more rapidly than ever now. Rask told him their experiment was working and the magical energy had to be channeled, and Kellen obeyed, because he didn't have any choice.

When he and Rask had been pulled through into this world, Kellen had hoped that perhaps the compulsion Rask had placed in him would no longer affect him. AURA had found and separated them, which had given Kellen even more hope, but the months Rask had spent away in Elvenhome while Kellen had stayed in New York learning of his new world had proved to him that he would never be free.

The elves called it fading, and Kellen agreed. That was exactly what it had felt like. As if he were becoming a shadow, fading and slowly dying. Even that had been preferable to how he had lived before the Event that had pulled him into the human world, or so he'd believed. When Rask had returned and found him, though, the crushing weight of despair had lifted, and Kellen had been relieved even as he'd wept bitter tears. There was no escaping Rask, and to refuse his wishes meant pain. And what did it matter really? His dust, the blood, the use of his body seemed small prices to pay for a life in which he was not chained, where he could help people every day and have friends like Tok and Tenzin, and perhaps even Sinistrus.

Kellen arrived to find Rask alone, which was unusual enough to put him on full guard.

"Where is the coven?" Kellen dared to ask when it became clear no one else was in the apartment.

"Someone has to procure the blood for tonight's ritual, since you failed to bring any," Rask told him.

Kellen paled. That was exactly why he had offered to bring the blood of magical creatures to begin with, so that no one would lose their lives to supply them. It was his fault, he should have thought of something.

"You can use my blood," he said suddenly. "You can call them in and just use mine."

Rask chuckled low, "You know that's not how this works. The blood has to come from sacrifice, given or taken doesn't matter, but it can't be from those who are part of the ritual."

Kellen slumped and felt a little sick.

Rask moved up behind him and lifted the braid of his hair, running it through his fingers. "Shawna hates you, do you know that?"

Kellen nodded slowly. He could feel his pulse suddenly in his throat.

Rask pulled the band holding the braid free and loosened it until his hair spread over his shoulders. "Her jealousy was amusing at first, but has started to grow tiresome." Rask bent and inhaled deeply just above Kellen's ear. Dread pooled into Kellen's middle. It had been a long time since Rask had used his body for anything other than as a conduit for the coven's magic and Kellen had hoped that Rask's other lovers were enough to keep him occupied.

"Your fear smells delicious," Rask murmured.

Kellen closed his eyes. He could endure this. He had before. Rask's cool hands skimmed the edge of his shirt and under, caressing lightly up his belly. Wildly Kellen thought of shoving those hands away, of yelling and screaming out all the dark and ugly things that Rask's touch made him feel, but refusing would only bring more pain than enduring. Rask's hand moved lower on his belly and Kellen did nothing to stop him. Lips, then teeth scraped the edge of his ear and Kellen shuddered.

"Rask! We've got it!" Shawna cried excitedly from the hallway.

Kellen thought Rask would pull away but he kept his hands where they were. "Master, please... Don't,"

Kellen murmured, knowing exactly what the game was.

"You presume far too much, *peshk*," Rask said.

Kellen moved his arms to cover himself and Rask grabbed a fistful of his hair, pulling his head back as Shawna came triumphantly into the room with Miris and Niles trailing behind her. She froze, holding aloft a plastic baggie of dark red.

Niles looked a little green, one hand against the wall for support, while Miris, who Kellen had thought of as the kind one, was stone-faced until she took in the tableau and Shawna's expression. Her lovely sylph features slid into an ugly grin, one she carefully didn't let Shawna see.

Shawna shrieked and threw the blood on the floor before taking two steps and slapping Kellen with a resounding crack. She drew back to hit him again but Rask caught her wrist and bent her arm back, making her cry out in pain and fury.

"Calm yourself," Rask said coldly.

"Fuck you! Get out! Get out of my house!" Shawna screamed.

A coldly calculating smile split Rask's lips and he twisted her arm harder, making her gasp, and he slapped her. "Your house? I think not," Rask said slowly. "No longer will you put on these airs, *slr'da*. This building belongs to me now, and so do you." He pushed her down as he spoke and when she started to rise, he hit her again, with enough force to stun and humiliate, but not do real damage. "Stay."

Kellen cringed as an oily feeling of power followed the word and twisted in his own gut. Shawna was cruel, vain and petty, but even so he would not have wished this on her, not upon anyone. The compulsion wrapped around Shawna and she struggled, then collapsed, writhing in pain. She began to cry.

"Pull yourself together. The ritual shall proceed tonight. What type of blood is in that bag, Niles?" Rask asked, as if the woman sobbing on the floor did not exist.

Niles pulled himself straight, his one glance at Shawna full of contempt. Oh, she hadn't made any friends here, but Rask would have made sure that his followers despised one another as much as possible. "It's flower fairy, sir. Otori trapped a troop of them. I'm afraid he may have eaten one."

The kitsune spun into the room at the sound of his name, twirling and pawing at the carpet. Red painted his jaws and his teeth when he opened his mouth to lick his lips. "Hot, hot, so hot and bright. Hot and bright."

Kellen swallowed hard and repressed the urge to be sick. What if he had known one of those fairies? A familiar feeling of hopeless rage bubbled slowly in his gut. Rask had somehow wrested control of Shawna's money from her, and although she didn't know it yet, she would soon realize he'd stolen far more from her. She would become his *peshk* in truth, or he would kill her. What little protection her jealousy and voracious sexual appetite had afforded Kellen was over. His life was about to become so much worse.

Chapter Seven

"For all the goddesses' sakes, Kai, stand still," Val growled as he tried, once again, to fasten the fussy orchid boutonniere on Kai's lapel. Typical drow, insisting on black and red for a wedding, though the orchid was a strange, luminescent green. Difficult to understand drow tastes sometimes.

"I am standing still!" Kai snapped, then appeared embarrassed that he'd been so loud. He lifted his chin and managed to stop shifting long enough for Val to affix the flower on his blood red jacket. "Val?"

"What now? If you tell me it's too far to the left, I'm pinning it to your bottom lip."

"Charming." Kai rolled his eyes. "No, I... Thank you. For standing up with me today. You're not, ah, family and you certainly didn't have to."

Val took him by the shoulders. "None of that. You and I, our families are far from here. And who else has been your friend so long?" The trembling under his hands concerned him. "Try not to faint."

"I most certainly will *not* faint." Kai sniffed in offense.

It was hard not to laugh, but Val managed. Today was not the day to wound Kai's prickly dignity. The music was starting and now Kai seemed rooted to the spot.

Quinn slipped up behind them seemingly out of nowhere and put a hand on Kai shoulder. "Are you ready? I can't hold the guests in circle much longer."

Kai turned his head but of course Quinn was grinning and winked at him. "I'm kidding. You look amazing, Kai. Take a deep breath."

The drow was doing as instructed, for once, and Tenzin appeared around the corner of the largest azalea bush to the left. Kai's breath choked off and Val wondered if he was going to have to call a medic. There were several present, and Kai looked like he'd forgotten how to breathe entirely.

The beautiful red and silver chrysanthemum-print sarong was stunning against Tenzin's white fur, brushed to gleaming. He was an imposing, gorgeous sight, with silver bells around his ankles, a mountain god stepped down from the clouds. Val couldn't help the chuckle as Tenzin reached out and tucked Kai's unresisting hand into the crook of his elbow.

"Beloved, are you well?" Tenzin whispered. "Please don't faint."

Quinn snickered quietly and Val turned his attention to his own love now that his charge was safely under the wing of his groom. Quinn didn't dress up often, so the dark gray suit was particularly unexpected on him, beautifully tailored and showing off his compact, lean physique. Val had the rather inappropriate stray thought that he hoped Quinn would take the jacket off later. That lovely backside had to be shown to best advantage in such closely tailored pants.

Quinn looked away from Kai and Tenzin and up at him, and the grin he wore turned slowly to something warmer and more seductive. He slid an arm around Val's waist and brushed a kiss on his lips. "Behave yourself, Captain Hartgrove," Quinn whispered.

Val raised an eyebrow at Quinn but he smiled. "I like the suit. You should wear more...suits." He let the last word trail off in a hungry growl.

If anyone else had suggested it, he probably would have gotten a sharp comment, or a snort of derision, in fact Val had expected him to respond with something about the discomfort of being 'strangled' by a tie on a regular basis. Instead Quinn surprised him with another tender brush of his lips and a, "We'll see."

"Then I will behave. So that there will be rewards." Val gave him a wink and tucked Quinn's hand into the crook of his elbow so they could precede Kai and Tenzin as they walked the path to the flowered arch where the priestess waited.

They took their places, then Kai and Tenzin emerged together. Their eyes were on each other rather than their guests or surroundings, but there were no missteps. Kai no longer looked like he might faint. In fact he looked as calm and beatifically happy as anyone could be, and Tenzin no less so.

This was the first AURA wedding in some time, the last being a much smaller affair for Lysander the faun counselor and his dryad assistant, Aesa. There had been only a handful of humans at that wedding, ones used to dealing with all manner of beings every day. Val had to wonder what all the humans attending today thought, their ranks swelled by government dignitaries and high-level city service folks. It wasn't every day, he was quite certain, that the wedding couple was flanked by elf, human and centaur on one side, and incubus, pixie and faun on the other.

The priestess in her shimmering robes reached out her hands to the approaching couple with a warm smile, taking a dark drow hand in her right and a huge furry yeti hand in her left.

The music faded and the crowd settled as she began to speak, intoning words of commitment and celebration, bringing the focus to the couple being joined together. "Friends, family, loved ones, today we celebrate the union of these two souls…"

Val listened but the words didn't seem as important as the feeling threading its way through the air, a feeling that was somehow both filled with love and anticipation. Being there with Quinn at his side, he couldn't help wondering if perhaps he should ask him if he'd also want a ceremony like this. Val felt not the least hesitation if that was indeed what his love wanted, but in his own mind their bond was already more than any words or witnesses could convey. Still, it was a legal recognition that they did not yet have. He tucked the thought away to discuss with Quinn later.

The priestess joined Kai's hand with Tenzin's, keeping her hands around theirs as she wrapped a bright red scarf around the couple's clasped hands.

"Bond mates, life mates, you are already joined in every way that matters, joined in hearts, joined in souls. But with this ceremony today, we make your union whole in the eyes of the law, so that every right and privilege of a legally wed couple now supports the promise of forever you have already made each other."

Val stood straight and still but he let his gaze wander—to Quinn, whose eyes were perhaps a bit too bright, to Nestor, who wiped tears from his cheeks in unashamed joy, to Sin, who stood chewing on his bottom lip, deep in thought.

Kai spoke then, a few words of love and promise. Drow ceremonies were not the same as Aelfe ceremonies, they tended toward a heavy, sober atmosphere even when celebratory, but Kai's words were surprisingly simple and heartfelt. Tenzin then sang first to him, then to the rest of the guests, and although no one knew the language or the words other than perhaps Kai, they all felt the magic in them. It filled the small, sheltered area with warmth and a light feeling and by the end, there was no one whose eyes were not shimmering with emotion.

Val hitched a breath, forcing back tears, and smiled down at Quinn when his lover put a hand on his arm. "I'm fine," he mouthed, and Quinn beamed up at him.

The priestess said the obligatory words about being empowered by the state of New York to pronounce them wed and prompted the newlyweds to kiss, though the way they gazed at each other with such tender joy, Val thought telling them was hardly necessary. With Kai's hands held gently in his huge furry ones, Tenzin bent and Kai stood on tiptoe to meet him, the kiss gentle and appropriate for company, but holding enough heated promise to make Val feel as if he intruded by watching. When they parted, the priestess smiled, gave them each a kiss on the cheek, and sent them off to their guests with a blessing from the Mother.

Kai and Tenzin were surrounded by friends and well-wishers, handshakes and hugs. A pavilion had been set up only a short distance from the ceremony. The guests and newlywed couple made a true wedding procession on their way over, followed by the music of a string quartet and a shower of petals from what seemed like every flower fairy in the city. Music, food and dancing were just the things everyone needed.

Kellen trailed the wedding party with a bemused smile. Tenzin was always efficient and serene even when chaos was bursting in through the doors to medical. He was certainly the kindest being Kellen had ever met, and he absolutely deserved the radiantly happy look on his face as he walked with his new husband. The song he had sung was haunting and beautiful but Kellen thought the way the people all around had reacted to it was even more wondrous. There was something in it that soothed an ache he'd hardly known was there, he'd carried it so long, and made the darkness he hid within a little lighter.

Surreptitiously he watched the flower fairies flitting around the guests. He didn't know them all but he counted those he did know and they were all present, which made him feel both relieved and disgusted with himself. The coven had killed last night, and here he was, celebrating with his friends and coworkers. This morning he had tried to make himself approach Sergeant Nestor and tell him, but the crippling pain of the compulsion had forced him to his knees until he'd given up.

The trapped feeling settled like a cloud around him and he drew away from the party, watching and enjoying their fun and merrymaking, but not feeling right in joining in.

Sergeant Nestor wasn't too far ahead of him, walking slowly, hand in hand with Sinistrus. When they had first started seeing each other, people had taken bets, rolled their eyes and made snide comments. Incubi couldn't have lasting relationships. It was against their very natures. And centaurs? The next nice piece of ass would show up, and they would gallop after it.

People had been wrong.

Nestor leaned down to kiss his lover's forehead, the gesture sweet and tender rather than in any way lascivious. It hurt Kellen's heart to watch sometimes, other people's happiness, though it helped him remember that all the world wasn't dark and all the connections people made weren't horrible. Watching them, watching Kai and Tenzin and everyone around them so happy, and some so in love, made Kellen ache. Even so, to deny himself the pleasure of watching others be so happy would have been worse.

There was dancing and feasting well into the afternoon and evening and Kellen truly enjoyed being a part of it, even if he was on the fringes. It made it all the more shocking when several of the AURA officers were suddenly glancing down at their phones almost as one. Kellen saw Captain Hartgrove answer, his face go grim, and just as he started to move through the crowd there was an ear-splitting clap of thunder in the distance.

"Ladies and gentlemen," Captain Hartgrove's battle-trained voice cut through babble of frightened voices. "We have Event sign. I'm requesting all civilians stay here, inside the tent. All AURA personnel, with me."

Kellen was close enough to hear the captain as he stopped briefly beside Kai. "Can you do it? A shield for the whole tent?"

"Go, *tesined*. Of course I can. It's a small tent and not a mounted battalion. Whatever this is, I will keep them safe."

Kellen wasn't sure why he followed. As medical staff he would ordinarily be instructed to go where there were wounded, but staying back with the wedding party and waiting it out never even crossed his mind. No matter how steady Captain Hartgrove's voice had been, Kellen still felt the underlying tension. Something big had happened. Something like the varg. Maybe bigger.

Even as he hurried after the officers, he glanced back in time to see Kai plant his feet just outside the tent, palms held toward the ground. His jacket removed for dancing, his black silk shirt stood out stark and ominous against the white of the tent. Green magic, drow magic, traveled up his body and coalesced in his hands. He lifted his arms and spread them, and the glow crept out to encase the entire tent, though Kai stayed outside with Tenzin. A shield, a circle of protection, and Kai, even on his wedding day, intended to hold it against whatever came.

He looked so like Rask, so much it was disturbing, and yet he was nothing like Rask.

That was when Kellen heard the first sirens. Another crack of thunder shook the sky and great black clouds started to roll in. Perfect. Just want they needed. A big storm on top of an Event.

"Kellen, come with me. We'll return to medical and get supplies," Tenzin told him.

Kellen nodded and started to follow him. They didn't make it back to headquarters, though.

Screams rose from the streets beyond the park and they started to run, the AURA officers already well on their way. The boom of thunder almost masked the boom of cracking concrete. Kellen stopped cold.

In front of them, people were running toward them in panic. The sky was pitch black with storm clouds and roiling angrily. The top of a building lay crumbled in the street, several cars crushed beneath. Kellen looked up and it took several moments for him to comprehend what he was seeing.

Its shape was that of a bird of prey, but its size was beyond anything Kellen had ever imagined a bird to be. One taloned foot alone was the size of a city bus. Its wingspan was enormous, but difficult to calculate because it appeared the wings and body were not just obscured by the storm clouds but part of them, or perhaps the creature itself was the storm. Well over a hundred feet, surely, maybe twice that. It pumped those great wings and a howling wind rushed down the street, blowing people right over. Its beak opened and more thunder shook the ground beneath their feet. When it launched into the air, another top of a building tumbled to the street below, smashing vehicles and people alike.

More sirens were closing in. This was more than AURA alone could handle, although they certainly would be expected to somehow stop what was happening. Kellen's feet were already carrying him forward, toward the wreckage and injured people, in Tenzin's wake.

"Tenzin! What is it? What is that?" Kellen yelled over the pandemonium.

A visible shudder went through Tenzin. "Thunderbird. This may be more than any of us can handle."

Captain Hartgrove had gathered his officers, not giving them time to consider and let fear creep in. He pointed to the second crumbling building. "That's mostly apartments on the top floors. We need to clear that building! If you can fly, you stay out here and wait for Hal and the rest of the aerial medevac team. He'll coordinate trying to take that thing down. If you *can't* fly, you're with me. We have to get as many people out as we can!"

His ground officers, mostly in formalwear, though some had joined them from the squad room, took off after him toward the building in question, dodging car fires and falling debris as they ran. Sin joined the sphinx and siren from the enforcement department, waiting for instructions as Hal the griffin swooped in under the boiling, unsettled clouds.

His deep voice carried easily to those assembled, waiting. "The governor has declared a state of emergency. She is dispatching the Air National Guard. We are to pursue and contain, if possible."

Kellen heard this dictate and looked at the officers standing ready, most flexing their wings.

"Tenzin... I can go with them," he said.

"No. Under no circumstances." Tenzin shook his head. "Your wings aren't meant for endurance flight through storms."

"There are only six of them and none have weapons to engage this kind of enemy... Tenzin, if any of them are hurt, they could be hours from help. Let me follow them."

Tenzin was obviously conflicted, his eyebrows drawing down. "All right. Please be careful, Kellen." He patted Kellen's shoulder and began picking his way across the street to the apartment building being evacuated. There were enough people there already who needed help and they didn't have any more time to waste.

Kellen strode over to the officers preparing to pursue, some of whom had already leaped into the air. Sinistrus was still on the ground, though.

"I'm following for backup medical," Kellen told him, pulling his shirt off.

Sinistrus looked him up and down as if assessing, then he nodded, snapped open his huge black wings and leaped into the air on a powerful down stroke.

Kellen jumped into the air after him, wings a blur. Tenzin was absolutely right that his wings were not meant for long flight, but that didn't mean he couldn't push himself into it when need be. At least speed was not a problem, he had plenty of that, and he arrowed after the rest on the tail of clouds and thunder.

Their goal was not to attack directly, but to harass and keep the beast from landing and causing any more destruction. It was a much more difficult task than it sounded. The thunderbird was more substantial than its cloud wings and body made it appear. It battered them all with winds and deafening screeches, looping and circling, never straying far from the buildings it wished to target. It seemed like hours before jet fighters engaged, but it was probably less than an hour.

The noise of engines joined the sounds of the storm. The blackness of the clouds intensified and rain sleeted down in great sheets. So far the bird had chosen to evade them, but now it wheeled in the sky, screaming its fury. The fighter pilots had outdistanced them and as the great bird turned, the clouds engulfed them. Red eyes lit from within glowed brightly, staring balefully at its pursuers and it opened its mouth to scream. Its head started to change shape, elongating and becoming thinner.

At first Kellen thought it was something the fighters had done, that maybe they had injured it and it would soon fall. He was partly right. They had injured it, but thunderbirds did not fall quietly. The huge body twisted and lengthened, and forks of lightning shot from its eyes and mouth.

Maybe it was because Kellen had dropped behind and to the left, separating him from the other flyers, or maybe it was because his body glowed against the dark clouds in comparison to the others. Whatever the reason, the thunderbird turned directly toward him, locking its strange, wild gaze with his. Lightning flashed…

A heavy body slammed into him, knocking Kellen aside, sending him tumbling. But the lightning missed him even though the air was suddenly filled with the stench of burned flesh and hair. Kellen righted himself in time to see Sin's huge wings folding as his unconscious body plummeted toward the ground.

Kellen dove, folding his wings straight back in a headlong plunge. He reached Sin, grabbed an arm, and snapped his wings out. While not fragile by any means, his wings were light, designed for short fast flights, not for soaring or breaking a fall like this. Sin's body weight was nearly double his own. The roar of the wind bent his wings back but he held on, got a grip with his other hand and strained with everything he had to keep his wings fully extended, slowing their fall. The thought occurred to him that Sinistrus could well be dead but even that did not intrude into his determination. If he wasn't dead, a fall from that height would surely finish him.

They hit hard, but only at a bone-jarring rate rather than a breaking one. Kellen lay gasping, trying to get a full breath, still clutching Sin's body to him, cold and inert.

Far above, the thunderbird raged and shrieked, smaller dark blots on the clouds darting in and out like blue jays after an eagle. The roar of jets turned and headed back. Kellen was certain it would be too late.

A terrific crack sounded to his left, and he whipped his head around in time to watch the slow collapse of the top four floors of the high-rise into which Captain Hartgrove had led his team. They were all going to die today. All of them in this strange human world none of them had been born to.

Kellen shook his head. *No.* That kind of defeatist thinking would help no one. He looked down at Sinistrus, sprawled on the ground with his wings spread out beneath him. The deluge of rain was plastering his dark hair back against skin pale as ashes.

"Oh, you foolish demon... Why? Why did you do that? You should have just let it strike me," he muttered as he checked Sin over quickly for obvious injuries. He wasn't bleeding from anywhere he could immediately determine and when Kellen pressed an ear to his chest, he couldn't hear a heartbeat or detect the rise of his chest. The rain, the wind and the sheer volume of the storm raging around them made him uncertain but he started CPR. He needed back up. He needed to get Sin to shelter. But none of that would matter if he didn't get him breathing and his heart beating again.

He counted the chest compressions, breathed into his mouth, more chest compressions. Had anyone seen them go down? Was anyone on the way? He didn't dare stop to try to call for help.

A human paramedic team finally arrived and took over. Better equipped, better able to tell if Sin had vitals, Kellen backed up and let them work.

"You with the organization, kid?" the male half of the paramedic team asked.

"AURA? Yes. Medical."

"Okay, look, I'm gonna need authorization for transport. There's no way AURA medical can take all these casualties. You gotta help us figure out who can go to a regular hospital and who needs your doctors and healers."

Kellen swallowed hard. All these casualties? What did that mean? "This one needs AURA facilities."

"I have a pulse. Spontaneous respiration," the other EMT said suddenly. "Let's get him in the truck. We're not waiting for authorization."

Kellen got into the back with them without asking. He had no idea who might be back at AURA medical or what they might be facing with Tenzin in the field and Sin out of commission. At the very least he had to make sure someone was there to handle incoming since much of the medical staff had been at the wedding, leaving only a skeleton crew on duty.

"When you said all these casualties," Kellen asked once they were underway. "Could you give me an idea? I might be manning medical alone for a while."

The human woman blinked at him. "You poor bastard. I hope you get relief soon. Most of AURA enforcement was reported near those top floors when they collapsed. We don't have a count yet. They're still pulling bo—casualties out."

Kellen felt the blood drain from his face and the freezing cold and wet finally caught up to him all at once. He might have been an outsider, on the fringe, even at work, but that didn't mean he didn't care about the people he saw every day. Most of enforcement… No, no, that couldn't be right. He refused to believe that. Not right now. Right now he needed to focus and do what needed to be done. He could think later.

He did just that, shutting down any part of his mind that wanted to natter at him about who might be injured, who might have been killed, how many of his coworkers would he never see again. As soon as those thoughts started to creep in, he shoved them to the side.

Medical was a zoo. There was no other way to put it. Tenzin was nowhere in sight and without his efficient leadership, the staff was running in circles, everyone trying to be everywhere at once. Triage was a nightmare. The pair of human EMTs wheeled Sinistrus in on a gurney behind him.

Taking a deep breath, Kellen grabbed the first nurse that he saw. "Janus, I need you to take over stabilization."

"But I was going to stitch up the patient in five — "

"If it's not surgery, it's not top priority. I need you to get an IV started, oxygen and run an EEG."

"But…"

"Just do it," Kellen said, giving her shoulder a squeeze. "One thing at a time, by order of urgency. The stitches can wait."

She nodded. "Yes, okay." Off she went with the gurney and Sin. Kellen had to trust that she would do what was needed.

One by one, Kellen assessed the current backlog of patient injuries and who was on staff and what they were doing. He reassigned care where it was most needed and soon the utter chaos started to become more of an organized chaos. Everyone worked with a sense of urgency but no one was running in blind panic. Patients were stabilized, wounds tended, those who could wait were given water and blankets and settled in the lobby. Someone gave him a scrub shirt, which he gratefully put on.

It was hours later before he heard news in the form of a battered and exhausted Halcyon, who came in with another wounded officer.

"The air force was called to stand down. A consultant found the proper ceremony to appease the thunderbird and it...dissolved. It came apart, lost its form in the storm, which is starting to die out now."

Tenzin finally arrived escorting an ambulance gurney on which lay Captain Hartgrove, barely recognizable through all the plaster dust and grime. He moved restlessly, despite the obvious multiple compound fractures, despite Tenzin's hand on his chest keeping him down.

"I have to go back," the captain whispered. "I have to go back. Ness is still up there. Ness... I have to go back for Ness."

"You can't, Val. It's over. Please rest. You can't do any more," Tenzin soothed, though his voice cracked and he limped heavily.

Kellen rushed to them, helping Tenzin to a chair and making sure Val was rushed off to surgery before he crouched by Tenzin. "Ness hasn't been brought in. Tenzin?"

The yeti buried his head in both hands, pulling in a deep breath that was perilously close to a sob. "They're still digging him out. He was ahead of everyone else when the ceiling collapsed. He— They're still digging him out."

Kellen took Tenzin's hand. "Are they bringing him in? Does he have a chance?"

"He's dead, Kellen. There was nothing we could do. He's... It doesn't seem... But he is. There was too much. He just wanted to help. To save everyone he could. Someone will have to tell Sin."

Someone. Yes.

Kellen released Tenzin's hand and placed it gently on his knee. "I'll tell him. He's here. He was injured." Kellen stood.

The walk down the hallway didn't feel real. AURA had faced many a crisis, some of them had taken lives, but this felt so much closer to home.

Sin was hooked up to an IV and heart monitor but otherwise he lay still and unconscious. Bandaging stood out bone-white against the leading edge of his wing, but otherwise it looked as if he could simply be sleeping. Kellen sank down numbly in the chair beside his bed. He had not felt tired until that point, but as soon as he sat, he felt the weight of all that had happened settle on him. There was still so much that needed to be done, so much to be seen to, but he couldn't have gotten back up right then if his life depended on it. He would rest, and wait.

Chapter Eight

The world seemed too quiet when Sin woke. He waited and listened, unsure of where he was and, more importantly, what was happening. Was the thunderbird still lurking nearby? Did he have to move quickly and soon?

No... Wait. There were soft beeps. Medical department beeps. He was on his back. His wing hurt like hell. So did his right side. What in the world had happened? It was hard to move and his head felt so fuzzy and... *Oh, crap.* Moving caused a wave of nausea. Bad idea.

He felt around on the sheets. There had to be a call button somewhere. Someone to tell him something. Anything. A soft sigh came from beside him and a rustle of cloth. Kellen, looking like three miles of oversalted, ice-cracked road after winter, dozed in the chair beside the bed.

"Kells?" Sin tried, his voice hoarse and scratchy. "Hey."

Kellen came instantly alert, or at least it looked like he tried to. His eyes popped open and he leaned forward quickly, but confusion clouded his expression for a moment. Then he blinked and took a breath. "Sin, you're awake. Don't try to move too quickly. You were injured. How do you feel? Would you like something to drink?"

"Yeah." Sin stopped and coughed. "Water's not a bad idea."

He waited patiently. *Oh, right, that's why they called it being a patient.* Ha. Kellen raised the head of the bed and went to grab some water, which Sin drank in grateful gulps.

"Lightning strike? Was that it?" Sin closed his eyes and tried to recall, but he was coming up blank.

"Yes. The thunderbird. It attacked. Y-you knocked me out of the way, and the lightning bolt hit you."

"Huh. I did that?" Sin shifted and thought better of it again when pain lanced through his wing. "When did I get all heroic?"

Kellen smiled faintly. "I don't know. Lie still. Or is it too uncomfortable on your back? Do you want to try to shift to your side?"

"Don't think it'd make much difference." Sin narrowed his eyes at Kellen, taking in the trembling hands, the gaze that flicked and twitched everywhere. "Hey. I'm doing all right. I mean, it's not fun, but I'm okay. Aren't there other patients? More urgent stuff than me?"

"Sinistrus, there were a lot of casualties," Kellen said.

Something in Kellen's tone alerted Sin. He was more than just exhausted, more than just concerned. There was grief in his eyes.

"How many? How bad is it…?" He sat up in spite of the pain and nausea. "Who was… Ness? Where's Ness? Was he hurt?"

Kellen put a hand on his arm. "Yes… He…"

Sin grabbed him, yanked him practically off his feet. "How bad? Where is he?" he demanded, ignoring the searing pain in his wing and along his side.

Kellen shook his head. "Sin, the building collapsed… Nestor didn't make it out."

"No, that's just stupid. Of course he made it. Ness survived a damn lich queen." Sin seized the railing and pulled himself up. "Where's my Ness, damn it?"

People were gathering in the doorway, looking uncomfortable and maybe scared. Was he being scary? Okay, great. His horns were growing. But someone just needed to tell him and not feed him nonsense.

"Clear out, folks." Flax's voice came from the corridor. "Go on. I got this. Everyone has plenty to do, I'm sure."

"Flax! Thank the goddess! Where the hell is my Ness?" Sin's arm shook from trying to support himself and he thumped back on the mattress. "Kells is spouting crazy shit."

Even Flax didn't look so good, his arm in a sling, a pronounced limp hampering his steps. He dragged his way into the room and Kellen gave him the chair, which he gladly fell into. "Sin, hon. I'm gonna tell you something and I need you to listen. And it's a hard thing and I'm so damn sorry."

"What the fuck? Flax, what's all this bullshit?"

"Hey. You gotta settle." Flax patted his arm, his face set in grim lines. "Ness went into the building. The apartment building where all those people were. The one Val said we needed to evacuate. He went first.

'Cause he's big and can get doors down fast. We started as close to the top as we could get. Hustling people out. The ones we still could since the top floor was already a loss. Ness handed me a little girl. I was on my way down with her. That's when the ceiling came down on us."

Flax pulled a too-familiar pendant out of his pocket, the silver wings glinting in the dim hospital lighting. "Ness was farthest up. He couldn't get out in time. We tried to reach him, but we all went down. It was too much. The concrete. The girders. Sin, I'm sorry. Ness died a hero, but he's gone. And I know that doesn't help. The recovery team gave me this. To give to you."

He handed over the pendant, the ruby cold and heavy in Sin's palm. A strange humming filled Sin's ears and he heard people calling to him from so terribly far away. "No. No. You're all lying. My Ness isn't dead. He's going to come through that door any minute. Not my Ness. No…"

There might have been tears. But they seemed to belong to someone else. None of this was happening. It just couldn't be real. It couldn't.

"Sinistrus… Sin…"

He heard his name being called by a soft, concerned voice, then there was a roar that made him wonder if the thunderbird had returned, only to realize the terrible sound was coming from his own throat. Everything went away. The room, the furniture, the people. None of it was real. None of it mattered. He screamed and there was pain. Hands tried to hold him, to stop him, and he flung them away, he swung wildly and smashed whatever was in his way, and finally the emptiness came to claim him and he embraced it.

* * * *

Drawers overturned, hangers strewn across the floor—Sin laughed at the odd thought that anyone would think the mess looked like a break-in. That was all right. He'd gathered all of Ness' clothes into a nest in the middle of the living room. He would sleep here until Ness got home. Yes. Surrounded by Ness' scent, he might sleep.

He could apologize to Ness later for the mess. Maybe even do some ironing. Wouldn't that shock the stuffing out of his centaur? Ness always did the ironing.

Such a ridiculous, small thought, but it set him crying again. Why was he crying all the time? It made no sense. But he hurt so bad, rocking on the floor, Ness' clothes clutched to him. Why wasn't Ness coming home? He should be home by now.

And damn it, he was hungry. Hadn't he just fed recently? Wasn't it...? No, he couldn't remember now. Ness would know. He'd apologize to Maggie later. Maybe. Why should he? He could feed wherever he liked, after all.

Fine. Sleep wasn't happening. He wandered back to the bedroom, dragging his wing. Stupid wing. What had happened? Stupid wing. Yep, there they were, in the back of the closet since he didn't wear his old clubbing clothes much anymore. He shimmied into the leather pants, wincing as the movement pulled on the burns up his side. Boots. Tight black shirt with the silver snaps to go around his wings. *Ow. Damn. Stupid wing.*

Out into the night. He would drink and feed and drink some more. And eventually, Ness would come and take him home. He wouldn't approve, but he would come and take Sin home. When he stepped out onto the street, Sin flung his head back and howled. People stared. Shied away. He didn't care. He was a night creature and he would reclaim the night as his. Until Ness came to take him home.

* * * *

"Yeah, no word," Flax said as he eased into the chair beside Val's hospital bed. "The apartment's trashed. The door was wide open. It just looks like he walked away. Witnesses say he came to Crossovers, started a fight, threw some furniture around, and then left."

Kai leaned against the wall, fighting exhaustion and his own spinning thoughts. "Can't you send out a bulletin to NYPD?"

"Oh, gee." Flax smacked his forehead in an exaggerated manner. "Why didn't the police officer think of that? Of course we alerted them. But the bar owners won't press charges, so it's not like they can arrest him."

Val struggled to sit up further, wincing and hissing at the pain. "He's not well. Someone needs to find him."

"Sin lived for years on the fringes, with only one arrest," Kai reminded them. "If he doesn't want to be found, he won't be found."

"We're still gonna look, you cold-hearted bas—"

"Flax. Enough." How Val managed a stern, commanding whisper was a mystery to Kai. "I know you're not at your best, either, but I need you to remain professional. We're all grieving and worried, but the world won't stop for us. I need you, Matt and Lisa to divide Ness' duties between you. Until I'm able to decide on permanent assignments. I'm counting on you."

"Yes, Captain."

"And remember that some people's grief is simply more private than others." Val closed his eyes, the whole interaction apparently too much for him.

"Yeah... Sorry."

Kai shoved off the wall and meandered toward the door. "Quite all right. We're all running on fumes, as the young humans say. Val, I'll send your *kalesi* down as soon as we've finished the staff meeting this morning. You need him. Badly."

The last thing he wanted was to have a staff meeting right now. Crawling home to bed, preferably with Tenzin, ideally so he could take some time simply to cry, would have been his preference. But he didn't have that luxury. Something wasn't right. A strange dread crept through his bones, something he should be remembering, something just out of reach. It was driving him mad. Data, he needed more data.

When he reached the conference room, for once everyone was already there. Probably because Kai was late. Well, he was the department head. He could be late once in his lifetime.

"Good morning. I won't ask if everyone's all right. None of us are. But we will carry on as best we can." He eased into his chair at the head of the table, running a hand back over his hair. "Quinn, I take it you still haven't had any success finding Sinistrus?"

Quinn shook his head, and that in itself was enough to make Kai look at him more closely. There wasn't anyone here unaffected by the tragedy, but grief was expressed in many ways and Kai knew for Quinn it often came out as sarcasm and determination. Silence worried him. The haggard look and hints of fear he thought he saw hiding in Quinn's eyes worried him more.

Vicki cleared her throat softly and slid a tablet over to Kai. "I've created a table showing our staff numbers and expected length of absences across all departments. The second column shows all the unfilled positions from before the last, ah, incident. We are now critically understaffed in both enforcement and medical," she said. Her words were plainly spoken but concerned and Kai appreciated her ability to come directly to the point even with such distressing numbers.

"Wait…" Kai said as he noticed something in the data table. "What are these numbers?"

"Those are former applicants."

"Former? So many? All of these failed recruitments?"

"No." Vicki reached over and tapped a few times on the screen. "Only two of these didn't pass standards. The rest have all voluntarily withdrawn."

Kai saw the column next to the names that listed reason for withdrawal of application and couldn't help a faint smile. Not only was she succinct but she was also thorough. She really had become the best in his research department since he had handed over more duties to her.

"Relocation… Relocation… Almost all of these applicants moved away?"

Vicki nodded. "There is a correlation between numbers of crossovers who have withdrawn due to relocation but it's inconclusive because the data pool is not large enough for determination and there are outliers."

Which was researcher speak for 'I think something's going on here, but can't prove my theory yet'.

"We should start more active human recruitment," Kai murmured as he filed the data away in his mind for later. "Sterling, Event analysis?"

"In your pile there, boss. The packet titled *Event Analysis*."

Kai raised an eyebrow at him but didn't snarl at the gentle sarcasm. His staff picked the oddest times to follow his example. "This is... Did we recheck these numbers?"

"I had everyone go over them, Mr. Hiltas. The data doesn't shift and it's not an error."

While the pattern wasn't entirely regular, it was a definite pattern. New York had always been home to regular Events. Large population centers tended to be and the city had a larger population of magic users than most. But this... The number of Events over time had begun to increase exponentially over the past year, with the increase accelerating in the past month. Volume, mass of beings pulled through, and the sheer power of those beings had all increased concurrently.

"There has to be a cause," Kai muttered half to himself. "This can't just *happen*. I want area analysis, what came through where. Precise locations. Let's see if we can dig a little deeper here. This is simply unsustainable for so many reasons."

Quinn rose. "If that's all you need right now, I need to get down to see Val."

Kai's head snapped up, a bit of guilt lodging in his stomach. He flapped a hand at Quinn. "Yes. Go, go. He needs you. I shouldn't have kept you so long."

"It's okay," Quinn said and left.

Kai watched him go and shook his head. Something wasn't right there either, but he didn't have time to wonder about that when there was so much else that needed to be done.

* * * *

Daylight became something Sin saw in rare glimpses. He holed up somewhere during daylight hours—abandoned basements, storage sheds—taking on the vampiric role humans had long assigned him. When the sun set, he reemerged, ready to prowl again.

Sometimes he returned to the apartment in the early-morning hours when he felt the need to feel clean again. But he did this less and less as the days went by, certain there were eyes on the building.

If they caught up to him, they would say he was ill and put him away. Maybe they would arrest him, since some of the things he had done could justify arrest. That couldn't happen. Ness would come for him soon and they would go home together. Then everything would be right again. He just had to wait for Ness to come.

He had lost track of days since the thunderbird had come through. Ten? Twelve? Sin stretched his wings in the deserted alley where he had spent the day. The injured wing still felt wrong. Maybe it would never heal correctly. He would have to test it soon, to see if he could fly again. Soon. Not right then.

For the first few hours of the night, he stayed to the shadows. Normal people still walked the streets, people who found his appearance startling and frightening. He lurked, watching happy couples on their way to dinner, groups of friends out for the evening. But closer to midnight, the crowd began to change, the true denizens of the night emerging, the outcasts, the fringe dwellers, his people.

Sin swaggered down the street, listening for the loudest club noise. When he found what he wanted, he flashed his sharp-toothed smile at the bouncer. The man moved aside for him, though he eyed Sin with dark suspicion. Inside were pulsing lights and writhing bodies, the heavy bass thump a heartbeat under his boots. A buffet so conveniently laid out for him.

Shoving his way through the crowd, he made his way to the center of the dance floor, slowly spread his wings and let his head fall back as he released his own special magic blend of pheromones into the air. He didn't need pickup lines or come hither looks. He just had to exist in a space with females and be hungry. The rest simply happened.

A redhead beside him turned first, giving him a predatory smile. She sidled up to him, rubbing along his body as he began to move to the beat. A dark-haired woman followed and let him shove a knee between her thighs as she gyrated against him.

Soon he was inundated, surrounded, nearly drowning in a flood of women, all desperately trying to get a handhold, trying to get closer to him. A human male rushed him, shouting and angry. Sin couldn't hear him above the music, but he had a good idea what the young man was saying.

"Sorry about your luck, pal." Sin gave him a lazy smile. "See, long as I'm here? They're all mine."

The human tried to grab his shirt and Sin punched him in the face. The women rubbing off all over him didn't even notice. They fed him orgasm after orgasm and he threw his head back, laughing. *Too much, oh, fuck, it's too much.* He was going to be sick later. But it was still amazing and he wanted... He wanted. He needed to fill up the empty dark and he didn't know how else to do it.

In a haze of overfeeding, he finally broke free of the crowd and staggered outside. Somewhere he had picked up a whiskey bottle. Perhaps someone had bought it for him or maybe he had stolen it. He didn't know. He made his way down the street to where he could be sick behind a dumpster in peace. Then he and his bottle wandered through the streets again, looking for the next place to hide.

Chapter Nine

On the one hand, having temporary medical staff on loan from various hospitals was a huge help to AURA. On the other hand, it wasn't a perfect or easy fit when the human nurses and doctors didn't understand the patients' needs or how the crossover healers worked. Still, the help was necessary and everyone was grateful for it.

After three sixteen-hour shifts in a row, Kellen was glad to be headed home and planned to sleep his entire day off. While his neighborhood had never felt entirely safe, ever since the varg attack, Kellen was on higher alert walking home. As he passed the place where the vargs had nearly caught him, Kellen couldn't help think of Nestor. He did every time he went by. Of course it made him think of Sinistrus, too, and wonder where he was, if he was all right, if there had been some way he could have cushioned the blow telling him about Ness.

The sound of shuffling movement ahead caught his attention. Someone was in the alley between buildings. Probably just a drunk, or someone looking for a place to sleep, or both. He walked quickly across, sending a fleeting glance down the alley just to make sure nothing was coming out, and stopped dead. The shape stumbling along was far too big for human because there were large wings mantling behind him.

In disbelief, Kellen turned into the alley. "Sinistrus?" Of course it was Sin, he could see that, but still he sounded doubtful to his own ears because this Sin looked far different than the last time Kellen had seen him. The horns were larger, and his eyes glowed vermillion in the dark. His dark hair was lank and he stank of alcohol and vomit.

The ominous shadow that was Sin stopped as well, staring at Kellen. His claws squeaked on the bottle in his hand as he clutched it harder and brought it up for a long drink. For a moment, he seemed to have forgotten that Kellen was there as he shambled out of the alley and plopped down on the curb to continue drinking.

"Hey, Kells. Nice night."

Kellen looked left, right. No one else was in sight. "Um, I suppose so." He moved next to Sinistrus and crouched. "Sin, where have you been? We've missed you at work."

"Can't go back to work yet." Sin shook his head, his curled ram's horns making the action look cumbersome and painful. "I have to wait for Ness. Soon as he shows up, we can go home."

Kellen's belly tightened and he bit his lip. "Sin, no one expects you to work but…we can help you. Why don't you come in?"

Sin held the bottle out to Kellen, who shook his head. "Yeah, cheap tequila's nasty stuff. Don't blame you." Despite that admission, he took another long pull. "I'll come in soon. Don't worry. Don't want you worried. Just have to wait for Ness."

This was not good, to say the least. Everyone had been looking for him. Now that Kellen had found him, drunk and delusional, he couldn't just let him wander off again. "It's late, Sin. I don't think he's coming, tonight. I live just down the street. Why don't you come and sleep on my couch? Get some rest."

"Couch." Sin said the word as if considering what it meant. "Yeah. I guess it is kinda getting there. Need to find a place to hole up anyway. You sure? Don't wanna get in the way."

"You won't be in the way. I live alone. You can stay as long as you like, as long as you need to."

What was he doing? He should be trying to convince him to seek psychiatric care, or at least remind him that Ness was dead, but neither of those seemed like a good idea. Maybe if he just got him in somewhere safe he could make a call, get him the help he needed. "Come on." Kellen offered his hand to help get him up.

Sin frowned at the hand, obviously just as puzzled as he had been over furniture a moment before. When he reached out, it was tentative, careful, as if he thought, perhaps, that he might break Kellen. "Okay. One night. Nice of you. But if Ness shows up, I need to go, right?"

Kellen couldn't quite bring himself to agree, but he nodded and took Sin's hand, although how much help he was in getting him on his feet was debatable. Once he did, Kellen got a better look at him and gasped. Now he saw why Sin was holding his wings at an odd angle.

The injured one was in a state, the wound looked infected.

"Maybe we can get you cleaned up a little too," Kellen suggested, leading the way to his apartment.

"Hmm." That might have been agreement or grumbling. Hard to say since Sin was drinking as he walked.

They did manage to make it to Kellen's apartment without any major stumbles and he breathed a little easier once he'd closed the door. It would be harder for Sin to bolt now, at least.

Kellen sat him down in the same chair that he'd sat Flax in and once again, retrieved his first-aid kit. From the look of things, he was going to need more than what he had on hand but he at least needed to make an attempt.

"That has to be painful. Will you let me take a look at it?" Kellen asked.

"What?" Sin twisted, trying to see where Kellen pointed. "Oh. That. Yeah. I guess. It's been pretty useless lately."

Kellen examined it and shook his head. "Well, maybe it's good you've been drinking. This looks pretty badly infected. I can clean it out, but it's going to hurt." He didn't give Sinistrus a chance to argue with him. Instead he began swabbing around the wound area with antiseptic solution. Sin kept twitching his wing until Kellen was forced to take hold of it by the upper pinion and hold him still while he worked to clean the wound. He pressed lightly from underneath and pus and blood started to run. That was good, though, had to get it out of there.

"Damn stupid wing." Sin wrinkled his nose in disgust. "S'okay. Hurts all the time anyway. You have nice hands, Kells. People prolly tell you that all the time."

No, people did not tell him that. Sin was the only one, as far as he could remember. What Kellen said, though, was, "Try to hold still. I'm almost done. It will hurt less once we get some of this infection out." It was going to need more than cleaning, but he would cross that portal later.

Sin hissed when Kellen pressed harder and he murmured an apology. He swabbed what he could away and grabbed a clean towel to express more. They were getting down to the meat of it now and Kellen held his breath as he washed away the mess with more antiseptic.

When Kellen had covered the still-seeping wound in gauze as best he could and released the wing, Sin turned in his chair. He wrapped an arm around Kellen's waist and laid his horned head against Kellen's chest with a weary sigh. "Thanks, Kells."

Kellen stood stock-still, his arms held awkwardly out. Sin didn't seem in any rush to let him go, though, and slowly Kellen brought his arms down gently around his head. Sin shifted and his uninjured wing flicked, then stretched to enfold him. His patient made a sound, something deep and grief filled, and Kellen wondered how deep the delusion that Ness was still alive really went. He had been so busy, kept himself so busy, with every waking moment, that he really hadn't any time to think about anything. He carefully stroked Sin's hair and hummed softly under his breath, soothing and healing. He didn't have the same magic as the elves, but his song was comforting, which could sometimes work as well.

Without warning, Sin jerked back. "Oh, goddess. I can't do this!" The wing wrapped around Kellen twitched away, knocking into the wall as Sin backpedaled off the chair and fell on his ass, his eyes wide and horrified. "I can't be doing this. What the hell would Ness think? I don't... Oh, fuck."

Head buried in both hands, he wrapped his unencumbered wing around himself and started to sob.

"Shh, shh, Sinistrus, it's all right..." Kellen hovered but didn't touch him. "It's all right. You weren't doing anything. You're just tired, and hurt, and there is nothing wrong with needing comfort. That's all it was. Just a hug. Now let's get you settled for some sleep, okay? Things will be clearer after you rest."

Sin nodded and let himself be led to the couch where Kellen tucked him in with extra blankets and those dazed red eyes finally closed. He dropped off so quickly Kellen had to wonder when the last time was that Sin had felt safe enough to sleep deeply.

He fretted and worried, fighting his own need to sleep, and kept watch over Sin for several hours while he decided what he should do. Sin was safe here, but for how long? He had a feeling that as soon as he woke in the sober light of day he was going to be off again. Cleaning the wound was not enough — it needed to be treated, and if Sin took off again, who knew how long it might be before anyone saw him again. The infection could render the wing unusable, or possibly even kill him. Kellen had no choice. Sin had to have help.

Reluctantly he went to his room and made a phone call.

"AURA enforcement, Kensington," the gruff male voice answered, sounding as tired as Kellen felt.

"Officer Kensington? It's… It's Kellen." He swallowed hard. This felt like such a terrible thing to do, even though he knew it was right. "From medical?"

"Hey, Kellen." A little shuffle probably meant Kensington was sitting up straight, coming to full alert. "What can we do for you?"

"I found Sin. That is, he found me."

"Sin? Holy sh— Where are you? Can you keep him with you?"

"He's asleep. At my place. I'll try."

"Do the best you can. If he takes off, just try to remember which way he went. We've got a squad car on the way."

Officer Kesington needn't have worried. Sin was still dead to the world when Officer Wolfheart and his two *kalesi* silently entered his apartment. While the two were still officially in training, there was a lot of looking the other way lately while everyone was just trying to get things done.

"Hey, Kells," Flax whispered as he gestured toward the sofa. "How's he doing?"

Kellen shook his head. "He's not well. He's obviously been drinking heavily, his wing's badly infected, and he says he's waiting for Ness to come."

"And you? Are you well?" The tall, silver-haired elf standing just behind Flax asked Kellen.

For a second Kellen felt like his eyes were looking right into him, right through to where he could hide nothing. His throat worked, then he shook the feeling off. "I haven't slept, but I'm fine."

A snort came from the sofa, a snore interrupted, and Sin surged up, suddenly awake. "Cops?"

Flax held his hands out wide. "Sin, it's me. It's Flax, damn it. I know I'm in uniform, but it's still me. You're okay, hon."

But Sin either didn't hear or wasn't processing the words. He leaped up and put the sofa between himself and the elves near the door. "You called the fucking *cops*?"

His trailing wing ruined his defensive stance as he turned frantically, most likely searching for an escape route. Then his gaze locked on Kellen. "How could you do that to me? I thought we were friends! How could you fucking turn me in?"

The last words came out as a terrible bass roar, Sin's eyes gleaming red. He lunged and punched Kellen in the face.

Kellen had been hit before but he was totally unprepared for the blow. It landed square on his jaw and sent him reeling back until he crashed into the opposite wall. For a second he saw only a field of black and stars dancing before his eyes. From far away he heard yelling and roars of rage. Gentle, firm hands took hold of him and his vision cleared. Flax and Sage had Sin pinned to the floor and were trying to wrestle him into handcuffs but were hindered by his wings.

"Don't hurt him!" Kellen said. "He's injured. Be careful!"

Flax let out a huff that was part bitter laugh, part exasperation as he shoved the wing battering his face out of the way and managed to get his shoulder against it while Sage secured the still free wrist. "Kells, we're trying. Sin's not making it easy."

They finally had him cuffed and Flax sat him up, only to be smacked in the head with Sin's good wing again.

"Sin, knock it the fuck off!"

The green-haired elf, his forehead wrinkled in confusion, asked Flax, "Do we Mirandize?"

Probably not the best thing to say. Sin lunged for Flax, sharp teeth sinking into his shoulder, and all three went down again in a heap of struggling limbs. Finally, Sin seemed to run out of fight and sagged between them.

"No. This isn't an arrest. You hear me, Sin? This is *not* an arrest. You're sick and people are worried and you need help, damn it."

"Then take the fucking cuffs off," Sin snarled.

"No. No way in hell. You're killing yourself out here. And we can't just stand by and let you do that."

"I *will* be fine once Ness comes," Sin said. "Let. Me. Go."

Flax looked from Sin to Kellen and Kellen shook his head slowly. "He keeps asking for Ness," Kellen said.

"Crud." Flax stopped trying to restrain Sin and instead hugged him tight. "I'm so sorry. I'm so damn sorry. Let's get you to headquarters, all right? That makes sense, doesn't it?"

Sin blinked at him, his expression blank. Then it suddenly cleared. "Of course. I've been so stupid. Ness is at headquarters. Of course he is."

He struggled to his feet, Flax and Sage supporting him on either side.

"I should've just called. That would've made sense. I just…just haven't been thinking straight."

Flax's jaw looked tight enough to break teeth, but while he looked like he wanted to sink into the floor, he didn't contradict Sin. "Let's get you safe, hon. And then you can talk to the healers about all this. It's gonna be all right."

As Kellen watched them lead Sin out, he shivered. He didn't think things would be all right. Not for Sin. The tall, silver-haired elf touched his shoulder and when Kellen looked up, he felt the weight of his stare again. "You work with the healers, I'm told?"

Kellen nodded.

"Get some rest, little one. None of this is your fault. Sinistrus needed our help."

He knew the words were meant to ease him but somehow the guilt threatening to choke him only became worse. After he closed the door and locked it behind them, Kellen sank to the floor and pressed his forehead to his knees.

Sin's burning look of hatred and betrayal before he'd hit Kellen played in his mind again and again. Had he really needed to call for help? Could he not have done more for Sin on his own? The way he had looked at him, it hurt so much. Sinistrus was right. He did not deserve his friendship. He was weak. Too weak to help his friend, too weak to break the compulsion binding him.

Chapter Ten

At least he's safe. Kai sipped his morning tea as he stared through the one-way glass into Sin's observation room. It was a nice room, bright, cheerful and comfortable, with a regular bed and a comfortable wing chair. Sin had soft pajamas to wear instead of a hospital gown, warm slippers if he wanted them, even a computer if he wanted to read or watch movies.

But Sin had draped a shirt over the back of the chair and stuck a book on top of the back and called it Ness. He had conversations with the chair and cuddled with it at night. While he seemed more peaceful, most of the time, it wasn't Sin. Not all of him, at any rate.

Warmth suddenly enveloped Kai's back, and white furry arms came around to hug him tight.

"Kai, my beloved, my own, you're not doing him any good like this."

He leaned his head back against Tenzin's bulk. Simply having Tenzi there took the edge off his persistent headaches. "I know. I do go in to visit. Though he doesn't always know I'm there."

"But sometimes."

"Yes. Sometimes." Kai gestured with his mug. "His horns have receded to normal. The wing is doing much better, they tell me."

"One thing at a time. We're addressing the physical first, since we believe all the pain and dreadful living conditions were only exacerbating his condition." Tenzin nuzzled at the top of Kai's head. "None of us are doing well. It's just that some of us are doing better than others."

"Oh?" Kai turned in his husband's arms to look up at him. "It sounds as if you mean something specific."

"Hmm. Ash said something odd today when he came down with Flax for a follow-up on his knee issues. He said that Kellen's energy is too dark. That his light is veiled in webs of black."

"Damnable elves. What in the world is that supposed to mean?"

Tenzin stroked his hair with a sad smile. "I presume it means that Kellen is terribly depressed. At least that's how it seems to me. I've asked him if he needs to talk. He says it's nothing. Though he has hinted at feeling guilty for Sin's detainment."

"He did the best thing!" Kai protested. "If he hadn't called in, Sin would be dying in some filthy alley."

"Of course, love. I know. Still. I've asked Kellen to take a rotation with Sin. Perhaps it will help to see that Sin is doing better here than he would be on the street."

Kai scowled thoughtfully. "Do you think that wise, Tenzi? I heard how our Sin was brought in, how he reacted to Kellen."

"We'll watch the first time. Sin's reactions don't always follow reasonable patterns at the moment. He may well have forgotten about the circumstances of his arrest entirely."

Kai made no further comment. This was Tenzin's environment and he often did know best how to treat his patients, even when the healthcare went beyond the physical. Still, he decided to stay for longer than he had intended so that he could be with Tenzin in the observation room when Kellen went in the room with Sin.

That entrance was a marked contrast to the too cheery nurses who had come and gone before to bring Sin's breakfast and check on him.

Kellen came into the room quietly, carrying a tray with bandages, swabs and tape. Kai couldn't decide if it would have been any smarter to send him in with a tray of hot food. He still looked quite battered himself and it would be interesting to see if the sight of his bruised face jogged Sin's memory any more than just seeing him at all would.

"Sin? I'm here to change your bandages," Kellen said.

"Yeah? Well I'm here 'cause you're a whiny narc twerp. You can take the fucking bandages and shove them up your uptight little pixie ass."

Kai's hand hovered over the call button for assistance, not that they would need more muscle with Tenzin standing right there. But Sin's invective was tired and grumbling rather than threatening and while he glared at Kellen, he hadn't moved from the bed. He did sound more reasonable and sane than he had at any time in the past two days.

Kai watched Kellen's shoulders hunch, and waited for him to retreat, but after a brief moment he seemed to come to some decision and stepped forward.

"You know the rules. You can either let me tend the wound, or they will send someone to force you to hold still."

"Let them send someone else. They won't have to force me. I just don't want *you* here."

Kellen faltered at that, but he took another step and lifted his chin. "Too bad. I'm what you got. I don't care if you don't like me. I have a job to do."

Sin turned his head, a frown creasing his forehead as he stared at the chair beside the bed. "Fine. Whatever. Since Ness feels bad for you, I guess I'll be a good boy and not bite you."

Kellen set the tray on the end of the bed and began to remove the old dressing. He cleaned the area gently and applied an ointment meant to both help heal the wound and to keep the membrane of his wing from stiffening. That was a bigger risk with a wing injury than the wound itself. An improperly healed membrane would hinder Sin's mobility unless treated properly. When he was done applying the bandage, Kellen cleaned up.

"I'm sorry, Sin. I had no choice. I couldn't treat this without help."

"That's 'cause you're a twerp." The insult sounded tired and devoid of real malice. Sin pointed to the mostly untouched breakfast tray on his nightstand. "Look, you really wanna help? I need to feed. Solid food's nice but only 'cause I need a little of that to keep up this perfect physique."

Kai nearly choked on his tea. Poor Sin was wretchedly thin, the bones in his wrists standing out as sharply as his ribs.

"And I can't ask the human nurses. They'd get all offended and crap. So, yeah. That would be helping."

"Y-you want to feed from me?" Kellen asked.

Sin snorted. "Really? You're that clueless? No. As in fuck, no. I can't feed from you. If I could feed from males, I wouldn't need to ask you. I have Ness." He waved at the chair. "Incubus. I'm a fucking incubus. Yeah. Pun intended. I need female sexual energy, even though it's not my favorite flavor. Kinda like human kids have to eat their broccoli."

"But...oh, never mind," Kellen said, clearly flustered. "Okay, I'll get... I'll arrange...something."

"Huh." Sin gave him an odd look, but he seemed to have shed some of the hostility. "Well, thanks."

Kai leaned his forehead against the glass, dizzy with relief. That had gone far better than he had a right to expect. Not perfect, but far better. He didn't have illusions about Sin getting magically better, but a good stretch of reasonable behavior was excellent progress.

* * * *

Of all the humiliating things Kellen had ever been put through, having to find Sinistrus someone to feed from was by far the least of them, but it still wasn't comfortable. He could have foisted it off on to someone else but that didn't seem right. Sin had been 'in custody' for over a week now and he'd not requested food from anyone else, so Kellen took the responsibility.

Considering Sin's mental and emotional state, he wasn't sure it would be wise to bring in someone from the outside, which meant trying to figure out which among the female staff would be willing to donate their…time. And wouldn't think he was some kind of pervert. He knew the medical staff better than anyone from the other departments, but he hesitated to ask anyone in medical for several reasons, the most important being that he had to work with them. If any decided to take offense, it could make things awkward later.

There were still several choices. He just needed to work up the courage to ask. He reminded himself that Sin had to do this all the time, and he never seemed to lack for female attention, whether he encouraged it or not. On top of his own discomfort, he also considered that humans were often confusing when it came to sex. They said one thing and gave off signals for another. Their mating rituals were baffling. Elves were at least more honest and easier to understand, but there were no female elves here at AURA.

He decided he would start with nonhumans first, and if he didn't find anyone, then he would venture into asking a human woman. His first stop was enforcement.

"So, you see, I thought perhaps, if you felt comfortable in donating?" Kellen felt the words tripping out of his mouth. Officer Aello was not looking pleased with him.

She tapped her pen on her desk, mouth drawn down, wings rustling in an agitated way. Across the room, Matt looked up from a file and made a gesture that could have meant *you need me over there?* She waved him off with a scowl and took a slow breath.

"Look, Kellen, I know this can't be easy to do. So I'm not gonna get mad. But there's so much no here. I can't even start on how much no. I have to work with Sin. On emergency calls. There's no way I can do this."

"Okay, it's no problem. I understand," Kellen said. "I'm hoping that you, that we, will both be able to work with him again. I'll let you get back to work then, thank you for your time."

"It's okay. Oh, hey. And maybe don't ask Cypria." Aello nodded to where the sphinx was doing an intake with a goblin gang suspect. "She's not real good with talking about sex."

Kellen nodded. The sphinx was absolute last on his list anyway, but he figured he would just cross her off entirely. He was sure that the flower fairies were off the list too, if for no other reason than the logistics of size.

His next stop was down in holding. This time he asked the officer in question, who happened to be a selkie, to speak to him privately. How that request had gotten so misconstrued he wasn't sure, but she ended up thinking that he was propositioning her or trying to trick her and he spent the next fifteen minutes explaining and apologizing. Needless to say, she didn't offer to feed the incubus.

The two nymphs in counseling said they had no interest in being a meal, but they offered to help him work out his frustrations, which only made Kellen more flustered and he left as quickly as he could.

Little hoof beats pelted after him as he turned down the hall away from counseling. "Kellen!"

He turned to see Lysander running to catch up with him, the little faun all proper and professional from the waist up in shirt and tie and in nothing but what the

Mother gave him from the waist down. It was always a little jarring, but fauns wouldn't dress any other way.

"Kellen, I couldn't help overhearing. We've been trying to think of a way for Sin to feed that wouldn't interfere with a later counselor-patient relationship." Lysander put a hand on his arm. "And I have a suggestion."

As giantesses went, Betty from accounting was average size. Meaning she was nearly ten feet tall, slender and shapely. She could have passed for human, if not for her height. She also was agreeable, which was even better.

"He was always nice to me," she told Kellen in her warm, gravelly voice. "And that's not as common as it should be. Besides, he's awfully cute."

Kellen could feel the blush creeping up his cheeks and hoped she wouldn't notice. Cute wasn't exactly how he would describe Sinistrus. Maybe to a giantess he was cute. But to Kellen he was... Kellen wasn't sure. Handsome? He was that. Even when he was fierce and angry, he was still handsome, by any standard. He supposed he had noticed that before. Maybe. Sin certainly had sex appeal. He was tall, broad in the shoulders and narrow in the waist. Even thin and ragged, there was a quality about Sin that spoke to carnal desires. He supposed.

The relief of finding someone for Sin to feed from over, Kellen realized it was more than just making the arrangement. She would go to him now, and they would do...whatever they were going to do together. It wasn't as if he were ignorant of sex. It had just been a long time since he'd thought of it in any way that didn't involve pain and betrayal and a disgusted feeling afterward.

He was not going to think about what sex with Sinistrus would be like. Sin didn't even like him for one thing, and…and Kellen would never be free to enjoy such a dalliance anyway. Would he enjoy it? Would it be different?

Kellen pushed those confusing thoughts away.

He walked Betty down to the rooms set up in medical as psych ward rooms. There were only two, perhaps the smallest ward in the city. Sin blinked at them as they came in.

"Ah, this is Betty. I think you know Betty," Kellen fumbled through the introduction. "And she, um…"

"Hi, cutie." Betty waggled her fingers in a little wave. "I hear you're getting a little famished. Just came to help out."

Sin rose slowly from the bed, his expression thoughtful as he nodded. "Hold on. Ness doesn't like to watch." He threw a blanket over the wing chair and held a hand out to Betty. "Thanks for coming. There sure is a lot of you."

"Okay… I'll, um…go…if you, er… Okay." Kellen stopped talking as Sin slid his arms around her and she bent down to kiss him. He fumbled with the key card and slipped out as quickly as he could, closing the door behind him. Thankfully there was no one else in the hall and he had a moment to compose himself. Embarrassing. That was all he felt, right? Embarrassed. He looked down the hall blankly. Jealous? He was not jealous. That was absurd. And he was not the least bit aroused either. Even more absurd.

Chapter Eleven

"So, you're not here to take them off our hands?" The NYPD officers Kai had spoken to had all been frustrated to greater or lesser degrees. This one letting him into holding was no exception.

"I do apologize," Kai said in a chill tone that implied his apology was mere professional courtesy and not actual regret. "But I'm afraid the holding cells at AURA must be reserved for the more dangerous crossovers at present. Or would you rather I take goblin and fairy youngsters and give you the varg and the wyvern we currently have down there?"

The officer paled, cleared his throat and pretended not to have heard. "There's just too many these days. And we can't keep them with general population. It just causes more fights."

Kai nearly choked when they reached the nonhuman cells. The first held ten young goblins in a cell meant for four. The NYPD never paid particular attention to crossover crime if they could help it. They had AURA to handle nonhumans. But this…

Four different braidings. Kai shook his head. "You do know that you're housing rival gangs in the same cell?"

The officer shrugged. "They're all goblins. All look the same to me."

Long ago, in another world, Kai would have made the man pay in pain for his racist idiocy. Now? He had to clench his jaw and pick his battles more carefully. "Cousins," he addressed the occupants of the cell in the common goblin dialect. "What has happened that so many are here?"

There was some shoving and some angry glares before the largest of the youngsters approached the bars. "Elder brother, we didn't start this war. The fairy scum did."

"Wolf Clan allies with Badger Clan? With Otter and Stag against the fairy?" Kai pointed with his chin to the cell's other occupants.

"Never." The young goblin shoved a stray lock of black hair behind his ear, a dozen gold hoops bright against his green skin. "There are no allies here."

Oh, wonderful. It's a free-for-all out there. "Your territories—"

"All treaties are broken, elder brother. Too many lines crossed. If you have come to negotiate a peace, as the AURA *tesined* has tried to do, you waste your breath."

"Understood. I came only to count. And to mourn."

The goblin gang members stilled. That wasn't the answer they'd expected. Kai turned his back and stalked down the row, taking count as he had said. Goblin, brownie, fairy—all the small tribal groups the human world had never understood enough to assimilate properly. Too many, far too many, and all of them far too young.

Uniformed officers fell back and made way for him when he stalked back out of the station, and he had no doubt that thunderstorms rode in his eyes.

Something was driving the escalation in violence. The gangs fought, certainly, short, nasty turf battles, skirmishes over obscure points of trampled honor. But not like this all out warfare. Something...just under the skin...just out of reach...

* * * *

With a regular feeding schedule, Sin was putting back on some of the pounds he lost, and the wounded wing was in good shape, nearly healed. If he were a regular patient, Kellen would be thinking of ways to get him rehabilitated and on his own again. What stopped him was not Sin's physical health. Although Sin had long periods of lucidity, he still would not accept that Nestor was dead, and he retreated into delusion when anyone suggested anything to the contrary. Not that many tried.

Tenzin believed that time and patience were what was needed, but Kellen was not so sure he was right in this instance. In fact, he was starting to think the longer Sin believed the delusion, the harder it would be to bring him back.

There was not much more he could do however, except to visit and coax Sin into conversation. If his questions pressed too hard Sin either yelled, or shut down, until Kellen changed the subject. He also thought Sin should have more visitors but everyone was so busy lately that sometimes Kellen was the only one who saw him during the day. He'd taken to eating his lunch with Sin, and he brought Lola with him so that he had some variety of company. Lola seemed to enjoy the visits too.

One day, several weeks after Sin's hospitalization, Kellen had brought Lola along with some of the nut mix she had been eating.

"C'mere, little tree rat." Sin held out his hand and Lola happily ran up his arm. "How's my big girl today? Good goddess, you're turning into a giant squirrel, aren't you?"

Ignoring his own lunch, Sin seemed entirely content to sit cross-legged on the bed, feeding Lola.

"She is," Kellen agreed. "She's almost ready to be out on her own."

Sin's head snapped up, his eyes suddenly filled with anguish. "On her own? Like, out there? Away from us?"

"Well," Kellen said slowly. "She wouldn't be completely on her own. But, Sin, she should be free, don't you think? To be with her own kind? Find her own mate?"

"Mate?" Sin held Lola up at eye level, shaking a finger at her sternly. "You're too young for a mate, young lady. Don't you forget it. You don't need some male squirrel bossing you around, making you promises, deserting you when the season's over…"

He trailed off, his voice cracking. Something had intruded on his insular little world.

Kellen reached over and gently patted his knee. "Not yet, no. She's still too young, you're right. But soon. Spring maybe. She'll want to be outside with the other squirrels. Maybe you could help me find a place for her in the park, if you're well enough."

"I don't want to let her go." Sin had dropped his gaze to the floor. "I don't...don't want to lose her."

The back of Kellen's neck prickled. He wasn't really talking about Lola, or at least not only about Lola.

"She has to move on from us sometime, Sin, and...you need to get well."

"I feel fine. I can leave right now. I'm not the one keeping the door locked."

"Yes, I know," Kellen said, careful now. "Sin, you have to face things before they'll let you go. That's not Nestor..."

Sin narrowed his eyes and put Lola on the blanket where she played happily. "What the hell is wrong with you? Of course that's Ness. He's laughing at you. You hear him. And they say I'm the one who's out of touch with reality?"

So close. He had been so close to a breakthrough. Kellen was sure of it. He had *felt* something happening, for a moment. Now he was right back into his delusion. He stood with a frustrated sound. "It isn't him, Sin. It's a chair. You have to face this." He shook his head and ignored the sudden stillness that came over Sin, the dangerous gleam in his eye. He walked over to the chair and sat down.

Slowly, Sin rose, a deep growl rumbling in his chest. The red glow that heralded his rage intensified and he balled his fists despite his claws elongating. "What the *fuck* do you think you're doing? Get the hell off of —"

Just as his voice rose to a roar, Lola decided she'd had enough of playing with the threads of the blanket and leaped to Sin's shoulder. He startled, his descent into rage interrupted by the fuzzy squirrel face nuzzling his cheek. For a long, terrible moment, he stood frozen, gaping, as if he had turned to stone. He stared at Lola, then at Kellen in the chair, shudders racing through him.

"No," he finally whispered. "No. Oh, sweet mother, no." With a cry of heartrending anguish, he fell to his knees, sobbing. "No, no, no, don't leave me. Don't leave me… Ness… Fuck… Ness… Don't *leave* me!"

Kellen's heart was beating so hard he could feel it pounding against his ribs. The wash of fear had come and gone and in its place was nothing but a deep sympathy. The last time he had tried to offer Sin comfort he had rejected it violently but this time the sorrow felt larger, consuming, heartbreaking. He moved to lay a hand on Sin's wing, already humming at an inaudible level. There was still every possibility that Sin would turn on him, but he hardly cared. Something had to bring him back, or he was going to be lost forever.

Sin grabbed on to him, but it was the desperate clinging of someone drowning rather than a physical threat. "Tell me it's not true. Tell me they were wrong. That Ness made it out. Tell me he's somewhere… Even if I can't see him. Please. Kellen… Please."

Kellen put his arms around Sin and rested his cheek on the top of his head. "Somewhere, yes. With the Mother, in the After. Somewhere that isn't here," he crooned soothingly. "You have to let him go, Sin. He wouldn't want you to not go on."

"I can't do this. I can't do this without him." Sin's wings wrapped around them as if to hide all three of them from the world. "I need my Ness. It wasn't supposed to… I can't. It was too soon."

The sobs wracked Sin's body, horrible, choking sounds as if he dragged them up from the marrow of his bones. Perhaps he had, since he'd buried his grief so long. The infection in his wing had healed, while the infection in his heart had festered.

Kellen didn't know how long they stayed like that, how long he held and soothed him while his grief poured out. Oddly, in the shelter of those great wings, things like time and duties and the rest of the world simply ceased. He shed his own tears for Sin's heartbreak, and he sang to him soft words of comfort and lament.

When Sin finally quieted to whimpers, he didn't seem able to move. Kellen helped him into the bed and tucked him in with only a half second's thought that it was a strange thing to do with a full-grown incubus. When Kellen left Lola went with him, as did the chair. No need to cause Sin extra anguish having to stare at it.

Tenzin met him in the hall and laid a gentle hand on his shoulder. "Well done."

Kellen shook his head. "It doesn't feel that way."

"I know. It's always hard to ride the storm of someone else's pain." Tenzin folded him close, something Kellen wouldn't normally have allowed. "But you did what needed to be done. What no one else was able to do. You and Lola."

Kellen chuckled weakly. "Yeah, I think Lola did far more than I did. Probably saved me from another punch too." He scratched lightly behind her ear.

"He'll rest. We'll watch him over the next day or two. But I think he may be able to walk out of that room this week."

* * * *

The apartment stared at Sin, lifeless and strange, as if their home had died with Ness. He picked the pile of clothes off the floor and transferred them to the sofa, emptied the dishwasher that had waited patiently for weeks, and put the drawers back in Ness' bureau. Gathering all of Ness' clothes into a nest pile? He didn't recall doing that, but he must have.

Sin touched the pendant he wore around his own neck in remembrance and tugged Ness' pumpkin-colored scarf from the clothes pile. It still smelled like Ness after all that time and he had to sit down for a bit and cry. Again. *Never seem to run out of tears these days.*

They had made him promise that he wouldn't take long. He was expected for dinner and was just here to pack a suitcase so he could stay with Kai and Tenzin. They worried about him living alone, which, yeah, he couldn't blame them. Being here was harder than he thought it would be, though, and he wished now that he had waited for Tenzin to get off shift as the yeti had suggested.

"I don't want to adult anymore, Ness." He picked up Ness' leather jacket and buried his face in the lining. "Not without you. It's too damn hard. It's just too hard."

While he didn't still think Ness was standing beside him, he couldn't help talking to his pony boy. Maybe he always would. Tenzin said that wasn't at all strange. But he felt himself sinking and he needed someone responsible. Kai would be home late. Tenzin didn't leave work for another two hours. Quinn was... Goddess only knew what Quinn was doing these days. He hardly ever answered his phone. Flax? No. That pointy-eared twit had so much guilt where Ness was concerned he just made Sin want to cry more, and Flax's boys didn't like him. Not one bit.

Sin pulled his phone out of his pocket and sent a text.

Kells? Are you off shift soon?

Within a few moments he received a reply.

Just leaving now.

It wasn't the easiest thing to do, asking for help, but he was supposed to. The counselors called it his support system.

Can you come to my place? Not doing so good?

The response took just a little longer but still within moments.

I'll be right there. Directions?

Through blurred eyes, Sin typed directions from the AURA building. It wasn't far. Ness had liked the proximity to work. Yeah... The apartment with its special accesses and facilities. All for Ness.

He was certain Kellen did not possess the ability to teleport, but it seemed like he was suddenly there after Sin had just sent the text. He might have lost some time. The soft knock on the door brought him back and he let Kellen in.

"Hi," Kellen said.

Sin took a deep breath and tried to explain. "I'm supposed to be packing some shit. To stay with Kai and Tenzin." He waved at the apartment, realized he still had Ness' scarf clutched in his fist and fell to pieces.

"Shh, shh, it's okay," Kellen crooned. He patted Sin's shoulder but not an awkward pat, more like a caress. "Maybe you aren't ready for this yet, Sin."

"I can't stay here." Sin hated that he was blubbering, but he couldn't seem to stop. "I have to… I just wanted to… And all of Ness' things…"

Kellen drew a deep breath and took him by the shoulders. Green eyes looked directly into his own, jewel bright and solemn. "Why don't I help you pack some things for yourself, to take with you? The rest, it isn't going anywhere. It will wait until you're ready. Okay?"

Sin managed a nod, still snuffling, and waved vaguely toward the back of the apartment. There was a suitcase back in the closet, wasn't there? Ness' scarf he kept hold of, simply unable to let go yet.

"I don't… I think there's…" But he found it while he was trying to form a whole sentence, the bag with the wheels. The bright red bag with the wheels that Ness had bought him for future travel plans. He cleared his throat and managed to pull it from the closet without more blubbering.

Kellen followed him into the bedroom. Sin noticed he was looking around in that way people did when they didn't want to seem like they were looking.

"What do you think you will need for a few days away?" Kellen asked him, probably because he was just standing there like he was waiting to be told what to do. Somehow Kellen made the question seem perfectly reasonable instead of like a counselor trying to talk him down.

"Um…clothes?" Sin sat on the bed wiping at his eyes. Great Mother of demons, this was ridiculous. "Toothbrush? I don't need a lot."

"Okay." Kellen sat down next to him, close but not too close. "Do you need help packing, or would you just like me to keep you company?"

"I just need someone here. So it's not so empty. And…empty." Sin rubbed both hands over his thighs. "I didn't think it could still hurt so much. I mean, of course it still hurts so much. But it's like the pain is still trying to jam all the signals. Ram straight through my brain down my throat so I can't breathe. I thought I could do this."

"It takes time, Sin," Kellen said. There was a familiar soft rustle as Kellen shifted beside him, tucking one of his legs up so he could sit on one hip and flick his wings to the side.

Sin nodded and something in that calm, quiet presence allowed him to move again, to get up and open a drawer, gather a pile of T-shirts and put them in the open suitcase. Had he opened the suitcase? Kellen must have. That was fine. Shirts. Okay. A few pairs of jeans. Some of his custom-made scrubs. Tenzin said he could come back to work part time soon. Socks. He needed socks, though he never bothered with underwear. Except for… No. Not thinking about that. Toothbrush. Hairbrush. Tenzin would have everything else for him.

He stood staring at the pitiful pile of things and felt as if his brain were filled with sludge. "I guess that's it? I don't even know."

"It looks like that should keep you in clothes for a while, yes," Kellen said. "Why don't you put the scarf in with your things and take it with you?"

"I think I'll hang on to it." Maybe that was stupid. It was just a scarf. But he'd loved it on Ness and it felt good in his hand. He fingered some of his T-shirts, all custom. All his shirts were custom. "Kells? Why do you cover up your wings?"

"It's easier to keep them out of the way," Kellen answered.

Sin frowned at that. The answer had been too fast, too pat. "Uh-huh. I've got these big-ass wings and they never get in my way. Not sure how your cute little wings would be a problem."

"Well, it's not like they're very useful. Not like at home. And people stare enough as it is."

"Wings are always useful." Sin shut the suitcase and zipped it. "They're more expressive than hands." He let his wings droop, then rustle, then snapped them out to full extension. "And you think people don't stare at me? Well, okay. It's 'cause I'm too sexy for my wings, but damn, Kells. You have *wings*. You shouldn't have to hide them 'cause some people are jerks."

Kellen's head was bowed but Sin could still see the way his forehead crinkled in thought. "I—I don't hide them, exactly."

Sin snorted and Kellen looked up at him, a confused little frown on his face.

"You think I shouldn't hide them?"

"I think wings as beautiful as yours should never be hidden," Sin said with only the tiniest quake to his voice. There, he could do this. He was managing to be not crazy.

"Well, could I maybe borrow one of those T-shirts then?"

Sin even managed a smile. "Of course you could." He unzipped the suitcase and looked at the pile. All black and dark green. That wouldn't do for Kells. The drawer had some other colors nearer the bottom and he fished out an emerald-green one that would go with Kellen's eyes. The letters on the front read *I Hope You Step on a Lego*. Okay, maybe not the best choice for such a nice pixie, but it would be a start. With a hesitant smile, Sin handed it over.

Kellen took the shirt from him and to Sin's surprise, took his own shirt off right then and there and put the borrowed shirt on. Perhaps Kellen was simply humoring him.

The specially made slits in the back were made to accommodate Sin's wings of course, so they were more than adequate to allow for Kellen's. The shirt itself was about three sizes too big and hung on him like a short dress.

"Good color on you. And you could wear it as a nightshirt and stuff," Sin said with a nod. "I'll give you the name of the guy who does mine. So you can get some your size."

"Thank you," Kellen said simply.

Sin looked at him curiously. He seemed far too solemn and sincere over a simple T-shirt. It was no big deal. The look on Kellen's face though, the hesitant smile, and the way he slowly flexed his wings, fanning them out in a comfortable-looking arrangement, was like someone had just given him back something he'd lost.

It didn't take a genius to figure out the little guy didn't have many friends. Damn it. In all his wallowing in his own dark places, he still could've seen that. Sin cringed at the memory of some of the mean things he'd said to Kellen. The little guy wasn't sneaky, he was shy and socially awkward because of bad stuff in his past. At least Sin could try to be a better friend. He could do that.

"No, thank you. For coming to save me from myself. I hate needing help. But thank you."

Chapter Twelve

Leading a double life. That was what they called it when you had all these secrets inside. Secrets Kellen had no choice but to keep. It hadn't seemed so terrible before, keeping those secrets. He had his own space, he had work that he liked to do and people he liked to be with, and it had been so easy to pretend that was his life and what he did for Rask and the coven was simply an unpleasant chore, best done quickly, and just as soon forgotten.

It was, however, becoming more and more difficult to pretend that what the coven did was benign. It was getting more and more difficult to have a friend, when he couldn't be honest with him. He wanted to confess more than anything. He wanted to tell Sin about the blood rites, and his part in them. How he didn't want to help, but he was bound by magic to Rask.

At home, even if he had managed somehow to break through the compulsion and confess, he would have been an outcast. Slavery was common among his people. Pixie dust was valuable and rare. Their colonies were often raided and captives taken into slavery. There was no shame in having suffered such a fate, and those who escaped were protected and cared for, but what had been done to Kellen was different. What had been done to him was a perversion. The bond that mates shared was sacred, a melding of lives and souls. Instead of a sharing of trust and love that would have created the bond, Rask had used blood and pain to force it, enslaving him with a corrupted, evil version of the mate bond and twisting it inside him until he was compelled to obey. Kellen's dust was the rarest of pixie dust types, and Rask had wanted to be sure he had no hope of returning to his family even if he did manage to escape.

Here he didn't know what he might face if anyone knew, but he would endure the recoiling, he would accept being an outcast, if he could make things right. He rehearsed the lines he would say in his head, but if he tried to utter them, excruciating pain seared through his body. If he tried to write them, his hand spasmed and cramped into a stone. If he tried to push through the pain, he only succeeded in passing out.

Rask found new delight in tormenting him now that he had Shawna cowed and under his control and the only reason there was any respite was Rask was more often than not lost in his projects.

Kellen spent as much time as he could with Sin, and he found as much comfort in being with him as the incubus did in having Kellen around. He wore his new scrubs made with slits for his wings, and he felt a warmth of pride that he'd never felt before when Sin complimented him. He spoke more at work, he laughed more, and when Sin told him that he liked the improvements, he glowed. At night when he lay down, and he brought to mind how Sin looked in profile, or how he could coax a smile from him, or how it had felt to have his arms around him as he wept, no one needed to know those thoughts.

That morning, Sin was at the front desk answering the phone and handling patient scheduling. Both Hal and Tenzin agreed he wasn't ready to go back to work with the medevac team, but half days doing clerical or lab work had been going well.

"Hey, Kells." Sin glanced up and managed one of those quick, half-distracted smiles when Kellen came in for shift. "You're nine o'clock is here. An hour early. And you've got a ten with a goblin family whose kids are losing their hair."

"Okay, anything else going on?" Kellen asked, taking a stack of folders and straightening them.

Sin shook his head. "Quiet so far. But it's early, right?"

"Right." He took the top folder, turned around, and nearly collided with Kai Hiltas. His wings flicked back and down involuntarily. He would have been startled no matter who it was, but there was that extra half second before his brain registered that it was only Kai. Who was now married to his boss, his friend, and was looking at Kellen like he was more than a little tired of dealing with him every time he came down here. "Sorry. Good morning."

"Good morning, Kellen." Cool, polite, Kai always was with him, but there was always that slight narrowing of those disturbing silver eyes, as if Kellen were a puzzle or a problem Kai needed to solve. "Sin, is your lovely supervisor available? He forgot his watch again this morning."

"He's back in radiology right now, but they're doing equipment stuff." Sin waved a hand back and forth as if *equipment stuff* referred to some sort of arcane magic. "You can go back, beautiful."

Kellen watched as Kai nodded then went down the hall toward radiology. He followed him with his eyes until he was out of sight before he asked Sin, "You think he's beautiful?" He almost bit his tongue as soon as the words were out. That sounded far too personal. Jealous, even. He'd only meant it to sound curious.

Sin cocked his head, automatically glancing the way Kai had gone as if he had to check. "He's gorgeous. Most handsome drow I ever met. Kinda helps that he doesn't really think so. Drow can be conceited bastards." Sin frowned, his forehead wrinkling as he considered something. "But, you know, asking an incubus if he thinks someone's beautiful is probably like asking a fish if they like water. Everyone's their own beautiful."

"Oh," Kellen said. Maybe that explained why Sin said things like he thought his wings were pretty. That was just the way he talked. "I better get going then."

"Hey." Sin finally looked at him directly. "You do know you're gorgeous too, right? I mean really gorgeous? Like some pixies are pretty, but you're really stunning. I mean, you have to know that, right?"

Kellen's face felt so hot he was sure he was blushing to the roots of his hair. He wasn't sure if Sin actually expected him to answer, but since he kept staring at him, he figured he needed to say something. "Y-you don't have to say that."

"Of course I don't *have* to. Did you ever know me to say shit just to be polite?"

"I— No," Kellen said. "I just thought, well, I don't know."

"You all right, Kells?" Sin's frown hadn't budged. "You're being a little weird this morning."

"Weird? No, I'm fine. It was just a question." He lifted the folder he was holding. "Really. I'll see you later."

"Okay. Yell if you need me." Sin gave him a wave as the phone lines began to ring, and if his cheer seemed a little forced, at least he was trying.

For the rest of the morning, Kellen's concentration was blown. He did everything he needed to do but every time he stopped for even a moment, his mind went back to the conversation with Sin. No, he had never known Sin to say anything just to be polite. Sin thought he was gorgeous? What did that mean, though? He played the conversation over in his head again and again. He had *sounded* like he was just being polite. And he did say he thought everyone was beautiful. It had to be just something to do with him being an incubus then, it didn't mean anything. He really wished he could convince his fluttering stomach of that.

"Kellen?"

"Hm? Oh, sorry. Did you need something, Jean?" Kellen looked up at the nurse who was holding out a clipboard toward him.

"Yes, I need you to sign this chart, please. You forgot to earlier." She smiled oddly at him as he took it, looked and saw he had indeed forgotten to sign it. He'd never done that before. He scrawled his name quickly and handed it back to her. "Sorry about that."

"No problem." She was still grinning at him. "Soooo, who is she?"

"She?"

"I know that look. You've been floating around here all day. So, who is she?"

Kellen twitched his wings and looked down to make sure he was standing on the floor still. Yes, feet firmly on the ground. He didn't remember any involuntary flights. "I don't understand?"

"Kellen! I'm asking who you're seeing. You look like a love-struck nymph," Jean chuckled.

"What? No! I mean, no. There is no 'she'."

"Oh, so it's a he?"

"No! There isn't anyone. I'm not seeing anyone. I was just a little distracted." Kellen's heart beat harder. Was he acting weird? How could she possibly know what he was thinking?

Jean smirked at him knowingly. "Right. Okay." She winked. "Well, you just let me know if that changes."

Kellen leaned up against the wall as she walked away. That was not good. He was going to have to be more careful. He didn't want anyone guessing…what, exactly?

Some pixies are pretty, but you're really stunning.

Kellen heard Sin's deep voice in his head and closed his eyes, groaning softly. He was just a friend. That's all he could ever be. He had to stop thinking about him like this.

* * * *

"Was it a good counseling session today?" Tenzin asked as he passed Sin the bowl of korma.

Sin appreciated that he never asked *did you actually go today?* The yeti simply trusted that he'd been responsible and had kept his promises. "It was good. Lysander says it's all right to be angry sometimes. That

164

I have to give myself permission to be angry. But I have to make sure I'm not misdirecting it."

"That's good for anyone to remember." Tenzin set the extra plate with Sin's bagel and peanut butter by his elbow. He insisted Sin needed the extra protein.

Across the table, Kai raised a snow-white eyebrow. "Was that directed toward me?"

"Not specifically, beloved, but it's something to keep in mind," Tenzin said in that serene way that implied that if the shoe fit... "Sin, dear, I do need to mention something more specific to you. Just something to keep in mind, and I don't want you to get upset."

"Oh?" Sin swallowed hard around his bite of bagel, the peanut butter making it difficult to respond. Not get upset? He wished people wouldn't say that. As soon as someone did, his stomach knotted.

"About Kellen." Tenzin put a warm, furry hand over his. "I'm so glad to see you two becoming friends. He needs a friend as much as you do. But I'm a bit concerned that he might be developing...more than friendly feelings."

"Why would you say—" Sin cut himself off, remembering the odd conversation that morning. "Oh."

"Yes, *oh*." Tenzin patted his hand before he picked up his sticks again. "Be his friend, but be a little more careful what you say to him. He's been solitary far too long, and he's vulnerable."

"Got it." Sin had to stare at his plate and blink back tears. Stupid things came at the weirdest times. He'd been so stupid, just worried about himself. Habit, really. Before Ness, he was used to worrying about one person—Sin. But, yeah. He really did get it.

"Kai?"

Tenzin's query apparently startled the drow, since he blinked and dropped his sticks on his plate. "Yes, dearest?"

"Bed right after dinner. You're distracted and exhausted. You can't even focus on conversation for more than a sentence at a time."

"But I need—"

"You do not. Whatever it is will be there in the morning. If you insist on overworking yourself, again, I will use force."

Sin dared a glance up from his plate and had to stifle a laugh at Kai's openmouthed, flummoxed expression. Hmm. By the scent, that suggestion had left his high and mighty drowness incredibly aroused too. Made Sin wonder how kinky they got in the bedroom. It was a pleasant, distracting set of images.

"You too, Sin."

Now he startled, his head whipping around to meet Tenzin's patient gaze. "Me too, what?"

"Straight to bed after dinner. No sitting up watching sad old movies."

"Yes, Mom," Sin muttered to his plate, but he *was* tired after working a longer shift today. Tenzin was almost always right about these things.

He helped clean up and said good night after a furry, enveloping hug from Tenzin and a kiss on the cheek from Kai. The drow was suspiciously anxious to get to the bedroom.

In the guest bedroom, a warm and comfortable space decorated in burgundy and gold, Sin stripped and climbed into bed, feeling once again like he'd entirely lost his status as an adult. He had people taking care of him, sending him to bed after dinner, for crying out loud. Not to mention the fact that he slept with a stuffed unicorn the size of a St. Bernard these days. Tenzin had won the ridiculous pink thing at a fair upstate somewhere and it was just a convenient soft thing to hang on to at night. He'd tied Ness' scarf around its neck, still clinging to the last bits of his beloved centaur's scent.

"I miss you, Ness," he said to the empty bedroom. "I love you, and I miss you. I'm supposed to think about good things. I'm trying. There were lots of good things. But it kinda makes me miss you more."

He hugged the stupid pink unicorn tightly and drifted off on memories of Ness in the park.

* * * *

Sometime later, he woke with a start to find Ness beside the bed, his horse half reclining on the floor, his human elbows resting on the covers beside Sin's head.

"Hey," Sin whispered, feeling dazed and stupid. "I thought you'd left me."

Ness reached over and combed his fingers through Sin's hair. "You know that's never really going to happen, don't you?"

"Well, um, yeah. It kinda did."

"I know, love. I'm so sorry about that. It all happened so fast." Ness kissed his forehead with a little sigh. "Wanted to come check on you and remind you that you're not good at being alone. I think you've proven that several times by now."

"Yeah, yeah. I know." Sin leaned forward to nuzzle against Ness's throat. "But I'm… I can't yet. I miss my pony boy too much. I… Gods, I miss you so."

"It's all right. Shh." Ness wrapped strong arms around him and held him tight. "It's all right to miss me. It's not all right to wallow and forget to live. You hear me, Sin?"

"I hear you. I do. Maybe someday. I'm trying. I really am."

Ness took Sin's face between his hands and kissed him tenderly. "I know. Keep trying. And remember I'll never really leave you."

Sin nodded, suddenly overcome with sleep as he drifted off in Ness' arms.

* * * *

He woke with a start again to see the clock read two in the morning. The room was empty, but Ness' scent hung there like a promise. Funny. He'd never really believed in ghosts before, and it was probably just a dream, but it was a nice thought, that Ness was still watching over him.

A bit of the ache around his heart eased, something dark lifting from him, a few shades, at least. He snuggled back in with the stupid unicorn and fell back to sleep.

Chapter Thirteen

Kellen suppressed the urge to flick his wings agitatedly. It wasn't that he minded having Tok over, or even that his sink needed repair, but he hated being late, and he was going to be this morning. He'd already called Tenzin, who had told him not to worry and to take his time.

"Too old, this one. Need to replace it," Tok said in his slow, methodical way.

"Okay. I'll leave it to you then," Kellen said.

Tok nodded. "No more dust."

"I'll have more for you soon. Look." He held out an arm to show how there was a faint opalescent sheen under the paleness of his skin. After he dusted, his skin was a smooth, pale cream color for a few days then slowly the sheen came back, but it wasn't noticeable until he was almost ready to dust again. From the color and amount of pearlescence, he could judge fairly well when it would happen. Stress or injury could bring it on early, like it had that one time at work with Sin, but usually he knew. "I'd say probably tonight," Kellen told him.

Tok nodded again. "Always my thanks. After you will go out?"

Kellen tried not to look surprised. He shouldn't have been. Tok didn't leave the building often, so he knew the tenants' habits. It wouldn't be hard for him to notice that Kellen always went out soon after a dusting.

"Probably. Yes." He tried not to sound defensive.

"Be careful."

Tok went back to removing the sink, and Kellen went to work, but now he had something else to worry about. If Tok had taken notice of his habits, had anyone else?

His day went from bad to worse. After arriving at work late, there was a backlog of patients, and they were already double and triple booked. Outside of injury, most of the crossover community was a healthy lot. Kellen had never seen so many sick fairies, fauns, centaurs and brownies. To top it off, Sin seemed distracted and preoccupied, not in a chatty mood. He left work that evening drained and disappointed. His dusting started soon after he arrived home, as he expected.

Carefully he collected the powder, reserving as much as he dared to give to Tok. The anti-magic properties were the only thing that killed most of the troll smell and made it possible for Tok to live so close to others.

He packed the rest of the pixie dust into a container and took the plasma bags from the refrigerator. More elven blood. It was all he could get. Rask kept badgering him for something more powerful but their elven blood stores were the most often replenished.

Rask was as unhappy as he had expected.

"I told you to get wyvern or sphinx, something powerful. Something worthy. And you bring me more watered-down swill," Rask spat, flinging the bags of blood down.

"I'm sorry, master, I tried. They keep a tighter guard on the blood of certain creatures." Which was sort of true, but mostly he didn't want to steal blood that was still viable for use. Not only might someone notice the theft, but what if there was an emergency and that blood was needed?

Kellen's head snapped back as Rask backhanded him completely without warning. He was so stunned he could do nothing but gasp when Rask grabbed him and shook him hard. "You will get something better, something stronger. The power is growing ever greater. We are on the verge of creating a stable portal, and this time I am not wasting it on a flea-bitten pack of vargs or an overgrown storm. Tomorrow, Kellen. I don't care what it costs you. Tomorrow you will bring the blood I need to release more power."

Kellen reeled as the words struck him like stones. The Events… They were random. What was he saying?

Rask laughed at the look on his face and dug his fingers into his arms. "Oh, come now, you can't be surprised?"

Kellen swallowed, speechless. Surprised? Yes. Shocked. How could he have been so foolish? So blind? The Events were random, yes, but how had he not noticed that the larger of the Events that had Captain Hartgrove and the rest of AURA so worried all seemed to happen soon after one of the coven's rituals? How had he not guessed that was what they were doing? What he had done? The vargs. The thunderbird. *No. No, it couldn't be.*

Rask's grip loosened, becoming a caress, and Kellen felt his stomach tighten in revulsion. He was responsible. He was responsible for Nestor's death. He was going to be sick.

"We will convene for the rite tomorrow night. Leave," Rask told the waiting coven coldly. He shoved Kellen toward the bedroom. Even the prospect of what Rask would do to him behind that door did not come close to the self-loathing he already felt, the coldness that was starting to numb him from the center outward. He could not let them cause another huge Event. He couldn't let them bring more destruction and death.

There must be a way. He had to find a way to break through the compulsion before tomorrow night. His mind tumbled and turned for a way as Rask pulled the clothes from his body.

* * * *

The workday was nearly over and Kai was looking forward to going home, simply going home and not thinking about the things he couldn't solve for a few hours, when Quinn appeared in his doorway.

Perhaps appeared would have been too strong a word, but Kai was so distracted that one moment Quinn wasn't there and the next he was.

"Quinn? Are you…? You look distressed."

"Distressed is a bit strong. More like concerned," Quinn said, not waiting for Kai to invite him before coming in and flopping down in one of the chairs by his office window. "And maybe a little confused."

"Aren't we all," Kai muttered at the data on his screen. "Is there a specific point of confusion? Or must I beat it out of you?"

Quinn didn't flip him off, not even a dismissive glare, and Kai felt the fine hairs on the back of his neck rise. He could count on one hand the number of times he'd actually seen Quinn this somber, and all of those times were in the midst of terrible things happening.

Finally Quinn sat forward, resting his elbows on the arms of the chair and lacing his fingers together in a thoughtful pose. "I've been thinking about how I couldn't find Sin when I scryed for him."

Kai tapped his pen on the desk impatiently. "Yes? I presumed it was something that Sin did to hide himself. You have something that indicates otherwise?"

"That's what I thought too. Only, this morning Matt said he'd lost a set of keys and asked if I wouldn't mind having a look on the other side for him. I did. I didn't find them. I didn't even find his building. It just…wasn't there. So I looked around some more, and it's like there are these pockets where things should be, things I know are there, and they aren't there in the spirit world. I can't see them. I can't sense them. It's like they died or something on the other side."

Kai rose slowly, though he needed the desk for support. A terrible dread lodged under his heart, one he couldn't name yet. "Show me," he whispered. "Show me one of these dead spots in the spirit world."

Quinn nodded, as if he had been expecting him to want to see for himself. Within a few minutes, they had a circle cast and Quinn pulled Kai's metaphysical body up above the AURA headquarters building with dizzying speed.

"There's a place near here I noticed. In the park, a place where some fauns and satyrs and nymphs liked to gather. They were working on turning it into a real Glade. But now, well, you'll see."

Quinn brought him to the place. Most of what they saw was the dulled grays and blacks with hints of muted colors mixed in that was common when using this type of sight. Except right in the middle, a blank space yawned. Not exactly a black hole—just an empty space where there should have been trees, grass and rocks. Instead it looked like the ground was covered in ash, and when they got closer yet, Kai could see fine lines of black around the edges of the place that disappeared into the ground below.

"No," he whispered, clutching at Quinn's spirit form. "We need to go back. We need to see this on the physical plane."

Quinn knew him well enough to save his questions and they both returned to their bodies far too quickly. Kai was too disturbed to scold, though he returned to a splitting headache. As soon as they were steady, he grabbed Quinn's sleeve and dragged him along, down the elevator, out of the doors, and down the street to the park. What began as a swift walk soon deteriorated to a desperate sprint. If this was what he thought, it was far worse than a mere shift in Events.

When they reached the spot, Kai couldn't quite stifle his cry of anguish as he got down on one knee to touch the blighted grass. The trees here had lost their leaves, not in glorious fall colors but in rusted browns spotted with black. The flowers—there had been flowers if the woodland folk had wanted a Glade—were gone, withered and died.

Quinn, consciously or not, stopped at the edge of the blighted area and refused to take another step. "What the hell is going on, Kai? It looks like something sucked this place dry."

"Something did." Kai rose, wrapping his arms around his ribs to ease his shaking. "Oh, Quinn, something did." He turned and stumbled, saved from falling by Quinn's hand under his elbow. "I'll explain what I can. But I need to explain quickly, and to everyone. Emergency meeting in the atrium. All department heads and all of Research. We need everyone there."

The proximity to the magic drain was making him nauseous, and he hurried them away again, trying to think how he could explain something so terrible.

The meeting room was packed. Extra chairs had been brought in but some preferred to stand. There was an edginess in the air as Kai paced, gathering his thoughts on how to deliver what he suspected, what Quinn's blighted spot on this plane and the other meant.

At last everyone arrived and quieted, giving him the floor.

He remembered all too well the doubt he had faced not that long ago when he had tried to tell Valerian that something sinister was happening within AURA's own walls. The fact that Val had been one of the first to arrive and stood with respectful attention should have felt vindicating, but Kai was too focused on what he now believed they were facing to feel much more than a slowly rising terror.

"I thank you all for coming quickly. I have uncovered vital information that threatens us all. For quite some time now, I have felt an unease that has been growing, certain incidents, certain data sets have all been pointing to something, but I could not put my finger on it until just now when Quinn showed me something I have not seen in many years."

Kai took a breath but he didn't give anyone time to interrupt or tell him to get on with it.

"Over the summer, incidents of violence have steadily increased, as I'm sure Captain Hartgrove and his officers in enforcement can attest. Not only have violent crimes increased, but the severity of those crimes have risen to an alarming level. This is not simply coincidence. It is part of a pattern. A sign, if you will. It wasn't the first, but it was the most obvious. The first sign was something less pronounced but has affected us all. Numbers of staff crossovers are down, and we are not seeing improvement in recruiting. A statistical analysis shows that more than half of those who applied since last winter have withdrawn their applications due to relocation. More and more crossovers, elves, fae folk, and the like, are moving away. The violence was the second sign, along with an increase in Events, ones that brought greater numbers and ever more powerful creatures into this world."

Kai stopped again, resting his hands on the table, steadying himself. "There are legends, some written as prophecy, even among the humans. But they are not simply stories. They describe a specific occurrence, and they give the signs as the people of those times interpreted them. The humans named these omens and gave them horses to ride. First the peaceful beings of the land sicken and flee. Next those of a warlike nature come. The third sign is the slow drain of life and magical energy from the land. A magical famine that will lead to a physical famine." Kai paused. "That is what Quinn showed me today in the park. The third sign. The one that allowed me to recognize the others."

"So, you're saying what, exactly?" Quinn questioned when Kai paused again. "That we're seeing the coming of an apocalypse?"

"Of a sort, Quinn. A localized apocalypse, for now. All of these signs point to a wizard tower being built in this city. It draws on natural magic, only towers do not give back to the balance. They only take. They pull all the magic in until everything within its reach is a dry husk and chaos reigns. It is the Suppression on a far more horrific scale and the only remaining power will lie with those who control the tower. If it isn't found and destroyed, the next sign is death on a scale we do not wish to contemplate."

"Kai, how do you know this?" Lysander's soft voice carried in the unnatural stillness.

"I have witnessed the devastation a tower can wreak. Even ancient towers still retain a blight on the surrounding land. The magic of the world sucked dry. A bane to life itself. The drow forbid few magic endeavors. This is one they do not suffer to occur."

Kai sat down heavily and that seemed to release the others' silence. For a few minutes, everyone talked at once as the news was absorbed and processed and questions raised.

"Well, that explains why our infirmary and holding cells are full."

"So where is it?"

"How do we destroy it?"

"Are we even sure that's what's happening?"

All of these questions flew around the room until Val called order and everyone settled again.

"If Kai says he's seen this before and recognizes the signs, I believe there is a plausible threat. What I'd like to know, Kai, is how exactly do we find it, how do we stop it, and until we do both, is there any way to stop the progression?"

Kai sat straight, his expression a mask of calm, though he wanted to crawl into Tenzin's arms and hide. "As to the last, no. The only way to stop the progression is to stop the person or persons building the tower. Every age has a mage or two who desire power to the point of madness. The tower is a giant magical collector, a storage cell, if you will. But too much power, and eventually it does begin to draw more and more, will have destructive consequences for the mage or mages involved. The power must be leeched on a regular basis and the increased regularity of Events in the city are the direct result of someone skilled and knowledgeable enough to know the power must have an outlet. We use the locations of the Events to find the perimeter. In the center will be the tower."

"How about the blight areas? Can we use those to help us find it?" Quinn asked.

"Of course, yes," Kai said. "We can also use the data for the relocations and incidents of violence."

"Good." Val nodded, his jaw set. "If we can put that data in the hands of our enforcement officers, now that we know there is a pattern to look for, we can try to put some preventive measures in place."

"If distance makes a difference, perhaps we can relocate those in the infirmary and holding farther from its influence."

"Until we know more," Kai spoke more sharply than he intended and modulated his tone. "Until we have a location, please keep what's been said this evening among those in this room. No one here wants to incite a general panic in crossover populations. And..." He paused, his gaze sweeping the room. "We've no idea how close to AURA this mage or group of mages might be. Let's not tip our hand early, as they say."

Kai's native drow suspicion told him he might be too late. The mage in question could be sitting here, among trusted staff. He could have given everything away already. If not, there was still no guarantee in a city this size that they would find the tower in time.

Chapter Fourteen

At the lab counter, Sin yawned and stretched. His first full day back at work and he'd done a third of a shift each at the front desk, assisting in radiology and playing lab tech. Easy work, really, doing preliminary screenings, labeling and logging specimens to be sent down to the real lab in the basement. Easy work and he was bone tired.

Kellen came to collect the blood work from the fridge to take downstairs, like he always did, like the thoughtful pixie he was, and Sin managed a cheery good night around another yawn.

"Oh, crud." Sin ran both hands back through his hair after Kellen had headed toward the elevators. He'd meant to ask if Kellen wanted to go grab a honey after work with him at the fae-owned honey and nectar bar across the street. Just a thank you and a chance to chat outside of work. Friends did that, right?

Trifon would want to talk for a bit, though, when Kellen reached the lab. He always did, the big goofball.

No panicking, then. Sin had plenty of time to finish charting, sign out for the night, and still catch Kellen downstairs. Good. If he missed the pixie today, he'd try to remember tomorrow, simple as that.

As it turned out, he went downstairs at just the right time. Kellen had just come up from the basement and they crossed paths in the lobby.

"Hey, Kells, I'm glad you're still here," Sin called to him and Kellen literally jumped a foot off the ground, his wings giving a little buzz before he settled.

"Oh, hi," Kellen said.

"Where are you going with that?" Sin asked curiously. Kellen had a red container in his hands and since he'd just come up from the lab, he didn't see why Kellen would still be carrying samples around.

"I, um, I'm just taking it out back for pickup." Kellen eyes darted nervously and his wings had flattened down his back.

Sin frowned. "For pickup?"

"Waste removal. They take it to the incinerator," Kellen explained.

It clicked for Sin. "Ah, so that lazy satyr talked you into doing his job, huh?"

Kellen looked around again. "Shh, not so loud. I offered to take it up. It's no big deal. He's supposed to do it but I don't mind."

"All right, I won't tattle." Sin gave him a wink. "He's probably all twitterpated about his newest nymph or something. You wanna grab a honey when you're done? I can meet you over at Birds and Bees?"

Those pretty green eyes seemed to light for a moment, and just as quickly a shadow fell across them. "I— That would be…" He paused and after a moment Sin was certain he saw a flicker of pain in his expression, and it wasn't merely an emotional type of pain. He winced like he'd bit his tongue. "I can't tonight, though. I'm sorry."

Something wasn't right here. Sin's finely tuned nose scented fear and sorrow. "All right, Kells. No biggie. I'll see you in the morning."

Uh-huh, like I'm gonna leave it at that. Sin waited until Kellen had turned a corner, then he followed to the disposal cage out back, wrapping the shadows around him. So, so not right, and he was Kellen's friend, right? If he was in trouble, he needed help.

Sin hadn't expected to see anything strange as he followed Kellen behind AURA. In the back of his head, he had it in mind that Kellen might be meeting someone later who was perhaps on the wrong side of AURA's view of positive crossover-human relations. Perhaps he might even need help extracting himself from an unhealthy situation. So he was perplexed when he watched Kellen set the bin down and open it rather than just pushing it into the containment area. His confusion only grew when he saw him remove two bags of blood before shoving the rest through for disposal. Confusion grew to concern as Kellen reached into his pocket and withdrew a syringe, injected something into the ports of each bag, then tucked them under his shirt.

What in all the hells was going on here? He tucked back deeper into the gathering twilight but it didn't seem like he need worry too much about being spotted. Kellen looked both hyper-focused and afraid, his mind wholly on whatever it was he was up to.

Relying on old habits and skills, Sin waited until Kellen was just out of earshot so he wouldn't hear the whoosh of wings, and took to the rooftops. Easy enough to follow Kellen that way until he got to the subway, and not the line that would take Kellen home. Sin landed softly and hurried after him, down the steps and barely making it onto the train one car back from where Kellen had boarded. Sin huddled in the corner, ignoring the side-eyes some of the humans gave him, and made sure he had a good line of sight into the next car. Again, Kellen made it disturbingly easy to shadow him. He slumped in a seat by the windows, completely oblivious to his surroundings.

When he got off, it was uptown, and Sin had to shove past annoyed commuters to scramble off the train in time. Plenty of shadows now the sun had set, so Sin followed on foot, more and more perplexed as Kellen stopped outside a swanky condo high-rise. He stood there for a moment and even at a distance, Sin's eyes were sharp enough to pick up on the rise and fall of his shoulders, as if he'd taken a deeper breath and let it out. Steeling himself for something?

Kellen took a step, then turned away from the doors and wandered a short distance. If Sin hadn't been watching him specifically, he wouldn't have noticed him at all. He was just another pedestrian. Only the way he hunched his shoulders, arms and wings both hanging limp, his head down, he was the picture of dejection.

That was enough for Sin. He had intended to follow him until he met up with whoever he was meeting up with, but if all the nervous fear and sorrow were being caused by whoever lived in that building, it might be better to show himself now and prevent him from changing his mind and going inside.

Sin let the shadows go and strode down the street. He probably looked strange enough in this neighborhood, still being dressed in his scrubs made him stick out even more. Still, Kellen didn't spot him until he was almost close enough to touch.

"Kells." Sin held up both hands, trying to be as nonthreatening as possible. "I don't know what's going on here. But I know you're scared. I know things aren't right."

Kellen's head came up and his eyes locked on Sin. All the color drained from his face and he was pale to begin with. "Sin, what are you doing here?"

"Trying to figure out how deep the shit is that you're in. It's something bad. I can see that. Kells, you have friends, resources, powerful people who could look out for you. I can even protect you if it's someone who wants to hurt you."

Kellen was shaking his head now. "You have to leave. Please, you have to go."

"Kellen, just tell me what's going on," Sin said, trying to not sound frustrated.

Kellen opened his mouth and immediately closed it again. His whole body went rigid, then relaxed. His breath was coming in short pants, a sheen of sweat on his brow. He shook his head and even that seemed to cost him something, he looked positively waxen.

"I can't. You have to go."

"Nope. Can't do that." Sin reached for his arm, but Kellen flinched away. "I wondered if you were in trouble. Now I know. I can't just leave you."

Kellen grimaced, he looked on the verge of passing out, or maybe finally telling him what was going on. Before he could do either, a man stepped up to them and put a dark hand on Kellen's shoulder. A drow. He smiled at Sin in the same way a shark would smile before it ate you. "Kellen, my dear, are you unwell? Are you being bothered by this…person?"

Sin barely contained the snarl that wanted out. "And who the fuck are *you*?"

The drow turned a proprietary eye on Kellen. "Kellen, introduce us."

Kellen looked at Sin, very still, his face a mask that gave away nothing. Only his tightly tucked wings gave any indication of his distress, and the paleness still in his face. "Rask, this is Sin. We work together." His voice came out even, if a little breathy. "Sin, this is Rask. He's my…"

He faltered and Rask stepped in, "Lover, is the word most of the humans understand, although it goes a bit deeper than that." He never took his hand from Kellen's shoulder as he spoke.

Sin watched the way Kellen leaned toward the drow. He didn't look any more comfortable, but he had stopped shaking. "Yeah, I'm so not a human, tall, dark and snooty. Kells, is this true? You with him?"

Kellen nodded slowly. "Yes. I'm sorry I didn't tell you before. Please don't be mad."

Rask laughed with absolutely no humor in the sound. "Why should he be mad? He's only a coworker."

"I'm a friend, your haughtiness." Sin fixed the drow with a cold gaze, not much liking what he saw. He had to admit that his impressions could have been overprotectiveness, though. "You know, a person you tell that kind of shit to."

Rask's expression didn't even flicker. "Well, perhaps not as good of a friend as you had thought then."

"That's not true," Kellen blurted out. If he had looked distressed before, he looked downright terrified now. "Sin, please, you have to go."

"Yes, I believe it's time for you to go as well," Rask said.

Sin backed a step, hands held up in feigned surrender. "Fine. Not 'cause you said so, drow boy. But I see you're where you wanna be, Kells. I got it. Sorry."

No, he wasn't leaving. But the drow had to think he was.

They turned to go, Rask's arm still possessively around Kellen's shoulders. Kellen looked back at him once but Rask kept walking. "Come, my silly pixie," he said, and Kellen followed.

Sin pretended he was going to turn a corner, but came right back once they'd headed inside. Back in incubus stealth mode, he stayed out of sight as they got on the elevator, which the indicator said went all the way to the penthouse without stopping. No way Sin was leaving. That was a drow brand on Kellen's hip and he'd bet his left nut and wing that the jackass he'd just met had put it there.

* * * *

Rask was silent as they rode the elevator to the top floor. Kellen was not at all fooled by the peaceful quiet or serene expression. He shook so hard he was sure Rask could feel it through the arm he kept wrapped around him. All he could do was hope that Rask thought his fear stemmed from being 'caught' talking to a friend, that he'd allowed himself to be followed. That certainly was part of the fear. Plotting to murder five people also had a great deal to do with it.

He must maintain control, no matter what Rask did, until the ritual tonight. After that, nothing else would matter. Zenicotti was a powerful tranquilizer made by the goblins, and Kellen had put enough in the blood to make sure none of the coven would wake from it. He had no idea if the compulsion would release him after Rask died, but either way he was bound to be arrested and sent to prison. That thought did not upset him half so much as the thought that Sin would eventually find out what he had done, that he was responsible for Nestor's death, however unknowingly. At least no one else would die, either as a blood sacrifice or because they pulled a powerful creature into the world.

Rask waited until they were in the apartment before he said, "If you have failed again—"

Kellen cut him off before he could finish the threat, "I haven't." He brought out the blood pouches and held them out. "It's from a griffin. It's the most powerful blood in the stores."

Rask took the blood from him and held it in one hand while he looked at him. Kellen let his eyes drop because that was expected, but he was careful not to look at the blood.

"You were followed."

It was a statement but Kellen answered anyway. "Yes, master. I'm sorry. I didn't know."

Rask reached out and grabbed a handful of his hair, forcing him down to his knees and slammed him down on the low table in front of the sofa. "Little fool," Rask snarled. "I knew allowing you that much freedom was a mistake. No longer. You shall stay here, where I can make sure you don't inadvertently give too much away."

At one time Kellen would have fallen into despair at those words, perhaps pleaded with Rask to reconsider, but after tonight he didn't imagine he would ever be

188 Angel Martinez and Bellora Quinn

able to return to work anyway, so it didn't hit him as hard.

Otori bounded into the room, tails waving madly. He bounced up to Rask and made a grab for the pouches. "Blood. Blood. The moon is up. The wind whispers and whispers. Dark leaves and dark clouds on the moon."

"No." Rask hissed. "Otori, down."

The kitsune dropped to sit on the carpet, gaze still on the blood pouches and Rask shook his head. "When I have what I want, Otori, you may have all the blood you like. But not this blood. Not before."

He traced a claw down Kellen's back. "And you, my *peshk*, my troublesome, sneaky little pixie, you will sit at my feet once more. Where you belong. They had no right to take you from me, these mewling creatures with their false morality."

Kellen didn't dare move, so he missed the moment when Rask had put the pouches down. He raised his hands before him, dark magic gathering to him from below. "Mine. And you will remain with me. I am tired of bowing to their weakling laws. In a drow court, the strongest rules and soon this world will be my court, a proper world with proper laws."

Pain seared over Kellen's ankles and he cried out as his feet were forced together, bound in glowing green rings that burned, the magic spearing into his very bones. The only comfort he had was that Rask couldn't maintain these magic shackles if he had to concentrate on other magic. It was simply a warning.

"You will crawl for the remainder of this evening. On your belly so that you will relearn your place."

Kellen dropped to the floor, trying to breathe through the pain. Otori had a hold of his wing before he knew what was happening and the kitsune bit him clean through the membrane. A new pain seared his nerves and he cried out again.

"Crispy. Crispy pixie," Otori said softly.

Rask chuckled. "Bad pup. No biting."

Otori sat back, tongue lolling, his mad eyes fixated back on Rask. "The winds whisper. Wings and wind."

Usually, everyone dismissed Otori's ramblings, but for him to repeat a phrase was unusual. Rask regarded him with narrowed eyes. He opened his mouth, probably to ask Otori about the wind, when a splintering crash interrupted him, glass shards exploding inward from the terrace's French doors.

"You pig ball-sucking bastard!" Sin roared as he charged Rask, his horns at their full curl, eyes blazing red. "You bag of troll shit! Let him go!"

"Sin, no! Oh no…" Kellen tried to rise, panic warring with the pain. *No, no, no…*

Rask lifted a hand, an ugly sneer on his face, but Kellen also saw the gleam of satisfaction in his eyes. He would only be too happy to hurt Sin. In desperation, Kellen flung himself at Rask's knees, trying to stop him before he cast the spell. He was already hobbled by the magic though and Rask easily sidestepped, kicking him as he fell to the floor again.

Green magic, drow magic, coalesced around Rask. The same green magic that Kai had used so valiantly to shield civilians, Rask turned to his own selfish, terrible purposes. A bolt leaped from his hand and struck Sin square in the chest. Sin gave ground, roaring, shaking his head, but the stubborn incubus charged again.

Jaw set, Rask hurled a lash of lightning that curled around Sin's ankles and jerked him off his feet. Sin slammed into the table and lay there, dazed, as Rask secured him in glowing manacles of his own. "Niles!

Shawna! Secure them! I want them both in chains. The pixie doesn't need to be free for the ritual. Merely present. And this one... Oh, this one is delicious. We will keep him for now."

Sin roared invective, thrashing about on the floor, rolling to use his huge wings as weapons.

Rask's expression hardened to one of disapproval. "Do something about those wings too. Hooks pierced through them would do. And make certain you gag him. What a foul mouth."

Chapter Fifteen

Kai's fingers flew over his keys. Unlike a ground campaign, in a city of tall spires and spikes of glass and steel, data needed to be gathered in three dimensions. As his staff compiled, he created the model on which to hang the data points, snarling when they brought him vague coordinates, entering madly as they brought him precise ones.

Beside him, Quinn existed in that neither here nor there state of scrying as he pinpointed spots of magic famine, every blank, dead space lighting up in red when Kai understood exactly where it was. No one was going home tonight. They needed to find the tower.

"I'll sleep when I'm dead," he whispered to his screen, and if he failed, he might well find death before sleep. They all might.

Towers were built on blood magic, some mages had even insisted it required live sacrifice, but any sacrifice would do, even a sacrifice as simple as the giving of blood. Among drow, blood magic was an integral part of court life. It fueled curses and revenge plots, constructed tireless workers and was the catalyst for certain types of necromancy. But a few specific uses were forbidden, on pain of terrible, slow and horrific death. The perversion of the bond between mates was one of these, where a mage used blood magic to bind another being to him, enslave them in a horrible parody of bonding.

The tower was the other, for with it came the draining of all magic and no sane drow wanted the magic ripped from the earth.

Sterling cleared his throat beside him. He'd probably been calling for some time, but all his staff were accustomed to Kai getting lost in his thoughts.

"Boss, we're going down the phone tree, trying to locate every staff member, like you asked."

"Yes?" Kai pushed back his chair to look up into Sterling's dark eyes.

"There are a couple we're still tracking down. People do go out sometimes. But we've got two who are just missing. Who should be somewhere and they're not."

"Why…" Kai scrubbed both hands over his face. "Why does everyone insist on making me *drag* information from them? Who, damn your eyes, man!"

"Kellen from medical. The maintenance troll in his building—"

That brought Kai's eyebrows up, but he didn't interrupt.

"Said Kellen sometimes goes out, but he's always back by now. And the other one's Sin."

"What do you mean *Sin*?"

Sterling pursed his lips, his usual good humor eaten away by stress and lack of sleep. "Tenzin went home to check on him. He's not there. He's not with any of his friends or at the usual watering holes. Missing, boss."

"Not again. Not now." Kai frowned. Sin had been doing so well. He had been doing *so* well, in fact, that this sudden disappearance made no sense. He would've at least left a message, a note, Kai was certain.

"Thank you, Sterling. We'll alert the captain. Have his officers keep an eye out."

He had returned to the desperate entering of data when Rudy hurried up to him with a worried satyr in tow. What was the young satyr's name? Tribeca? Trilobite?

"Trifon? What brings you up here so late?"

The satyr wrung his hands, his eyes wide and flicking about with either distress or guilt. "Mr. Hiltas, we got the memo that we should report any odd shortages in blood supply to you. There's griffin blood missing, sir."

Kai pinched the bridge of his nose between thumb and forefinger, willing his temper down. "How much?"

"Two bags."

Yelling at the youngster would do no good at all. It might make Kai feel better... No, under the circumstances, it really wouldn't. "Thank you, for letting me know."

Griffin blood. Infused with powerful magic even *outside* the griffin. It couldn't really be any worse. No, no, one never said that. Things could always be worse. But this was bad on a scale of shark tornado bad.

"There is one more thing, sir," the satyr said reluctantly. "It was in the inventory yesterday. No one has checked any out, and there have only been two people in storage today. Myself and Kellen."

* * * *

Sin pulled and yanked on the cuffs, praying to the Mother that maybe they were cheap ones. But every yank pulled on the damn chain they'd attached with hooks to his wings and all he was managing to do was cut bleeding grooves in his wrists and ankles.

You're no hero, Sinistrus. Why the hell did you think you were?

He hadn't rescued Kellen. From the sounds in the front room, he'd made things worse and he winced as Kellen cried out again. Damn, damn, damn. Sin slammed his head back against the wall. At least his horns in their curling, angry versions made nice holes in the drywall. It didn't help, but it was satisfying to cause a bit of destruction.

Kells… Why didn't that drow fucker leave off? What could Kellen have done that was so terrible? Not that it probably mattered. Rask was obviously a sadistic bastard and hurting Kells was probably his idea of fun.

Although it felt like abandoning him, Sin took a deep breath and tried to block out the sound. Listening wasn't going to help Kellen or anyone else. He had to get his head clear and think. What did he know?

Kellen didn't live here. He had his own place. Sin had been there, and it was about as opposite from this apartment as it could get. Did that matter? Who knew. Kellen wore a drow branding mark on his hip and even if Sin hadn't been able to read it, he knew exactly what it meant. The scar was old. Old enough that it had almost certainly been given to him before he crossed over. It could have been put there by anyone. Sin was only guessing it was the same drow doing horrible things to him in the other room right now. It was however, a damn good guess.

What were the odds that the same drow had been pulled over in a separate Event and had happened to find Kellen? Very unlikely. So, had they come through the same Event? That seemed a more likely scenario. Then what?

At least he could do something about the gag that spindly, frail human boy had shoved in his mouth. Sin concentrated on getting the cloth between his sharp teeth and began to chew. *Bleh.* Someone had kept the damn scarf, or whatever it was, in a drawer with one of those patchouli-scented sachets. Really, really disgusting.

What else did he know? He knew Kellen had been trying to tell him something. The pain and frustration on his face as he tried pointed to some sort of spell or curse laid on him, keeping his silence.

Chew, chew, chew.

He knew Kellen had taken blood destined for the dumpster and brought it here instead. He also knew Kellen had put something in that blood. Drow were strange about blood magic. They embraced it, but it was shrouded in secrecy and constrained by laws. He had no doubt that whatever the blood was intended for could not be in any way good.

Good. He was through the disgusting cloth. Thank the goddess for sharp teeth. He spat the thing out and worked his jaw since the humans had tied the damn thing so tight. He knew... He knew... What had Kai tried to tell him about forbidden blood magic once? Damn it. Sin had probably been drunk during that conversation and he didn't remember much beside the unhappy, disturbed expression on Kai's face.

Things had quieted in the other room. He wasn't sure that was a good thing, not at all.

* * * *

For all that Rask liked to torment him, he was not usually prone to prolonged bouts of violence. He would slap or hit Kellen, pull his hair or shove him down, but then he would move on, secure that those minor punishments were enough to cow Kellen. He was truly furious tonight and seemed to take quite a bit of enjoyment in the beating he meted out. His eyes gleamed with a twisted pleasure and there was a swell at the front of his pants.

Aching and bruised, Kellen huddled on the floor after Rask at last grew tired and left him to prepare for the ritual. He could bear the pain. He had no choice, but at least the knowledge that it would soon all come to an end soothed him.

It seemed all too soon, though, when Rask came again and dragged him into the ritual room. The candles were lit, the ointment made from his dust prepared. Rask forced the vial between his lips and Kellen let him pour the drug into his mouth. This time he did not swallow the liquid but held as much as he could in his mouth. They began to chant. Kellen waited, biding his time. He fluttered his eyelids, as if fighting the effects of the drug, then let his head loll forward and opened his mouth, letting the potion dribble out. He went limp, as he always did, and the chanting grew in strength, the magic gathering around him. He watched through slitted eyes as Rask poured the tainted blood into the chalices.

Rask passed them around and the litany in Kellen's head changed to *drink, drink, drink.*

Otori twitched his nose and his tails, sniffing at the cup, his chanting halting.

"Spoiled," Otori announced. "Not for drinking. Blood should be blood."

No, no, no, this can't be happening. Kellen did not twitch a muscle. *Please, please, drink it! Don't listen to him!*

"Spoiled?" Rask said slowly. He brought his own chalice to his nose and inhaled. "I smell no rot."

"Tricksy, mixy things." Otori put his down and crossed his arms over his chest. "Won't drink it. No, no, no."

Rask narrowed his eyes on the kitsune. Kellen held his breath. After a long, thoughtful moment, Rask turned and looked down at him. The kick when it came was vicious, the roar of anger enough to shake the walls. The energy gathered was thick with tension and Kellen watched in horror as Rask threw the chalice, splashing blood across the wall.

Rask was wrapped head to toe in tangles of thick green, as if a giant creature from the deep sea writhed around him, lashing out in all directions. Rask screamed in rage and thrust the magic at the altar, smashing the heavy marble. Kellen scrambled back, as did everyone else. The wild magic in the room was thick, whipping around, and Rask did not look in control at all. Terrified, Kellen cowered on the floor and waited for the final blow.

"You!" Rask yelled, pointing at him. "You miserable little worm! What did you do? What did you *do*?"

Kellen shook his head. He could torture the truth out of him but telling him now would only mean his certain death.

"Get him out! Lock him up! Get him from my sight!" Rask raged.

The rest of the coven was only too eager to comply, dragging Kellen from the room as quickly as they could.

* * * *

The yelling and magic explosions from the other room couldn't be anything good. At first, Sin had hoped maybe rescue had come and he envisioned the valiant Captain Valerian slinging firebolts everywhere. But no, the drow douchenozzle was screaming again. Ten to one about Kellen, since the poor little guy was obviously the whipping boy here.

His paper-thin shreds of hope died when the minions shoved Kellen into the room with him, shackled just like Sin was, though at least they'd left his pixie wings free.

"Hey, Kells." Sin cleared his throat to rid his voice of its rasping growl. "Hasn't been the best night, huh?"

Kellen lay where they had dragged him, curled into a little ball. What Sin could see of him didn't look good. There were bruises on his face and throat and his expression was etched with pain. When he opened his eyes, they were deep wells full of fear and despair.

"I'm sorry," he croaked in a hoarse whisper. "I tried to tell you but I couldn't."

Sin latched on to something that had been niggling at the back of his brain. Kellen's struggle to speak outside, his inability to come to anyone for help, even Tenzin, all pointed to something more than feeling threatened. "When you say you can't tell me, you really mean you can't, don't you? Physically, you try your hardest can't?"

Kellen hesitated, looking uncertain, then nodded.

"Well, that kinda explains some things, I guess." Sin blew out a breath and shifted to lean a shoulder against the wall. With his wings chained and his hands cuffed behind him, there was no way he could lean *back*, but this would have to do. "Damn drow duck fucker and his damn compulsion spells. 'Cause that's what this is, am I right?"

Kellen hesitated again and Sin saw him move his head a fraction before he stopped. He paled and a flash of pain scrunched his face.

"Hey, easy. Sorry. Me and my mouth have caused tons of pain over the years. I'm an idiot." Sin banged the side of his head on the wall, just to make more holes in the drywall. Not that he was still trying to vandalize the drow's home or anything. Yeah. Okay. He was. "I'm gonna try to ask you yes or no questions, hon. And you maybe…rustle your wings for no and just kinda stare at me for yes. Wanna try it?"

Kellen gave him a wary look but he nodded. This was going to be difficult. The compulsion spell would prevent Kellen from answering yes or no if he got too close to the truth, but if he gave Kellen an out with no answer at all if the answer was yes, perhaps it would work.

"Good stuff. Twenty questions. My favorite game." He smiled for Kellen, trying to ease some of the fear in those beautiful green eyes with jokes. "Okay, so duck fucker's obviously got this compulsion thingy hold on you. Did you know him in your home? Where you came from?"

Nothing. Not a twitch from Kellen.

"Hot damn. This might actually work." Sin stretched his shackled legs out and pointed down with his chin. "You want a lap for your head?"

Kellen was shackled too, but he was not chained to the wall either so he was able to inch his way a little closer until he lay next to Sin and could put his head on his thigh. Most of his hair had come loose and strands lay across his cheek, making Sin wish he had his hands free so he could smooth them back.

"I don't suppose you can tell me what made him go ballistic just now?" Sin asked.

Pause. Rustle.

"No. Okay. So you can't talk about what goes on in this apartment."

No answer. That was correct.

"Did it have something to do with the blood you took?"

No answer. Again, correct.

"Can you tell me what you put in it?"

For a moment Sin thought he wouldn't be able to answer but then Kellen murmured, "Zenicotti."

"Whoa…" Sin blinked down at the little guy for a minute as the implications sank in. They used Z on the medevac runs for the worst trauma patients, in small amounts. The stuff worked faster than morphine and had fewer side effects for crossovers. But that was the kicker—in small amounts. Kellen had injected full syringes of the stuff, so he hadn't been intending on putting people to sleep. "That was a pretty badass thing to try. Guess they caught on before they actually drank it though, huh?"

Again, Kellen simply stared back at him. Another direct hit.

Sin took a moment to assess what he'd learned or confirmed. Kellen had known Rask before they crossed over, that was confirmed. He was compelled not to speak about anything that happened in this apartment.

Also confirmed. This had to have been going on a long time, whatever 'it' was. But Kellen had just tried to kill them.

"Something happened, didn't it? Something changed?"

Kellen was silent, but wore a look of frustration now. Yes, something had happened, but he couldn't tell him what. Something bad enough for him to want to poison five people.

"What were they doing just now? With the blood? Something magic? Are they working together?"

No answer.

"Okay, sorry. That was too many questions and not yes and no-y enough."

Voices murmured from the hall, at least they were quieter voices, no more bellowing and thundering. The shuffle of footsteps on thick pile carpet stopped at the door where Sin and Kellen were being held.

"Sir? Could we wait until I can get you a proper altar?" That was the skinny kid. Sin seemed to recall some name starting with N.

"My dear, beautiful boy. You've never failed me, unlike the others, and I do so appreciate your wanting to see to all the details. But it must be tonight. The influx of power is at its peak. If we have a robust enough ritual this evening, we *will* create that final Event." And that was duck fucker, of course. Damn drow.

"But without the blood? Sir? I don't—"

There was more rustling of cloth, and a soft moan. Even through the closed door, the sexual energy made its way through to Sin and his stupid cock responded. *Down boy. This is so not the time.*

"Niles, my Niles. We have what we need right here. That slinking worm of a pixie brought us a live sacrifice for this final ritual. The tower will be complete, its continuing influx of magic will hold the portal open, and we will draw from the power of two worlds. We will be unassailable after tonight, my dear. No more need to hide."

"Yes, sir," Niles whispered.

Wait…what? The meaning of what they were saying finally sliced through the pheromonal haze. Events. Blood magic. Ever increasing power. They had…holy Mother…

"You cocksucking bastardized frog fuckers!" Sin roared. "You did this! You killed my Ness! I swear when I get loose, I'm gonna rip your balls off and stuff them through your eyeballs!"

Sin's threats did not go unanswered. A moment after he started yelling the door opened and Rask and Niles came in, the former cool as ice, and the latter looking flushed and annoyed.

"Someone slipped their gag, I see," Rask said. "Maybe I should simply cut out your tongue."

"I'll bite your fucking fingers off, you pissant, trumped-up little mage. Then go try casting spells," Sin spat out. He knew it was stupid, in some still sane part of his brain, but the rage burned white hot. Ness' death hadn't been an accident. It hadn't been caused by heroic misfortune. It had been caused by *this* fucker, this petty tyrant who wanted to make himself bigger.

"Niles," Rask said, holding out one hand. Niles placed a small dagger in his palm. "It would be neater to use a needle to collect your blood, but the old-fashioned way will still work."

Sin shoved back even as Kellen scrambled away from him, out of the way. His growl rattled the floor as he tried to get his back against the wall for leverage. Rask circled, knife in one hand, collection vessel in the other, and Sin kicked out with both feet. He connected with the drow's wrist, and there was a satisfying grinding of bone, but not the snap he'd wanted.

Still ice-cold and calm, Rask merely sent his tendrils of magic to hold Sin down. He struggled and spat, cursing his captor, but the more he squirmed, the more the tendril around his throat tightened until black spots danced in his eyes.

The boy, Niles, shoved him over onto his face and a sharp, quick pain sliced into the crook of Sin's elbow, the scent and warm trickle of his own blood reaching his fading consciousness a moment later.

Not dead yet. They want blood. For the new altar. Not dead yet.

Sin woke with no sense of time having passed. He could have been out minutes, or days, although he expected it was closer to the former. He was still face down on the floor, chained, and he could hear softly distressed weeping nearby. He turned his head and a wave of dizziness encroached. A blurred image of Kellen crouched near him wavered in his vision.

"Sin? Oh, damn, Sin," he whispered urgently. He tried to say something else, but it must have been related to what this misbegotten coven was doing and the compulsion prevented him. Sin didn't need Kellen to tell him, though, he could guess well enough that things had gone from bad to worse.

When Kellen could breathe again, he looked at Sin with shimmering tears in his eyes. "I'm sorry, I'm so sorry, I tried to stop them." He was shaking. "I have to get you out of here."

"Sweetie," Sin said partly to the floor. "We need to get *us* out of here."

"You don't hate me?" Kellen whispered. Fresh tears came to his eyes. "I-I didn't know. And Ness." The words choked off as he got too close to saying whatever the compulsion kept him from saying.

"No, I don't hate you. If you had a part in it, I don't think you did so willingly, or knowingly at least," Sin said with a sigh. "Too bad they were smart enough to take my phone. Could've called for the cavalry, right? Hey, they didn't happen to leave your phone in your pocket, did they?"

Kellen shaking his head miserably smashed that last bit of wishful thinking into jagged pieces.

Sin heaved himself onto his side and dragged out another smile for Kellen. He just looked so miserable and hopeless. Maybe part of him should have blamed Kellen for the whole disastrous last couple of months. Kellen had been supplying these idiots the blood they'd been using. Yeah…he just couldn't. There was no way Kells had had any choice in the matter. He just hadn't been able to figure out a way to get free of the drow, and that wasn't his fault.

"Listen, Kells. I'm gonna ask you to do something and you're not gonna like it. But I think it's the only chance we have right now. I can't reach the hooks in my wings, but you could pull them out—"

Kellen made a horrified sound.

"No, listen! Far's I can feel, they're only wrapped around the wing joint, not attached to it. If you pull the hook through, it'll only tear the membrane. I've suffered worse damage and still flown. It won't be pleasant but you can do this. It's our only choice. Get us out the window and get help, right?"

Kellen still looked horrified and reluctant but Sin could see how the possibility was already running through his mind, and they both knew that if he didn't at least try, then the only other option was to sit and wait until Rask came back and made Sin the sacrifice to whatever dark magic he was working.

Kellen's hands were also bound behind his back, but he was flexible enough to use them while looking over his shoulder. It was by no means ideal or easy but they had to try. Kellen reluctantly got to his knees and moved over to Sin's back. He could feel the gentleness of Kellen's fingers as he ran them searchingly up his wing membrane until he encountered the hook wrapped around the supporting finger. Sin pushed his shoulders back as far as he was able to try to give him some slack, but there really wasn't much.

"Take a deep breath," Kellen advised quietly. Sin did, and gritted his teeth as Kellen started to pull on the hook, drawing it away from the bone. The membrane around it tore. The warmth of his blood dripped down from the wound as Kellen continued to pull. The membrane tore more and suddenly the pressure was gone, the chain sliding free.

The second hook was still embedded in his other wing, but they were no longer tethered together. Sin sighed in relief as he let his wings droop. Could he fly with the second hook still in? Maybe?

They had no time to celebrate their success however.

Sin had not even gotten to his feet or made an attempt at the window before the door swung open. All three of them startled and froze. Kellen was the first to break the silence.

"Niles, please. Say nothing. Let us go."

It was a long shot and it didn't work.

"Rask!" Niles called out.

"You little swamp rat," Sin growled as he struggled to get his shackled feet under him. If he could just get to the damn window, he could use his horns to break it. *Kellen's* wings were free. They could both get out. It wouldn't be a fun flight and landing would be a cold-hearted bitch, but they could get away.

The magic hit him in the back and stole his breath with its force. Even with hands and feet free, he doubted he would have been able to struggle through to freedom.

"What's this? Our birds are trying to leave the nest?" Rask laughed humorlessly.

Sin tried with everything he had to twist free but the magic drove him down, pinning him once more to the floor.

"I have had just about enough of your willfulness, *peshk*," Rask said, grabbing Kellen. "If we were home, you would already be dead for your treachery. You have forgotten your place and need reminding."

Sin could not fully see from his position what was happening but Kellen suddenly landed face down in the center of the room, a foot planted in the middle of his back. He craned his neck and saw Rask draw the same blade he'd used earlier to bleed him.

"Hey, put the knife down," Sin said.

Rask glanced at him with a dismissive sneer and wrenched one of Kellen's wings back. The dragonfly wings looked like spun glass but Sin knew they were tougher than that. Still, having a wing pulled back like that hurt, he knew from experience.

"The little bird needs his wings clipped, so he doesn't get any more ideas." Rask plunged the knife down, slicing where skin turned to membrane and Kellen screamed with agony.

"No! Get off him, you fucker!" Sin thrashed and struggled, trying desperately to free himself from the magic pinning him to the floor. Bright blood coursed over Kellen's pale skin. Blood on the snow. No one should be allowed to ruin something so beautiful and fine. Sin roared in his frustration and impotent rage.

It went on forever. Rask hacked and sawed and Kellen screamed and writhed until the wing was severed. The blood ran and soaked into the carpet and as soon as the horror was done, he grabbed the other wing. It couldn't have been as long as it felt. The knife looked wickedly sharp and the surface area where the wing was attached to Kellen's body was not that great, but he took his time at it. Played with Kellen. Made him suffer as much as he could.

Mercifully Kellen's screams stopped before he had the second wing severed. After that, Rask lost interest in his sick game and finished the evil deed with a last slice.

"Bind the wounds, Niles," Rask said, as coolly as if telling him to take out the trash. "We still need our little familiar for the ritual."

Niles looked more than a little green around the gills but he at least attempted to staunch the flow of blood from Kellen's shredded back while Rask wiped his blade clean. Sin caught the tremble in the young man's hands just before more screams rent the air from elsewhere.

"What in the cursed mother's name…" Rask hissed.

The door flew open so hard it bounced against the wall as the rest of the coven rushed into the room. The smell of troll wafted after them.

"Kellen?" a cavern-deep, thick voice boomed in the front room. "Kellen!"

The kitsune bounced around the room on the balls of his feet, eyes wide in fear, whispering, "Troll, troll, troll, troll."

"Yes, pup," Rask spat out. "Rather obvious. Our traitor pixie has been far more trouble than he's worth and will pay for this. His screams will be never-ending."

Sin managed to shift. The drow's concentration was slipping. This drow, this fucking drow, who had murdered the love of his life, had ruined Sin's life and damaged his sanity, *he* was the one who needed to pay. For Ness, for all the innocents murdered, for poor, beautiful Kellen who just wanted a normal life.

Slowly, carefully, he turned so he could see more of the room, size up the ones nearest him. Not the human boy. Too frail. Not the sylph. She didn't weigh more than a dandelion tuft.

Heavy footfalls stomped through the front room, the troll calling out for Kellen. It had to be the maintenance troll, a phrase Sin never thought he would have in his head, from Kellen's building, Tok. What other troll would be here calling Kellen's name?

Tok smashed through the bedroom door as if the doorframe were papier-mâché, leaving a troll-shaped hole in the wall, and Rask, give the drow points for courage, rose to meet him, hands up, green magic gathering in ropes around his arms.

That was it. The distraction Sin so desperately needed. The drow had too much going on at once and his hold on Sin slipped. Gritting his teeth against the pain, Sin swung his wing, the one still attached to the hooks and chain. The free hook swung like a grapple and embedded itself into the kitsune's shoulder. As Sin hoped, the kitsune yelped and tried to pull away, letting Sin pull himself half-upright. He yanked back with his hooked wing, ripping the hook out of the kitsune in a gout of blood and wrapped his free wing around the human girl, who stood just behind Rask, using her as a fulcrum for a swing and release.

Sin propelled himself forward on the momentum of his wings and smashed into Rask's back, bearing the much lighter drow to the floor. No sane or reasonable thoughts scurried through his head any longer. There was only rage and blood and prey.

The drow had time for a single frightened cry before Sin dropped his head to Rask's throat, fastened sharp teeth around his windpipe, and tore a chunk away, roaring his triumph and his bestial delight.

The room around him was in chaos. The human woman was chanting, throwing magical arrows against the troll, apparently to no avail. It was telling that she tried to save herself first rather than attack Sin to try to save Rask. The troll sniffed the air, ignoring the magic slung his way.

"Blood," he said, and spied Kellen.

The walls shook with the troll's roar and Sin heard the snapping of bones as heavy fists meted out punishing blows.

Sin managed to roll away, spitting out gore and blood. He wedged himself into a corner, dazed and ill, trying to make sense of things. Rask was dead. So very dead. His last rattling breath had ghosted over Sin's hair. His attack had been vengeance-fueled, for his beloved whom he would never see again, never hold tight, never wake up to when the sun rose. That bag of blood and bone now lying inert on the floor had stolen Ness' life, a life full of promise, of bright intellect and unfailing compassion. Rask had stolen all of the moments, all of the long years he should have had with Ness. So why didn't he feel any better? Why did he only feel empty, hollow and nauseated?

Tok had backhanded the human woman across the room. The boy, Niles, lay crumpled against the opposite wall. And Kellen... Kellen lay unconscious in the middle of a melee, still bleeding into the carpet. Sin wormed his way over, a modified shackled low-crawl under the magic still being thrown in futile bolts around the room. He reached Kellen's inert form, folded a wing over him, and pulled him in close, determined to protect the pixie with his own body and hope that, perhaps, the troll would tire of battle and might help them soon.

The roars and the shrieks and explosions took up too much of his hearing, so he was startled when he heard the trample of booted feet racing down the hall. Oh, damn. Reinforcements for the coven? Seriously?

But the figures who appeared suddenly in the ruined doorway were uniformed in the familiar black and gray of AURA, the faces ones he knew.

"AURA enforcement!" Captain Hartgrove bellowed, his magic sword at the ready. "Stand where you are!"

A crackle of magical lightning sizzled through the air from Niles' fingertips and struck the troll directly in the chest. It fizzled and singed the air around him, doing absolutely nothing. As far as Sin knew, trolls were not impervious to magic, but this one sure seemed to be, and a good thing too, or he would have suffered some serious damage already. Tok picked Niles up and threw him across the room at Valerian.

"Tok!" Sin called out. "Stop, please! These are Kellen's friends. They've come to help him."

Val had broken Niles' fall and looked ready to charge but he stopped when he heard Sin's voice.

"Sinistrus? What in the gods' names are you doing here?"

"Trying to be a hero. I suck at being a hero. Damn it, Val, Kells is hurt bad." Sin lifted his wing to let them see the wounded pixie. "I'll explain everything. Just please, he needs help first."

Tok had left off his rampage, mostly because everyone in the room was either dead, dying, wounded, or simply doing their best not to draw his attention now. He moved toward Sin and Kellen.

"Kellen is hurt," he said, as if he hadn't just heard Sin say that very thing. "Which of these hurt him?"

"The one that's dead, Tok. There, by your feet." Sin tried to point with his chin. Great mother, he was tired and he hurt and he just wanted this all over and done.

Tok grunted and bent his bulk over. He took Sin's elbow and pulled him up to sitting as if he were handling a child, then snapped the chain on the manacles binding his wrists.

Val came into the room slowly, wary of Tok, but he sheathed his sword and spoke into his radio instead. "We need medevac here. I have several civilians down."

Stepping around him, Flax eased into the room as well, not as quick to put his knives away. "Sin, give me a hint here. Who're the bad guys?"

"Um, well." Sin flinched as Tok snapped the chain between his ankles as well. He did that a little too easily. "The big baddie's dead there on the floor, the mud-fucking bastard. The only not bad people in this room, I guess, are me, Kells, and the troll. This is Tok. He's the maintenance troll from Kellen's building."

"Oh, um, hey, Tok." Flax gave the troll a less than comfortable wave. "We sorta, kinda met when I was at Kellen's place. Just stay there for me, okay? Appreciate it."

Flax moved toward the bleeding kitsune with handcuffs. Val's radio squawked. "Captain, research has urgent intel they need to relay over the phone."

"Copy that." Val pulled out his phone just as it rang. "Yes? Kai, I'm a little— I see. Would you repeat that address? Yes, I have it." Val's handsome face paled, his gaze sweeping around the room again and landing back on Rask's gruesome corpse. "Already there as things stand. Responding to a call of troll disturbance. Ah, Kai? I think we may have things resolved. I'll call you back."

Flax had the cowed and whimpering kitsune cuffed and was moving to the sylph, who was the only other member of the coven still conscious, though she was curled in the corner, weeping softly.

"Who killed this one, Sin? Who is he?" Val asked softly.

"I did."

"You did what?"

Sin cleared his throat, wondering now if he was going to jail. "I killed him. Val, that motherfucker killed Ness. He's been torturing Kellen. He was trying to kill everything from what it sounds like. Or something."

Tok had settled cross-legged on the floor beside Kellen, so Val followed suit. "Why don't you start from the beginning, Sin. Tell me what's happened here."

From the beginning might have been a bit much, but Sin started from when he'd found Kellen stealing blood and had followed him. He let everything pour out, about the blood magic and the compulsion, and the

Events, and eventually how he had killed Rask. He supposed he couldn't really feel bad about that, but he still dreaded what might happen next.

While he explained, wingbeats sounded out on the terrace, the smaller members of the medevac team making their way into the apartment.

The tengu who had recently joined the department knelt by Kellen, bird feet scraping on the carpet. Sin regarded his beautiful, undamaged feathered wings with a twinge of jealousy. It would be some time before either he or Kellen would fly comfortably, if Kellen ever flew again. He took Kellen's hand while the tengu worked to apply pressure dressings before getting the pixie ready to move.

"We're safe, Kells," Sin told him softly, unsure if Kellen would hear. "You're safe. He's dead and, I hope, gods I hope, that you're free. Hey, I still owe you that honey, right? So you need to be okay for me. Can you do that? Please?"

He didn't get a response, but perhaps that was for the best. Kellen had already suffered enough. The rest of the injured were triaged quickly, and Sin's injuries, while they hurt like hell, were ruled as noncritical. Kellen was flown out first, followed by the two human mages, both in bad shape. The kitsune was escorted out by enforcement, in cuffs, to have his injuries seen to under guard while the sylph, mostly uninjured, was arrested and read her rights.

The AURA coroner came for Rask and finally Val turned to Sin and offered him a hand up. "Tok, I assume you'll be heading home?"

The troll nodded with a grunt.

"Stay close in case we have questions for you, please." Val put a hand under Sin's elbow and shook his head.

"Sin, I'll take you myself. For now, consider yourself in custody until we get this mess straightened out."

"I'm being arrested?"

"No, not officially. But there will be an inquiry. And you do need to get to medical."

"Oh." Sin let himself lean against Val as they made their slow way to the elevator. "Val?"

"Hmm?"

"Drow tastes terrible."

Chapter Sixteen

Kellen slowly opened his eyes. He had been dreaming of something. He couldn't quite recall all of it, something about being caught in a storm and having nowhere to hide from the driving rain and lightning. It took him a second to realize he wasn't in his bedroom, and another to remember. Rask, the coven. Sin! He sat up, or tried to. He made it about as far as lifting his head and one arm and groaned. He felt so weak it was frightening. He was lying on his back. It felt strange and more memory came to him. His wings…

"Kells? You really awake this time?"

He turned, his heart racing at how calm that familiar voice sounded, calm and almost…aggrieved. "Sin?"

"Hey, gorgeous." Sin was sitting propped up in the bed next to his, both wings and wrists bandaged, a skin magazine open on his lap. "How do you feel?"

Kellen swallowed and tried to sit up again, this time more slowly, with much the same results. "Weak." It was the only way he could think to describe how he felt.

He wasn't in nearly as much pain as he thought he should be. "I can't get up."

"Nah. You probably shouldn't." Sin waved a hand toward the bed rail. "There's a remote control thingy there. The white thing. Raise the head of your bed that way. But they kinda have you drugged up a little. And you lost a lot of blood."

Kellen of course knew about the controls for the bed. It took Sin to remind him, though, before his fuzzy brain figured it out. He pushed the button to raise his head and carefully shifted, looking over his shoulder. There was nothing behind him but the bed. Completely gone. He couldn't quite believe that yet so he pushed it away.

"What happened? How did you get us away?"

"Oh, hon, I would love to tell you I was your white knight all valiant and daring with the swoopy, cool last-minute rescue. But it wasn't me. There was the maintenance troll. And then Val came. Though I may have kinda killed Rask before that part."

Kellen blinked, trying to absorb what he said. "You killed him? He's dead?" He hardly dared believe that any more than he wanted to think about his wings being gone.

"Yeah." Sin dropped his gaze to his lap. "I may have lost it a little when he...when he was hurting you. And when Tok came, I went for Rask. I, um, it was pretty awful."

"Tok?" This was sounding more and more unreal. Maybe he was still dreaming. Maybe Rask had killed him and this was something his mind was making up as he died.

Sin nodded, still unable to meet Kellen's eyes, apparently. "Tok... He's not a regular troll. Not by half.

He got worried when you didn't come home. And then, as he puts it, he sniffed for you. Followed your trail all the way to that damn coven and smashed the door down."

Kellen tried to push himself up further but his arms were like wet noodles. "What? He did what? Is he all right?"

"He's good. It was weird stuff." Now Sin looked over, his eyes weary but steady. "I mean, he crashes through the doors like someone yelled *Hey, Kool-Aid!* and the whole coven is firing magic at him. Just pop, pop, pop, all over the place, magic sizzle everywhere. But Tok? Didn't faze him. Nothing touched him, like it just slid right off. Kai got hold of him after and you know what he said? He said the troll was protected 'cause he was wearing some pixie dust concoction as armor. Imagine that."

Kellen stared at him. Pixie dust armor. He felt his lips twitch. Tok was okay. Sin was okay. Rask was dead. Relief washed into him and he slid down, blinking back a sudden surge of emotion.

"Kells?"

He glanced over to find Sin watching him uncertainly, his bottom lip caught between his teeth.

"I'm glad you're okay. Or you will be. I hope. So how long were you his...whatever that was? Under his thumb?"

Kellen's lips parted and his throat locked. *Almost ten years.* He thought, and there was no pain. "Almost ten years," he murmured. No pain. He looked at Sin with wide eyes. "No pain. I said it."

"You did." Sin managed a crooked little smile for him, and that vulnerable look nearly stopped Kellen's heart. "You're free, Kells. The nightmare's over."

Over? Was it over? That didn't feel any more real than the rest of it had. He tried to say a little more, waiting for the pain to grab his mind, but a word came out, and another, and nothing stopped him. "I didn't want to take the blood. If I didn't take it, though, they would have gotten it themselves, hurt people to take it. I tried to run away, but Rask found me. If I was away from him too long, it felt like…like what the elves call fading."

Sin frowned and even that expression on him was handsome. "Kai said…well, he said a lot of things, shit about drow magic and court laws that all kinda went blah-blah-blah in my brain. But he did say that AURA separated you from that duck fucker when you came through. That he got sent to Elvenhome for, what did Kai call it? Assimilation training? Which obviously didn't work. Did he… Sweet mother, I almost feel dirty asking this. Did he fade when he was away from you too?"

Kellen frowned. "I don't know. I just know when he came back, that feeling went away. He didn't say why he came back. I just thought it was because of the—" Kellen stopped. He'd already said too much. There were things he wanted to explain, why he'd done the things he done, how he hadn't wanted to do any of it, but he was not ready to face the revulsion he knew he would see when people realized how tainted he was.

"Hey. Look at me." There was a soft demand in Sin's voice. "You don't have to tell me crap. You might have to tell investigators more stuff, but me? Only the stuff you want to."

"Investigators?"

Sin looked at him and nodded. "The coven, those of them that are still alive, are all in custody. There'll be an investigation into what happened, and it'll all come out, all the shit they were doing. Though Kai and his crew have already figured it out. They'll still need to corroborate evidence and all that stuff that cops do. You'll have to tell them what you know, what you saw."

There was something Sin was holding back from telling him but Kellen figured he knew what it was anyway. "Will I be arrested? Is Tenzin angry? I'll resign, if he hasn't already fired me."

"Okay, whoa there, little cowboy." Sin held up both hands, flinched and set them back in his lap. "First off, we're both in medical custody, pending the decisions from the United Council. 'Cause, you know, crossover on crossover crime, the human courts won't touch it. I'm in custody 'cause I kinda murdered someone, so there's that. You're just here 'cause they need information. Well, I mean, you're *here* 'cause you can't really move yet, but you know what I mean. Tenzin's worried sick, but he's not mad. And nobody said anything about firing your snow-white little ass."

"You didn't have any choice. Rask would have killed you. He was going to use your blood," Kellen said. The thought of Sin being in trouble spiked his anxiety. If he hadn't followed Kellen, he wouldn't have had to do what he'd done.

"Yeah, well, I kinda know that." Sin glanced away, his mouth twisting in a grimace. "I don't *think* I'm gonna be charged. Gave my deposition and the AURA lawyers took it to DC to the Council. Kai went, too, and probably Val. Maybe. I dunno. I've been stuck here. But they should be back today. We'll know soon what's gonna happen. Kai took a blood sample from you. Said he could prove something or other with it." Sin shrugged, his bandaged wings lifting and falling with his shoulders. "They said not to worry too much. Either of us."

Kellen was worried, though. He had been prepared to face whatever consequences might come to stop Rask from hurting anyone else. Sin shouldn't have to face any consequences because of him. However, he hadn't the energy to worry for too long. He was already fighting to keep his eyes open after just a short conversation.

Kai took his blood? Why? What would it tell him?

* * * *

Kai Hiltas, head of AURA's Research department, former seeker to his drow queen, exhausted husband of a most-likely worried yeti, leaned against the empty elevator wall and groaned. He hated going to Washington to stand before the United Council. Half elected body, half government appointees, the Council passed for an actual governing body for crossovers, at least regarding those matters the human governments wouldn't touch.

And they were a blasted bunch of pretentious, overblown bureaucrats, regardless of age or race. It had to be something about the city. Seemed to do that to people.

His part was done, though. There would be wrangling about new procedures and new policies, but he didn't care one half blade of grass for all that. The hearing was finished. The important rulings had been handed down. If it had been mere policy and, goddess forbid, funding issues, he would have gone home and crawled into bed. As it was, he had people waiting for news and he wouldn't make them wait longer.

He stepped off the elevator at Medical and strode through the front doors, sparing only the slightest hint of a wave for the young human at the front desk. She made no move to stop him. Down the hall to the patient rooms, to a particular room where a deep, smooth as sin voice conversed with a higher, more musical one.

"Gentlemen," he said as he turned the corner. "Glad to see you both awake."

Kai was somewhat heartened to see that Kellen did not flinch at the sight of him, although he did lower his gaze for a moment. His mannerisms, his fear, they made sense now in perspective. It did not make Kai wish it wasn't so any less.

"You're back already? That only took, what? Five days? I figured you'd be mired in bullshit for at least two weeks," Sin said.

"Yes, well." Kai put his portfolio down on the bed and turned the armchair that sat between them so he could face them both before he collapsed into it. "There was much bullshit. And there will be a quantity more. I simply don't have to stay for the rest."

"Did you tell them it was self-defense?" Kellen asked. "Sin had no choice. They were going to kill him."

Kai raised an eyebrow at this outburst, but it was said so breathlessly and earnestly, he couldn't possibly take offense. "I told them many things, among them, that. Testimony from several officers and even from the kitsune helped in that regard. Officer Wolfheart called it self-defense against a loaded drow."

A strangled sound came from Sin, the incubus trying to muffle a laugh.

"Yes, yes." Kai flapped a hand at Kellen's continued anxious expression. "Sin has been cleared of any charge. It was, indeed, a clear case of self-defense. That he managed it at all, shackled and so on, says something for the survival instinct."

"Not really what I was thinking at the time," Sin said with a frown.

"*Survival instinct* is what I told the Council, and if you say anything differently now, I refuse to hear it." Kai laid his head back against the seat cushion. "Do *not* tell me of a need for vengeance or justice or anything of that nature." He rolled his head to the right to fix Kellen with his gaze. "And you, young pixie. Well, your case was more complicated."

Kellen dropped his eyes again and Kai could almost see, as if they were a shadow behind him, how his wings would have dropped a degree. Surprisingly he did not start making excuses or claiming his innocence. He rushed to Sin's defense, but not his own, which told Kai any number of things.

"I stole the blood. You couldn't tell them that was self-defense. Are they going to put me in jail?"

Kai heaved a long-suffering sigh. "No one ever lets me tell a story from start to finish. It's really rather tiresome."

"It's 'cause you take too long, pretty drow boy." Sin didn't quite snarl but it was close. "Get to the point."

"No, Kellen. You will not be put in jail. You certainly did commit crimes, some directly and some indirectly. Theft of medical supplies. Accessory after the fact to the murder of flower fairies." That part still gave Kai a bit of a turn. Odd, since a few years ago, he couldn't stand flower fairies. "Aiding in the perpetration of deadly, forbidden spells. However, there were extenuating circumstances, despite the fact that one Shawna Cosgrove attempted to, as they say, throw you beneath the bus."

Kellen seemed to hunch in on himself a little more with every charge leveled. "What does that mean? What did she say?"

Kai had the odd urge to reach over and pat Kellen's foot reassuringly, but he had the feeling that from him, it would be no comfort at all. "She claimed that you were Rask's willing accomplice. That you had been lovers for years. That she had photographic proof of your…entanglement with him." Kai had to stop and swallow against his own rising nausea. That drow, that revolting, twisted— He had to stop. The bloody idiot was dead and unless Kai wanted to resort to necromancy, raise him and kill him again, there wasn't anything he could do to him now. "However—"

"Holy hell, Kai," Sin murmured. "How can there be a however to that? I mean, that's a she said, she has the pics to prove it thing, right?"

Kai gave him a jaded smile. "Yes and no. I did take the liberty to obtain a blood sample from you, Kellen. And had one from that—" He did stop to swear in drow, but only for a moment. "Rask's body. The *peshk* bonding, hardly a true bond, of course, leaves certain traces in the blood for a time, even after death. Certain magical patterns. Only a drow would know this, though now I tell you. And when I produced these samples and showed them the identical pattern in your blood and his, there was no more talk of *willing* in that council chamber. You were under a compulsion so dire that you were unable even to ask for help. I will tell you, though perhaps I shouldn't, that the elvish members of the Council required a recess to, ah, get some fresh air."

Kellen paled as white as the sheet beneath him, he looked more than a little sick himself. Under the pallor was a stain of red high on his cheeks. "I never, never, wanted to do any of that," he said in a strained murmur. "I was taken in a raid and as soon as Rask knew what my dust could do he…he bound me to him so that even if I escaped, I would be an outcast, and he would find me no matter how far I ran."

"Even so. It is a revolting thing that he did to you." Kai did reach out for an absurdly awkward pat this time before he sat back in his chair. "But he wanted more than merely your dust, didn't he? He used you in all his magic."

Kellen nodded. "The coven needed a familiar. Someone they could push the magic through so it didn't blow up in their faces. Niles said I was like a flow restrictor."

"Indeed, an apt comparison." Kai nodded in grudging approval. "Your dust, your use as a magical ground and your abject submission. And even with all of this, he wasn't satisfied. But you aren't to blame in this. I know how this works, this perversion of bonding, and you truly had no choice."

When Kellen said nothing in return to this, Kai went on. "At any rate, the Council is now aware you were under a compulsion and took that into consideration. At some point a delegate may have more questions for you directly, seeing as how you managed to keep this tower from imploding or creating further damage such as the one did at Berkeley."

"What do you mean the one at Berkeley?" Sin asked.

"Hasn't anyone told you yet? Our research into the tower here led to the discovery that a failed tower was originally responsible for creating the RARE. Shawna

Cosgrove was the niece of one of the practitioners who died."

"Um, sorry." Sin shook his head slowly. "I don't get it."

Unpack, Tenzin always told him. *You know what's in your brain. No one else does.* "The students at Berkeley, the ones who caused the original magical accident that set off the chain of magical explosions that became the RARE? Those students were foolishly attempting to construct a wizard tower. But they had no idea what they were doing and simply caused a localized catastrophe. That failed tower is still drawing power, though in a rather random and unusual way, so the community directly around Berkeley is largely unaffected. Its discharges are what cause Events, and why the Tower itself acts as a signal for them."

"Okay," Sin said slowly. "But those mages are all dead. What's that got to do with this Shawna person?"

"This Shawna person, being one of only two magic users in the family, was in close contact with her aunt and was able to learn from her the basics of what they were trying to attempt through a magically enhanced computer matrix. Apparently, she had been attempting to puzzle out what had gone wrong for several years before she met Rask. And, either in an effort to impress him, or perhaps because she believes the nonsense that all drow know everything about dark magic instinctively, she shared the information with him."

"And the duck fucker figured out what they had done wrong, and was using Kells to fix the problem," Sin said.

"Something like that, yes. And using a coven of relatively powerful mages, though not too powerful, mind you, to help him build it rather than using a computer," Kai said. "Though he wasn't simply attempting to build a tower. He wanted to rip a permanent hole between planes, to connect this human world with one where, he hoped, magic would be available in higher concentrations."

"And now?"

"Now, we work on a way to destroy both towers." Kai slumped farther in the chair. The thought made him even more tired. "I do have staff on rotation at Rask's apartment already, bleeding off bits of magic. If we don't, we'll have another Berkeley."

"But he's dead," Sin said, scooting around to sit on the edge of his bed. "The tower shouldn't be doing shit anymore, right?"

"No. A tower becomes a self-perpetuating system. It will keep drawing magic out of the world until it's dismantled. And while I understand the theory, I've never dismantled one before."

Sin nudged his shoulder. "Hey, you can do it. You're the great and powerful Kai. Kinda like the Wizard of Oz."

Kai snorted and closed his eyes. "Not a good analogy, my dear. I do sincerely hope I'm more than a charlatan with special effects."

"Hey." Sin nudged him again. "Don't go to sleep yet, beautiful. You never said what happens to Kells now."

"Ah." Kai cracked one eye open and found Kellen studiously not watching him. "My apologies. I thought I did. Because of the clear compulsion set on Kellen, he has been cleared of all charges except one. That of improper medical waste disposal, which comes with a fine. The Council insisted that while you were compelled to collect blood, you weren't compelled to collect *expired* blood. I believe there will be paperwork forthcoming, Kellen, to garnish your wages. Small payments until the fine is paid."

"I can pay them now, if that's okay," Kellen said quietly.

"Well, I'm sure that would be acceptable to the authorities, Kellen, but it may be quite a substantial fine," Kai said.

"I have it. Unless it's over five years of my wages," Kellen said.

Kai's eyes snapped open. Sin was staring at Kellen as well.

"Five years of wages? Your full wages?" Kai asked just to be clear.

Kellen nodded. "Maybe a small amount less, but pretty close to everything goes into the account. As maintenance troll, Tok gets an apartment, but he prefers to live in the basement, so he lets me have it. Honey isn't cheap, but I don't eat much, and I live close to work. I don't really need money, not much anyway. I'll give them all the money I have if I can still work here."

"My dear, don't be so quick to throw away your savings," Kai said in the softest tone he could manage. "You never know when you might need extra funds. I'm sure the fine won't be quite *that* enormous, at any rate."

Sin slid off his bed and perched on the edge of Kellen's, one still-healing wing spreading behind Kellen to fold around him. "Hon, you're missing the really important part here. You pay a fine. Not jail, right? You're freaking free. And of course you get to keep the job. I'll take on anyone who says anything else."

Kai tried desperately to suppress a smile. "You know that's not your decision. But Tenzin has no intention of terminating employment. That was never even mentioned."

What was he seeing here? What did Sin's reactions mean? He was a physical being, yes, and gravitated toward physical affection any chance he had, but he was judicious and careful with touch. Feedings, certainly, and the occasional seduction, otherwise he required trust to get so close. Kellen had certainly been afforded time and opportunity to grow that trust, as co-parents to an orphaned squirrel, as Sin's rescuer, then caretaker, advisor and friend.

But this fierce protective streak, this desire to offer someone more than comfort and reassurance? This was something Kai had only witnessed where Ness was concerned. Interesting. Though he shouldn't read too much into it. Shared trauma was a more than reasonable explanation.

C h a p t e r   S e v e n t e e n

Sin's fingers caressed the willow's leaves on the short bits of branch he'd cut. While many of the trees had dropped their leaves by now, the weeping willows in the park still held on to their bright yellow. Waiting, it seemed, though he didn't know what willows waited for.

"Sin?" Beside him, Kellen shivered.

He'd agreed to come, though Sin was having trouble explaining this little outing to him. Maybe that should've been a sign of how stubborn he'd become about all this. He'd missed the funeral because he'd been in cuckooville and he still had angry moments over not being there to say goodbye to Ness, to see all the officers in uniform who'd come to pay their respects, to hear the, by all accounts, incredibly moving eulogy Val had given.

Don't you have rituals of parting? Tenzin had asked him. *From your home? Rituals of remembrance and farewell?*

Because it was time. Ness had come to him in the night again, so real, so solid, so *present*, and reminded Sin that while he would always be there, nestled against Sin's heart, he wasn't going to be walking through the door at the end of the day. *You're a hard-headed incubus,* Ness had told him. *Though you're my hard-headed incubus and I love you. But you can't live this way. You need to open those clenched fists and let me go.*

"It's okay, Kells." Sin dredged up a smile for the companion beside him. "I'm not gonna do anything stupid or dangerous. I just need these, and we're gonna head to the Hudson. I'll even splurge on a taxi if you're cold."

"It's okay, I don't mind the walk." Kellen paused. "Unless you wanted the taxi?" He bit his lip. "I'm doing that thing again, I'm sorry."

It had taken Sin a while, longer than it should have really, to notice how Kellen always deferred. He supposed ten years of hiding that you even had an opinion wasn't going to be undone in a few weeks.

"Make you a deal." Sin slung a wing around him as he turned them both toward the street. "You get through the rest of the afternoon without apologizing and I'll buy you a warm milk and honey when we come back from the river."

Kellen lifted his chin to look at him and he smiled, just a little smile that turned the corners of his mouth. "Okay."

The walk wasn't far, by New York standards, and Sin wove the willow branches as he walked, humming old snatches of half-forgotten tunes, songs from taverns back home. He'd been here so long, he didn't often think of home, of the less complicated and more dangerous, in some ways, place he'd been yanked from to come here. Kellen watched him curiously as he shaped the willow, leaves and all, into a sturdy hoop, and he smiled reassurance at his friend.

They walked close, Sin wanting to shelter Kellen from the wind as they made their way up Seventy-Ninth Street, past the yacht club, out to the boat basin and upriver a bit to get past all the moored playthings of wealthier people.

Finally, Sin stopped on the bank. It really should've been ocean waves lapping at his feet instead of little river fingers licking the shore, but it would do. The Hudson didn't travel far from here before it met the Atlantic. If someone had asked why it should've been the sea, Sin wouldn't have been able to explain. It just was. The tidal pull, the song of the waves, were important to his kind.

"I met Ness in a bar," Sin started with a slow smile that pulled at his aching heart. "He doesn't...didn't remember that first meeting. Not really. Because he was a young officer, green and new to the city. And everything was overwhelming still. I remember. He was beautiful and not just in the way all centaurs are beautiful in their power and their grace. He *shone* because his eyes took everything in and, hell, devoured everything he saw. Like he wanted to learn about everyone and everything – not judge. Learn."

Sin had to stop a moment, his throat closing up, his eyes watering. Kellen put a hand on his shoulder, and he found he could go on. "But the meeting Ness remembered was in the hospital, after the lich queen, both of us broken and, yeah, not at our best. They'd left me in a private room. Alone. And we both know that's not a good idea for a scared, wounded incubus. I crawled out of my room, desperate to find someone, anyone, to be with. And he called to me. Coaxed me into his bed. He claims he loved me from that moment."

The wind picked up, soft fingers caressing his face as if it tried to dry his tears.

"I loved him. So much I thought my heart would explode sometimes. Oh, I loved him so. People saw a freak, a centaur nerd, someone who didn't really fit anywhere. All I saw was Ness. Glorious, compassionate, kind Ness, who wanted to devour the world with his eyes. I still love him, of course. I'll always…there's no way you can just *forget* that life gave you a gift like that. But he's gone. And I'm still here. And even he comes to me in dreams and says I need to stop holding on so damn tight. 'Cause I'm still here. And he insists that I need to live."

Sin held the willow hoop up as if he could see other worlds through it, and whispered into the open circle, a strangled whisper meant to reach across to death itself, "*Ness.*"

Then he threw the circlet as hard as he could into the water, making certain the current would take it, carry it to sea where the waves would take his words.

They stood on the bank for a long time, not speaking, just watching the river. The wreath had long since been carried away out of sight when Sin noticed the warmth at his side and under his outstretched wing. Kellen still stood close, his face somber and his eyes glittering with unshed tears.

"I know we made a deal that I wouldn't say I was sorry anymore, so I won't." Kellen told him softly. "But I feel your grief and your loss. Your words were beautiful, Sin. I'm sure Ness would be proud of you."

Well, that tore it. Sin buried his face in both hands and wept, not caring one bit if someone was nearby to hear.

After another long while, Sin felt arms around him and heard a sweetly lilting voice through his tears. Kellen was holding him while he sobbed, and singing softly to him, which was becoming something of a habit. Oddly though, this time the tune he sung didn't seem directed at him. The notes held something mournful under the soothing comfort they wove, and seemed to lift out and over the water.

A hymn for Ness, he realized, and he wrapped his arms around Kellen in return, as much a thank you as a need to hold on to his warmth. "Thanks, Kells. That was beautiful. And thanks for coming with me. I'm…glad you did."

"You're welcome," Kellen said.

Sin waited, but that was all he said and he managed a little smile, his tears finally stopping. Simple and direct, that pretty much summed up the way Kellen spoke most of the time.

"Hey, you're shivering." Sin kept both arm and wing around Kellen as he turned them away from the water. "Let's get you back to civilization and some warm milk, okay?"

Kellen nodded and they started to walk up the bank. By the time they passed the yacht club, it finally registered that despite Kellen's shivering, he was toasty warm beside him. He could feel the heat under his wing like a little radiator.

"Do you feel all right, Kells?" Sin asked.

"I feel fine," Kellen answered.

They wound their way up to the street and Sin was wondering if maybe it was something to do with pixie physiology, radiating heat when they were cold, when Kellen tripped and would have gone sprawling if Sin hadn't caught him. He was practically limp, his eyes glassy.

"Kellen?"

"I'm okay." Only he obviously wasn't okay because Sin was still holding him up. He looked more on the verge of passing out than 'okay' or 'fine'.

Sin swept him up into his arms, a twinge tugging at his insides at how light Kellen was. "Hon, we're gonna have to talk about this not telling people when you're feeling like shit thing. I'm hailing us a cab. We're getting you back to Medical right fucking now."

Kellen didn't argue, but Sin suspected that was more because he couldn't argue than he didn't want to. He had gone from standing and seemingly fine to nearly unconscious at an alarming rate. Before Sin could find a cab though, Kellen was squirming in his arms.

"Take it easy, it'll be okay," Sin told him.

Kellen shook his head. "Hurts." He groaned and Sin suddenly smelled blood, although he couldn't see any on him.

"Shit." Sin went down to one knee in the grassy stretch beside the road and yanked out his cell. "This is Sinistrus. Medical emergency, end of Seventy-Ninth, just past the yacht club. Male, pixie, barely responsive, fevered, vitals are racing. Possible internal bleed."

There, that would bring them running, or flying rather. He cradled Kellen's shuddering body against him and settled in to wait.

He put his hand behind Kellen's back to support him and touched wetness. Gently he turned him and there were two bright red spots soaking into the back of Kellen's shirt. Frowning, Sin pulled the back of the shirt up. The wounds on Kellen's back should have been well on the way to healed, he'd seen the stitches himself, seen when they had been taken out too. There should be nothing but healing scar tissue. Instead he saw a new set of stitches in two neat rows on Kellen's back, both were seeping blood and looked red and angry. Swollen. So swollen the new stitch work was straining, digging tightly into his flesh.

"Double shit." Sin replaced shirt and jacket, handling Kellen like he was made of angel hair pasta. Damn, his brain did weird things when he was scared. And he was. How had the wounds reopened that they needed new stitches? Why the hell weren't they healing? He wished his own wings were along far enough that he could just fly off with Kellen and get help.

It wasn't long before the heavy wingbeats of the medevac team reached his sensitive ears, though, Hal leading the pegasus, Parnassus, and the new tengu medic in a V-formation. The huge griffin circled once to find a landing spot for his bulk, back winged and settled to the grass nearby.

"Sin! Can you bring him? Is he stable for transport?"

"He is, boss," Sin called back as he rose with Kellen in his arms and made his way over. "Permission to come aboard? I'll hold him steady."

"Up you come." Hal gestured with his beak to his own broad, lion-furred back. "I think every moment counts with this one."

With the tengu's help, Sin climbed aboard, Kellen held tightly across his lap.

By the time they reached AURA's medical unit, Kellen had gone from warm to hot and he was writhing in Sins arms as he carried him through the doors. Tenzin was there, directing him to take Kellen right in, although Sin was heading toward the first empty exam room anyway.

"I was worried something was badly wrong when I restitched him last night," Tenzin said. "The wounds had already closed over and there was no reason they should have reopened like that."

Sin shook his head. "It's more than that. The area looks infected, but like...I dunno. Like something's swelling from the inside, not just under the skin."

Kellen made a soft cry of pain when Sin set him down on the exam table. He reached out blindly and latched on to Sin. His whole body was trembling even though he was burning up. "It hurts," Kellen said hoarsely.

"I know, sweetie," Sin murmured, removing one of the hands clenched in his shirt so he could start getting Kellen out of his jacket. "We're here now. It's gonna stop hurting soon. Tenzin's here. Come on, help me get you set here so they can have a look at your poor back."

Kellen either didn't hear him or was incapable of helping. Sin managed to get his jacket off but Tenzin used scissors to cut his shirt up the back. The yeti made a crooning sound at the sight of Kellen's back. The vertical cuts held by the stitches were nearly purple and so swollen now they were raised in two ridges. He leaned in and sniffed. "I don't smell any infection."

Those large white furred hands were astounding in their gentleness as Tenzin probed along the gashes. Kellen twisted and cried out, burrowing into Sin's arms.

"We need to get the stitches out. Get one of the doctors in here to do some exploratory, I think. There's something terribly wrong here." Tenzin hurried to get gloves and instruments to remove the stitches while Sin did his best to soothe Kellen, murmuring to him and stroking his hair. He was crap at the actual healing part. No nice songs or spells to make people feel better. Just a field tech, all he could really do was get people stable enough to move them to where real help waited.

He remembered thinking, rather derogatorily, about how Kellen was no good in an emergency. His wings weren't strong enough that he could carry anyone and fly so he was not on the medevac team. How stupid he had been. Being the first one to jump in, deliver first aid, give transport, those things were what Sin was good at, but no less important was the ability to give comfort and act in a confident, efficient manner.

Tenzin spread a sterile pad on the table next to Kellen and placed the items he had gathered. The most useful of which were a pair of scissors, which he used now to begin cutting the stitches.

Carefully, oh so carefully, Tenzin snipped with the scissors and tugged the nearly strangled thread free with a pair of tweezers, sometimes having to use the tweezers to lift the thread before he could snip. Kellen cried out softly with each tug, his pain knifing through Sin's heart.

"It's all right, gorgeous. It is." Sin moved Kellen's hair out of the way so Tenzin could work. "Two more stitches on the right. Now one. Doing good. So good."

Snip. Tug. Snip. Tug.

Desperate for something to say to Kellen, Sin started babbling. "You've got the most incredible hair, you know that? So damn thick and soft. Always smells just a hint of honeysuckle. Don't like a lot of flowery scents, but I like that one. Beautiful color too. All coppery burnished and stuff."

Kellen's soft cries edged toward a scream when Tenzin had to cut a thread out of his skin that was embedded too deeply.

"Great Mother, I'm sorry, Kells." Sin held on tighter. "I should've seen something wasn't right. I'm so sorry."

As Tenzin cut the last stitch on the one side, the ridge of skin split. There was blood, but not nearly as much as there had been when the wound had originally been made. Tenzin touched carefully to the side of the wound, peering at it, perhaps trying to see if there was a deeper pocket of abscess. "Hmm…" Tenzin made a soft sound of wonder as the layer of healing skin split open further and the thin edge of a membranous wing uncurled, protruding just beyond the surface of the skin now that it was freed.

"Ah. I see." Tenzin put his hands on either side of the split skin, helping the wing emerge. "Sin, you stay right where you are. This won't be pleasant."

"What do you…?" Sin trailed off when Tenzin put his hands on either side of the other gash and began, slowly, carefully, to split the skin. He had to lean his hip against the exam table and clutch Kellen to him as the pixie thrashed.

Not pleasant was a massive understatement. Kellen was limp and drenched in sweat by the time Tenzin had coaxed the protruding edge fully free and carefully helped it uncurl. It was wet and bloody and plastered to Kellen's back, but it was a fully formed double dragonfly wing, identical to the one he'd lost, and there was still another to go on the left side.

"I wish we had more complete manuals on different crossovers," Tenzin murmured as he coaxed the left wing set free. "We should never have stitched you back up again last night, Kellen. Your wings were trying to fight free."

Tenzin began to chant, a two-note throat singing that washed over both Sin and Kellen, stealing pain, easing the bleeding. Now that the yeti didn't have to concentrate so hard on removing stitches, he could concentrate on his healing song instead.

A little over an hour after Sin had carried Kellen through the doors, both wings were freed and drying, the area where they had emerged looked raw, but wasn't bleeding and they appeared firmly attached and strong. Kellen himself was utterly exhausted, sore, but no longer in excruciating pain. He also stubbornly wanted to go home.

"I won't prevent you from leaving, but I do wish you would reconsider and stay at least overnight, Kellen," Tenzin said.

"I sleep better at home," Kellen said. "I feel much better already."

"Okay, I get the whole not wanting to sleep in a hospital bed. Again." Sin stepped around the exam table to settle Kellen's jacket over his shoulders. "But you're not going alone."

Kellen looked up at him and there was that little smile again, the one that just touched the corners of his mouth. "All right."

"Really? That simple?" Sin felt like someone had smacked him in the head with a tire iron. "No giving me crap? No, 'oh, no, Sin, I'm fine, you don't have to'?"

Kellen carefully slid off the table, holding on to the edge for a moment then letting go. "No. Unless you would like me to give you crap? I can try."

"Damn. Even the pixie wants to be a smartass today." Sin took him under the elbow, not at all confident about how steady he was. "Just not used to getting such a nice, easy yes out of you."

There it was again when Kellen looked up at him, that little twitch of his lips, that almost smile. Something in

Sin's chest lurched and slid sideways when Kellen leaned against him. Poor little guy. He'd had quite a day.

Sin made good on his earlier promise of hailing a cab. No way in several hells was Kellen going to ride the subway home. When they reached his apartment building, Sin paused before heading up the stairs.

"Do you go say hi to Tok first, usually?"

"Sometimes. Most of the time, yes. Unless it's very late, or early."

"Feel up to it now, or you wanna head upstairs?" Sin slid an arm around Kellen's waist, ready to support him on either set of stairs. The only other time Sin had been here, he'd been just a little screwed up. Yeah, okay. He'd been completely batshit crazy. But he did remember which apartment was Kellen's.

Kellen hesitated then turned toward the basement stairs. "I should say hi. He worries."

The strong smell of antiseptic cleanser greeted them when Kellen opened the door and led the way down the pristine stairwell. Tok must have heard them, or smelled them coming because he met them at the door. Filled the doorway was more like it, and he didn't look happy. He looked over the top of Kellen's head and narrowed his already small eyes on Sin.

"Kellen, are you well? I smell blood."

"I'm okay, now," Kellen said. "Sin made sure I was taken care of. Look…" He fluttered his wings gingerly.

Tok grunted and nodded. "New wings. Good."

Sin watched the exchange with renewed amazement. Sure, he knew a couple of civilized trolls. Usually rock trolls. Enforcement had one and they weren't intellectual giants, by any means, but they managed. Tok, though… Tok was a forest troll. They tended to be meaner and generally nasty in habits and temperament. It knocked him sideways to watch him, again, being so protective of Kellen.

"Hey, Tok." Sin held his hand out, bracing for a too hard handshake and possible broken fingers, but Tok just stared at the offered extremity. "Yeah. Um. Thanks for saving us. For saving Kellen the other day. I didn't get a chance to say it."

Tok nodded his head slowly. "Kellen says people don't like trolls when they are mean. Those others, they were like mean trolls."

Sin had to nod in agreement. Few words, but such true ones. "Yeah. They were probably worse than any mean troll I ever met. Trolls where I came from wanted to eat you or smash you. Those people…what they wanted was so much worse."

"Worse," Tok agreed. He pointed a very large blunt finger at Sin. "Be nice to Kellen."

"I will. Promise."

Kellen said his goodbyes and Sin helped him up the stairs. *Be nice to Kellen.* He hadn't always been. In fact, he'd kinda been a real shit to Kellen in the past. But it wasn't the threat of a troll guardian that had changed it.

"That was odd," Kellen said as he let them into the apartment. "He doesn't usually talk much to strangers. Are you hungry? I don't have a lot on hand, but there is some canned soup in the cupboard. I'm starving."

"You need me to run out for anything?" *Canned soup? Dear goddesse*s. "I can get us some takeout. Go down to the market?"

"Only if there is something you want. I have what I need," Kellen said, going directly to the kitchen, which was only a few steps into the apartment. He opened the cupboard and took out a mason jar of dark honey. His hands were shaking as he unscrewed the lid. He tipped back the jar like he was chugging a beer, holding on to it with both hands.

"Hey, hey…" Sin took him under the elbows and guided him into a chair. "At least sit down, hon. No, I don't need anything. Some days I'm not hungry for, you know, food. It's been a little off and on. The food thing."

He watched with some concern as Kellen guzzled honey, though he managed to get one hand and then the other free to help Kellen out of his jacket. Closet…closet… There didn't seem to be a coat closet, but there were three neat hooks by the door. Sin hung the jacket up on one of those, then returned to Kellen and took off his shoes.

He got himself a glass of water and sat in the chair opposite, keeping an eye on Kellen as some of the pink returned to his cheeks. "Scared the hell out of me today. That's not an easy thing to do to an incubus."

Kellen set the jar down and licked his lips. "Why?"

"What?"

"Why were you scared? I was okay."

"You were so not okay. I thought you were dying."

Kellen frowned at the jar, which was a little over a quarter gone already. He started to say something, then stopped. "I'm—" He stopped again and shook his head. "I would have been scared too, if I thought you were dying."

That stopped Sin a moment. They were friends, right? He did care that his friends were all right. But the way Kellen said it, in that soft, hesitant way…he was saying something else? Wasn't he? Sin's emotional compass

242

had been on the fritz since his last trip to crazytown. Had he really been missing something obvious?

"Kells," he started, then stopped again. "Do you… Don't you still think I'm annoying as fuck? That I'm a terrible person? Like you used to?"

"I never thought that," Kellen said. "You made me angry sometimes. Mostly I was just worried because you were right about me. I was being sneaky. I did hide things. I wished all the time that I could just tell you."

"And instead of trying to help you, 'cause I knew things weren't right." Sin reached over the table to cover one of Kellen's hands with his own. "Instead of helping, I taunted you. Made you miserable. Kells, you may say I don't have to say it, but I'm sorry."

Kellen dragged his eyes up to look at him. "No, you don't ever have to be sorry. Not to me. If I hadn't done the things I had…" He shook his head a looked away again. "I can never be sorry enough for what I did, Sin."

He couldn't stand the devastation on that beautiful face. Sin flung himself from his chair and landed on his knees beside Kellen, still clutching his trembling hand. "Don't say that. It wasn't your fault. You tried the best you could to limit damage, to keep people from being hurt. You didn't have a choice. He *stole* that from you."

After a long moment, Kellen looked at him again. He didn't deny that at least, but he didn't agree either. His wings were fanning gently behind him, something Sin had picked up on before. He did that when he was unsure what to say or do. Sin was sure he didn't even know he was doing it.

Kellen lifted his free hand and gently touched Sin's cheek. "I don't know if I'm ready to believe that yet."

"Then I'll believe for you. 'Cause it's true." Sin used the force of his eyes. He knew their impact. "And I'll keep telling you until you do." He rose up on his knees so he could cup Kellen's face between his hands. "You're lovely and kind and you want the best for other people. You're absolutely crap about taking care of yourself, but you'd give the world your heart on a platter if you thought it would help. That's a wonderful thing. And so rare. And I…"

He what? What did he want to say? What the hell was this that he had… That he felt with Kellen?

Slowly Kellen closed the distance between them. He brushed a soft, hesitant kiss on Sin's lips.

Oh, yeah. That's what this was. He liked Kellen. More than liked. He wanted him. His body yearned for him, and he hadn't acknowledged it except in ever-increasing little touches.

"Kells," he whispered, and moved in to press their lips closer, gently, tenderly, exploring without attacking.

Sweet, honeyed kiss, quite literally. Sin had shared many kisses, with many different people in his life. Some lusty, full of passion, some full of love and need. Kellen's kiss was like melting into sugar. He seemed to follow Sin's every move, his lips caressing back when he pressed forward, or hesitantly exploring when he drew back slightly.

Sin took both of Kellen's hands and turned them to kiss each palm. With little flutters of trepidation in his stomach, he sat back on his heels to gaze up into spring green eyes. "It's kind of a cruel joke, you know. Being a gay incubus. What I need to survive, I don't really want. And what I most want, usually doesn't want me, 'cause my sexy superpowers don't work on males. So I'm careful. And I ask. Kells, do you want me?"

Even as he said it, the flutters turned to a strange tumult inside. He'd just said his goodbyes to Ness and there was guilt raking its nails through his lungs. Everyone told him to live, to go on, and for an incubus, sex was life. But could he? Did he want to? Could Kellen even conceive of wanting to, since Sin was certain he'd been mistreated in every way possible?

"Yes," Kellen said, leaning back in to slide his slender fingers into Sin's hair and pull him back for another kiss.

"Sweet Mother," Sin whispered against his lips. Carefully, as if Kellen might spook, he slid his arms underneath and lifted Kellen to continue the kiss, more urgent now, devouring Kellen's lips, his tongue pleading for entrance. Kellen opened to him and Sin moaned as he shoved inside to explore that sweet, heated cavern.

If Kellen had seemed hesitant before he certainly didn't seem so now. He returned Sin's kisses with a heat that had nothing to do with the fever that had taken him earlier. Had that only been this afternoon? Maybe he should slow things down. He had pulled Kellen from the chair and he'd slid astride Sin's lap, his legs wrapping around him and his arms holding just as tightly. Did he think that Sin might change his mind?

Sin broke the kiss. "Hey, easy. I'm not going anywhere."

Luminous green eyes regarded him. Kellen's lips were slightly parted and looking very kissable. The look of confusion that followed was almost too cute. His grip around Sin's neck loosened slightly. "Did you not want this as well?"

"Yeah, we can take our time, though. No need to rush."

"Oh." Sin could feel the way the tense muscles of Kellen's back and thighs relaxed a degree, but the confusion remained in his expression, then he brightened a little, giving him a small smile. "I want to learn all the things you like."

"Honey," Sin let his voice drop to a sultry murmur, "that might take a few months. I like a lot of things."

Kellen was light enough that Sin could stagger up from kneeling on the floor with the pixie in his arms. He took a quick glance around the shabby apartment. No, that sad little sofa wasn't going to hold up to any hard use.

"Bed?"

Kellen pointed to one of the two doors in the hallway. Sin opened it to a neat if sparsely furnished room. There was only the double bed, no dressers or chairs, but the bed did have a frame, which was better than a mattress on the floor.

Sin hesitated in the doorway on the sense that he was about to leap off a cliff and he wasn't certain his wings would hold. *Ness would be proud of you,* Kellen had said. More than one person had told him Ness would want him to go on, to take care of himself, to live. *You've never been good on your own*, Ness' voice echoed in his head. It was something ghost Ness had said, but it was something they'd talked about when Ness was still alive too. It wasn't *Ness'* permission he needed here, though. His beloved centaur would've wanted him happy and safe. Sin needed his own permission to do this, to take that final plunge, that final admission that Ness was really gone.

"Sin?"

The anxious note in Kellen's voice tugged at his heart. Sin glanced down to meet eyes filled with uncertainty and want. He wasn't the only one in need here, damn it.

"It's okay, Kells. We're gonna do this one thing at a time, you and me. We're both on a little bit of shaky ground, but we're in this together."

He set Kellen on his feet, and Kellen took a couple of steps, pulling his shirt off carefully. The skin around the wing joints on his back looked a little tender, but there was no more blood. They were almost as good as new after being released. His jeans went sliding down narrow hips to the floor and he stepped out of them, lithe and naked before he turned around then stopped.

"Too fast again?" he asked.

Sin shook his head and closed his mouth when he realized it was hanging open. "You're so beautiful. It's like you have a little sun living inside you and it makes you shine."

Kellen came back to him, just two small steps, but Sin's eyes caught on his every move. Had he really never noticed before how he moved like rolling water? Only when Kellen touched him again, putting his hands on his chest and caressing upward, did Sin realize he was still standing in the doorway.

"You can come in, if you like."

"Thank you." Sin walked them in, his hands caressing Kellen's wrists as he gave the pixie a wink. "You have to invite an incubus in, you know. Or we can't cross the threshold."

"Is that true? I thought that was just a myth," Kellen said.

"It's so not true." Sin chuckled as he started undoing his shirt. "I did breaking and entering in a former life. Not proud of it, but I couldn't get a job here."

As soon as he bared his chest, Kellen leaned in, kissing along his collarbone, his fingers trickling down his ribs to his waist. He found the button of his jeans and rested there. "Is this okay?" he asked, murmuring along Sin's skin.

"That's more than okay." Sin gave him a little smile. "I like being unwrapped."

Kellen pulled the button free and unzipped him then pushed his hands down over Sin's hips, tugging the snug-fitting jeans down. When they only went so far, Kellen grasped the waist and sank to his knees, taking them down with him. For someone who was usually so reserved and uncertain of himself, he didn't seem so shy now. He had Sin hobbled around the ankles with his own jeans and his hands came back up Sin's thighs, caressing inward, cupping his balls gently in one hand as he kissed the base of Sin's cock.

"Mmm, that feels so good." Sin tried to spread his legs, frustrated and turned on even more when he couldn't.

Warmth and wetness suddenly engulfed Sin. Kellen's hands moved featherlight over his thighs, hips, abdominals and back again.

For a moment, Sin combed his fingers through Kellen's thick auburn hair, head tilted back, drinking in the sensations. Part of him, the selfish, hedonistic part, wanted to stand there and take what Kellen offered so sweetly. But the scent of Kellen's arousal wrapped around him, and he knew he couldn't do that.

Gently, he pulled Kellen off and whispered, "We've had a long day. Let's get in bed."

Kellen looked up at him, that earnest look of wanting mixed with threads of confusion again. "Did I do something wrong?"

"No, hon. As sweet as this is, you on your knees for me, I'm a greedy bastard and I want more." Sin pulled him up by the arms and kissed him, passion and tender promise, while he toed off his shoes, socks and jeans.

Kellen wrapped around him like a vine, his mouth soft and inviting. There was nothing soft about the way he pressed up to Sin, though. The bed dipped as they both sank down on it. Kellen slid a leg over Sin's hip, wriggling into his lap. "I like the way you kiss me," Kellen said when their lips parted breathlessly.

"I like the way you kiss me too," Sin said on a chuckle. He let his hands rest on the top curve of Kellen's ass, letting his gaze wander down between them. "Our boys seem to really enjoy it too."

Kellen looked down too and his hand followed, fingers drifting over Sin's chest and down to curl lightly around his shaft. He rolled his hips, pressing the undersides of their cocks, rubbing them tentatively together. "This is okay?" Kellen whispered huskily near Sin's ear. "It feels so much better this way."

"Mmmm, that's delicious," Sin got out in a husky murmur. He rolled his hips in time to Kellen's stroking, leaning in to lick a wet line up Kellen's throat.

The pixie tipped his head back, closing his eyes and stroking them more firmly. A soft groan that was more like a trill vibrated in Kellen's throat against Sin's lips. His hips thrust a little faster and he ground harder. "I like the way you touch me too, this feels so good." Kellen rubbed his cheek next to Sin's ear and flicked his tongue there lightly.

Sin wrapped his wings around them both, shivering with pleasure as Kellen's silken wings fluttered against his. "So good... Oh, you don't even know."

He'd never had a winged lover before and the sensations were amazing. He leaned his head on Kellen's shoulder, letting the base of one horn rub against Kellen's chin and thought he might die of sensation overload.

Kellen must have noticed the sudden surge of pleasure because he tilted his head, using his cheek to brush lightly along the horn. His lips nuzzled into his hair and he kissed at the base, sending another wave of delicious shivers through Sin. "Do you want to be inside me now?" Kellen asked softly.

"Hmm, what?" Sin's lust soaked brain took a moment to process the question. He scooted them both farther up onto the mattress, only too happy to let their eager cocks bump together before he flopped down on his back, taking Kellen with him. "You know what? No."

"No?" Kellen's hesitance had returned and he'd stiffened again, as if he might be afraid he'd done something wrong.

"Nope." Sin wriggled his hips, grinding up against Kellen. "I want you inside me."

Kellen went totally still, the look on his face unfathomable. He was silent so long, braced on his arms and looking down at Sin that Sin was just about to ask if *he* had done something wrong.

"You want…but…" Kellen floundered for a moment. "I've never done that before."

"Then it's about time, right?" Sin said in mock sternness. He nuzzled at Kellen's throat. "Nothing I like better than a cock inside me. And you've a lovely one. Please say you will."

Sin could tell that he'd thrown Kellen by the suggestion, but he was not completely put off by the idea, if the hard cock poking him was any indication.

Kellen's responses thus far were both telling and raised questions, but those questions could wait. He shifted a leg and Kellen's slender frame fit nicely between his legs.

Kellen kissed him again, his lips touching down sweetly tender, warm and seeking. Sin rested his hands on his hips, drawing them up the small of his back, feeling the way the fine muscles there flexed under the skin with each wing twitch. He ran his hands down to cup the curve of his ass and Kellen moaned softly into his mouth, nudging down more, wriggling into position.

"That's it, sweetheart." Sin spread his wings out on the bed to keep himself steady as he bent his legs up, thighs parted as far as he could manage. A little out of practice maybe, but he was still damn flexible for someone his size. "I'll help you, guide you. You just do what feels good."

For a human, maybe they would've had to have stopped and searched for lube and all that other nonsense. Though maybe not. Sin knew enough human males who liked it rough and raw. Not that he thought Kellen would get rough, exactly. He reached between them and grasped Kellen's cock, positioning him right at his entrance.

"You're gonna have to push. Don't be afraid. You can't hurt me. Push hard."

He perhaps needed the reassurance more than the instruction as he proved by swiftly sliding into Sin without any fumbling about or false starts. He held for a moment before slowly drawing back a fraction and rocking his hips forward again in a delightful way. So, he knew what he was doing even without the experience. That too was telling. Sin resolutely pushed

Angel Martinez and Bellora Quinn

those thoughts out of his head, easy enough to do with the way Kellen was kissing him, his fingers caressing into his hair, stroking gently along his horns while he thrust between his cheeks.

Tempting, so tempting to spread his arms and let Kellen simply have his way, but he suspected that Kellen would be a bit dismayed if he did, perhaps even frightened. Instead Sin wrapped his legs around Kellen's waist and used the leverage to meet him thrust for thrust, slow and gentle at first, though Sin hoped he would lose control. He let his hands wander Kellen's back, careful around the tender skin, caressing those lovely wings, all silky membrane and delicate veins, unlike his own giant, brutish things.

That must have been a sensitive place because Kellen groaned and his hips kicked, spearing deeper and faster into him. Kellen broke the kiss, his breath fanning across Sin's cheek and throat as he bent his head and sucked a little kiss there. "Oh, this feels...mmm..." Kellen nipped at the tender skin where neck met shoulder.

"Kells, that feels so good." It had been so long. Too long since he'd let anyone hold him like this, too long since he'd joined with anyone so closely in the ancient dance. Tears started in Sin's eyes and he wasn't sure of the source. He needed. So desperately. He held Kellen tighter and whispered, hoarse and broken, "Harder, sweetheart. Please."

To Sin's surprise, Kellen slid his hands up his sides, under his arms, bringing Sin's arms up above his head and grasping his wrists. Kellen's lean body arched over him and he spread his knees, drilling down into Sin in a pulse-pounding rhythm.

252

Another time, with another lover, Sin might have fought and wrestled, played at combat. But here, with Kellen, this was what he needed, so badly and he *surrendered* on Kellen's rising tide. Head flung back, only his hips answering Kellen's thrusts, he gasped and moaned and forgot how to speak, until...

"Oh, goddesses... Kellen!"

Kellen bent over him, smothered his gasps in a smoldering kiss, his fingers tightening around Sin's wrists. He didn't slow, didn't stop until Sin was shuddering, quaking with the rush of release, only then did he feel Kellen go taut, buried deep within for a few precious, throbbing seconds.

He released Sin's wrists and Sin clutched him tightly, his lungs heaving as he fought against sobs. This was supposed to be about Kellen. He'd wanted something better for the pixie to replace what had to be terrible memories. When had Kellen turned it all upside-down?

Kellen was murmuring soft soothing things, kissing the tears on his cheeks, even as he lay panting on Sin's chest. His hands moved to tangle in Sin's hair and for a while that was all either of them could do, just hold on to one another.

"Couple of wild babes in the storm," Sin whispered when he could speak again. He let his legs down but made no move to get out from under Kellen. Not that the pixie was any burden at all, a comfortable weight on his chest. "You all right, hon?"

"Mm." Kellen snuggled against him, his wings lying folded to his back now. "That felt really amazing. Thank you."

"Ha. He's thanking me. The boy takes me and turns me inside out and catches me when I'm falling, and he thanks me." Sin combed his fingers through long auburn strands, Kellen's braid a bit of a mess now. "It was wonderful. Thank you."

Kellen lifted his head, gazing at him with half-closed, sleepy eyes and that sweet little smile of his. "I'm glad. I didn't know if I could please you this way."

"I am quite pleased," Sin rumbled in a lordly voice and grinned when he got a little snicker from Kellen. "Seriously, that was wonderful. And now I'm gonna be a terrible guest and fall asleep in your bed, 'cause I don't think I can move."

The room was already growing dim as the light faded outside the window. Kellen reached for the blanket that had been shoved down toward their feet and pulled it up around them. He slid to Sin's side, moving away, but Sin rolled and pulled him back close. "Is it okay if I hold you like this for a while?" he murmured, kissing the top of Kellen's hair.

"Yes," Kellen said, snuggling into his arms. "I'd like that."

Sin put his wings behind him as he lay on his side, gazing at the beautiful pale skin, those sleepy green eyes. "I'm here, Kells. Even when I'm not in this bed with you, I'm here. You need someone, even just to talk to, I'm here."

Kellen covered one of Sin's hands with his own, the one he'd pressed to his chest. "Will you stay? Here? Not only tonight, but as long as you like."

"Hmm. That almost sounded like 'Sin, would you move in with me?' Is that what that was?"

"I like when you are with me," Kellen said, pausing. "I like talking to you, kissing you, touching you…and when we're apart I miss you."

Sin looked about the sparse apartment, then thought of his own, in a better neighborhood, better furnished, and with more space for honey. "Kells, I worry about you living here. I know it's been a good arrangement for you, in a lot of ways. But I'd be happier if we could live somewhere better. Together. Not that this is bad, really. I mean, I've lived in dumpsters and in abandoned tool sheds. But…"

Yeah. There's a big thing hanging there that you haven't said. My apartment. Ness' apartment. With all the custom stuff sized for a big strapping pony boy. Would it be too weird for Kellen? Would it be too weird for him?

"Sin, I will go with you wherever you want to go," Kellen told him. "And until you want to go, we can stay here."

"Whither thou goest, I will go, is that it?" Sin kissed the top of his head, nuzzling at his soft hair. "For tonight, here's good. Maybe tomorrow, we can go to my place. And this weekend? I think we need to go apartment hunting."

Epilogue

"Are you ready?" Kellen asked.

Sin nodded, threw him a mock salute, and they both tensed.

"Set... Go!" Kellen shouted and they launched off the rooftop. Kellen snapped his wings back and arrowed toward the right while Sin pumped powerful wings to gain lift over the top of the neighboring building. He lost sight of Sin as he came around the edge of the high-rise office building and made a slight adjustment that carried him within a hair's breadth of the next building. He twisted again, his wings blurring, arms and legs tucked in tight. He caught sight of Sin again as he turned from Thirty-Seventh Street onto Seventh Avenue.

"Shit! Shitshitshit!" Kellen put his chin down and put on another burst of speed. Madison Square Garden was just ahead and he didn't even slow to take the turn onto Thirty-Fourth Street. He lost Sin again as he flew for all he was worth toward Fifth Avenue. The distinct and familiar sight of the Empire State Building came into view and Kellen pulled up, shooting down the street like a rocket for the top.

He had yet to lose a race, but Sin was fully recovered now, and their little challenges had done a great deal to help them both in regaining their strength. He saw dark wings shoot up from between two buildings just ahead of him. It was very close. He gave it everything he had, and he almost beat him, but Sin was over the top just a second before he was.

His friend and lover let out a loud whoop and circled, turning in an aerialbatic spiral. Kellen grinned and laughed, darting through the loop he made. "You win this time!" he shouted over the sound of the wind.

"About bloody time!" Sin called back, laughing. "Losing to your tiny little dragonfly wings was just about beating my pride into the dust!"

Kellen zipped back toward him, hovering for a moment before darting back and forth and around him. "I'm made for speed and maneuverability. You're made for long glides. Of course it's going to be hard to beat me."

He felt rather than saw Sin roll his eyes over the yards separating them. "I'm made for lots of things, little bit. Most of them involving endurance."

Kellen looked over at him and shot him a mischievous grin. It had not been all that long since the day that Sin had said goodbye to Ness and Kellen had asked him to stay with him. Just a few days short of a month actually. In that time they had found a new apartment together, healed together, and grown closer that Kellen would have ever thought possible. He could not imagine his life without Sin now. So much had changed, but those first stirrings of something he couldn't even define when Jean had asked him if he was seeing someone all those weeks ago, that hadn't changed. Only now he knew what it meant.

"Cocoa?" Kellen asked.

"You know the way to an incubus's heart." Sin flashed his bright, charming grin and turned back toward home, his huge dragon wings beating a more leisurely rhythm through the air. "And cake?"

"Honey cakes," Kellen agreed. He'd developed quite a fondness for them, and put on another burst of speed.

"Hey! I thought we were done racing!" Sin's aggrieved voice chased him along with his heavy wingbeats thumping close behind.

They arrived back at their building and Sin mock-tackled him as they landed, laughing and rolling with the leftover momentum of flight. Clouds were gathering, though, and it was time to get inside before the snow started. Sin removed the brick they used to prop the roof door open and they both scurried in, shivering as the wind picked up. Their third-floor apartment on Sixty-Sixth Street was only a couple of blocks from the park, a five-minute flight to work in good weather, and had an old poplar tree just outside the window. It had been the perfect find and more than affordable for the two of them together.

As soon as they'd closed the apartment door behind them, Sin hurried to the window and flung it open, something that might have appeared quite mad considering the coming snowstorm, but Kellen knew what he was doing. The incubus leaned out, clicking his tongue rapidly behind his teeth in a special call and a chitter soon answered from the street. The poplar branches shook, remaining brown leaves rustling. With a final cheep, Lola launched herself from the branch nearest the apartment and landed on Sin's outstretched forearm.

"There you are, tree rat daughter of mine." Sin laughed as he brought her inside and shut the window. "Better stay in with us tonight. Looks like it's gonna get nasty out there."

Lola jumped from his arm and scampered to the kitchen where her bowl of nuts, always kept full, waited for her on the table. Most of the things had come from Sin's apartment since Kellen's had been sparsely furnished, but the warm honey-colored table where they had breakfast together most mornings they had purchased together.

Kellen shrugged out of his jacket and went to the kitchen to start cocoa while Sin stopped to blow a kiss to the picture of Ness in his dress uniform on the living room wall. Sin had expressed concern that Kellen would be uncomfortable with the portrait there, but Kellen wanted to honor the memory of Sin's love and of the brave police sergeant who had once saved him from being varg dinner.

Kellen rubbed a finger between Lola's ears and crooned at her while she looked over her hoard and selected a nut. Waiting for the milk to warm was always the hardest part. Sin teased him about his impatience with the process but Kellen had to admit he did like the taste of the cocoa. He only needed the honey, and perhaps a drop of milk to survive, but a nibble of cake and a sprinkle of cocoa once in a while were a nice treat. And Sin said that was what life was about, finding those treats, those moments of enjoyment that made life worth living.

When the milk heated enough, Kellen added the chocolate and poured it into mugs. He took them, plus a plate with a couple of honey cakes, into the living room where Sin had the TV on the channel that was just a picture of a crackling fire. He said it was a ridiculously human thing but he liked it anyway.

Sin made short work of his honey cake, then leaned back on a contented sigh, mug in hand, feet propped up on the coffee table. He put his arm on the back of the couch behind Kellen in wordless invitation for Kellen to snuggle close.

Still licking his lips, Kellen put the mug down and scooted closer, tucking up under Sin's arm. Having Sin's arm and wing around him was the most contented feeling he'd ever experienced. He still sometimes felt like it couldn't be real. A few days after his wings had grown in, he'd suffered what Lysander called a 'panic attack' because he'd suddenly been sure that Rask was not really dead and would find him again. He hadn't had another since, but both Sin and Tenzin had insisted that he should talk to Lysander a couple times a week for a while. He didn't think he needed to but he'd agreed to make them happy. Oddly, the sessions of just talking seemed to help.

There were other things he'd had to learn. It wasn't long after the first night they had spent together that Sin had explained that when they were intimate together, it wasn't all about Kellen pleasing him, as much as he enjoyed that. It had been something of a confusing conversation because Kellen felt lots of pleasure when they were together, no matter what they were doing. It took him a while to see how much of his behavior was drawn from his only experience of being with someone who used him more as a sexual thing than treating him as a real person.

After he understood the difference, and several exceptional blow jobs during which Sin had refused to allow him to do anything but feel had helped, Kellen worked hard to reject his training and relax, and mostly he succeeded. Talking more and not weighing every word had been even harder, but he'd made strides there as well.

Sin kissed the top of his head and Kellen tipped his face up to kiss him back. "Thank you."

"For what?" Sin asked.

"For everything."

Sin's smile was somehow full of both warmth and irony. "Sweetie, you saved me, from myself, from sliding into the dark. I should be thanking you."

Kellen smiled back. "How about if we thank each other then?"

"That's what all this is." Sin waved a hand to the apartment. "Thanking each other every day." He sipped at his cocoa, his gaze suddenly distant, and Kellen was afraid he was remembering painful things again when he suddenly grinned down at him. "Hey. I'm thinking we should have a Yule party. What do you think?"

"I think...I think I'd like that," Kellen said. The concept of allowing people he knew, friends, into his life was still hard for him as well. He liked it though, not having to keep everyone at a safe distance to hide his secrets. Little by little, he no longer felt so much like he was standing outside looking in. He watched Sin for a moment, watched him take another sip from the mug and the way his tongue licked his bottom lip.

He turned toward him more, and slid one leg over Sin, straddling his hips. He grinned at Sin's look of surprise and kissed him. Not a little kiss, but one that made sure he could taste the sweet flavors of honey and chocolate on his tongue.

"Flying races get the blood going, do they?" Sin chuckled and reached awkwardly around to set his mug down. In those first few days together, Sin would have already been stripping, desperate for contact, for physical connection. Now he just folded Kellen close with a happy hum.

"No, you get my blood going," Kellen said, sliding his hands up into Sin's hair. He kissed him again and pressed closer, chest to chest, so he could feel Sin's pleased hum vibrate all the way through him.

Sin's hands threaded into his hair as the kiss caught fire. For Kellen, who had been isolated and bereft for so long, having Sin's arms around him, his hands stroking him, and the warmth and tenderness he exuded wrapping him safely was more than he'd ever dared dream. It wasn't a dream. It was real. Sin had told him the nightmare was over and now he was finally awake. This was happiness, this was life, and if it all did turn out to be a dream, he'd gladly stay right here, dreaming with his incubus.

About the Authors

Angel Martinez

The unlikely black sheep of an ivory tower intellectual family, Angel Martinez has managed to make her way through life reasonably unscathed. Despite a wildly misspent youth, she snagged a degree in English Lit, married once and did it right the first time, (same husband for almost twenty-four years) gave birth to one amazing son, (now in college) and realized at some point that she could get paid for writing.

Published since 2006, Angel's cynical heart cloaks a desperate romantic. You'll find drama and humor given equal weight in her writing and don't expect sad endings. Life is sad enough.

She currently lives in Delaware in a drinking town with a college problem and writes Science Fiction and Fantasy centered around gay heroes.

Bellora Quinn

Originally hailing from Detroit Michigan, Bellora now resides on the sunny Gulf Coast of Florida where a herd of Dachshunds keeps her entertained. She got her start in writing at the dawn of the internet when she discovered PbEMs (Play by email) and found a passion for collaborative writing and steamy hot erotica. Soap Opera like blogs soon followed and eventually full novels.

The majority of her stories are in the M/M genre with urban fantasy or paranormal settings and many with a strong BDSM flavor.

Angel and Bellora love to hear from readers. You can find their contact information, website details and author profile pages at http://www.pride-publishing.com.